Poppy's gaze narrowed. "You don't believe I have what it ~~takes to be a field agent like~~ you. Well, I d~~are you to watch me~~ going to do it."

The events of tha~~t night were ancient histo~~ry, but Poppy bore the scars.

He'd thought taking a bullet would've cooled her jets about undercover work but it'd only made her more determined than ever.

That'd been the beginning of the end for them.

Now it was happening all over again, and he was supposed to just let it happen because now it wasn't any of his business?

Talk about a messed up déjà vu.

But it is what it is.

They weren't dating. They hadn't even spoken to each other since the night she bailed.

Up until yesterday when Poppy walked into the debriefing, she'd faded like mist from his life.

So...whatever.

Shaine hailed a cab, telling the cabbie, "Take me to the hottest nightclub in Miami," and leaned back to get his head on straight.

Time for a little research.

Game play level: professional.

* * *

Dear Reader,

Stories with intrigue, danger and sexual tension are my favorite kind to write. There's something about immersing myself in a world where bullets fly and the potential of death lurks around every corner that really gets my creativity going.

When I envisioned *Deep Cover*, I knew it was going to be a wild ride and I hope you agree.

The Kelly brothers are the best kind of men—hot, stoic and protective—which spells danger for the women in their lives.

Set against the sultry Miami background, the idea of two agents, one FBI and another DEA, going undercover to catch a violent crime lord was too tantalizing to pass up.

I hope you love my newest Harlequin Romantic Suspense as much as I do.

I love hearing from readers. Connect with me on Facebook, Twitter or drop me an email. Or you can also write me a letter at PO BOX 2210, Oakdale, CA 95361.

Happy reading,

Kimberly

DEEP COVER

Kimberly Van Meter

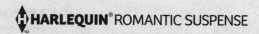
HARLEQUIN® ROMANTIC SUSPENSE

ISBN-13: 978-0-373-27996-8

Deep Cover

www.Harlequin.com

Kimberly Van Meter wrote her first book at sixteen and finally achieved publication in December 2006. She writes for the Harlequin Superromance, Blaze and Romantic Suspense lines. She and her husband of seventeen years have three children, three cats and always a houseful of friends, family and fun.

Books by Kimberly Van Meter

Harlequin Romantic Suspense

The Sniper
The Agent's Surrender
Moving Target
Deep Cover

Harlequin Superromance

Family in Paradise

Like One of the Family
Playing the Part
Something to Believe In

The Sinclairs of Alaska

That Reckless Night
A Real Live Hero
A Sinclair Homecoming

Harlequin Blaze

The Hottest Ticket in Town
Sex, Lies and Designer Shoes
A Wrong Bed Christmas
"Ignited"
The Flyboy's Temptation

All backlist available in ebook format.

Visit the Author Profile page at Harlequin.com for more titles.

Chapter 1

"The kids are calling it Bliss," began FBI chief Patrick Hobbs as the PowerPoint presentation began in the darkened conference room. Special Agent Shaine Kelly and Special Agent Victoria Stapp were the only ones invited to this debriefing, which told Shaine they were about to get into something interesting. "It's ten times more potent than Ecstasy and ten times more addictive. Whereas X used to be the drug of choice for trust-fund kids partying on Mommy and Daddy's money, Bliss is cheaper, easier to find and, as evidenced by the bodies in the morgue with the junk in their system, *deadly*."

Chief Hobbs switched to the next frame.

Dead college kids, by the look of their clothes, white drool frozen on their curled lips, as if they'd died in immeasurable pain.

"That's not a good look on anyone," Shaine said, eliciting a nod of agreement from Victoria.

"Watch the wisecracks," Hobbs warned before moving on. "The drug is a ticking time bomb. Users say the high is like an opiate high, without the extreme lethargy. It's simply...*bliss*."

Stapp, a short redhead with a stereotypical redhead's temper, said, "Sounds better than Xanax. Explains why kids are dying to get their hands on it. So did they OD?"

"In a matter of speaking. That's what makes Bliss unique. It doesn't kill you right away. Similar to LSD, the drug remains in the system far longer than the high, which then builds up until the body goes into painful convulsions, ultimately giving the user a massive heart attack."

The lights flicked on and Shaine briefly squinted against the light. "So where's it coming from?" he asked. "Colombia? Mexico? Guatemala?"

"Miami."

"Florida?"

Hobbs nodded. "We suspect someone known as El Escorpion is in charge of the manufacturing and distribution, but we haven't been able to get proof. No one can get close enough to infiltrate the operation."

"El Escorpion... Spanish for *The Scorpion*," Victoria murmured with a wry grin. "Sounds like the kind of guy you wouldn't want to screw around with."

"El Escorpion is the worst kind of criminal—smart, rich and *anonymous*."

"What do you mean anonymous?" Shaine asked.

"No one knows who this El Escorpion is. Anyone with that knowledge is either dead or missing. He or she is a ghost with a helluva presence."

"Convenient. This person could be operating in plain sight, thumbing their nose at authorities," Shaine said. "So how are we supposed to catch him?" Victoria cleared her throat meaningfully and Shaine dutifully corrected himself, saying, "Or *her*."

"Since no one knows who El Escorpion is," Hobbs said, handing out dossiers, "we're putting a small, elite, multiagency team together to infiltrate the Miami scene. This undercover detail is highly classified, dangerous and top priority."

"My favorite—" he started to say, but the door opening stopped him.

Shaine didn't know the man who entered, but it took all of one horrible, gut-grinding second to realize he knew the woman.

Intimately.

Poppy Jones.

Tall, lithe and built like a Norwegian supermodel with long, straight limbs and blond hair pulled into a tight ponytail, Poppy was hard to forget.

Shaine's expression remained impassive, though every muscle had just been pulled taut.

"Agents Stapp and Kelly, meet DEA agents Poppy Jones and Marcus West. The DEA will be one of our partner agencies for this operation."

"Pleased to work with you," Marcus said briskly, extending a hand out of professional courtesy to both Shaine and Victoria. Of course, Poppy did the same.

Since it was bad form to be openly rude, even if the Queen of Hell had just walked in, Shaine offered a perfunctory greeting, "Yeah, likewise," and accepted a quick handshake from each.

Two high points of color jumped to Poppy's porcelain

cheeks the moment their hands touched, but otherwise she remained perfectly professional.

As if they hadn't maintained a covert operation of their own, unbeknownst to their superiors while Poppy was still with the FBI.

As if they hadn't spent hours bathed in each other's sweat, reveling in their own stink like drug addicts hunkered down in a run-down hotel, except their drug of choice had been each other.

Prior to this moment, two years had seemed a lifetime ago.

Now…it seemed like yesterday.

Marcus and Poppy took their places at the table and opened their folders. Poppy took point, talking first.

Not surprising.

Poppy had always been a little aggressive.

Shaine had enjoyed that aspect of her personality, particularly between the sheets.

But he hated it any other time.

Particularly on the job.

"From what we've been able to ascertain, El Escorpion is working the college-aged users, likely recruiting young college coeds to push the product. We believe with the right undercover agents, we can gain access to the inner circle and find out who El Escorpion is, and how his organization is manufacturing and moving the product."

"And just who exactly are the right agents for the job?" Shaine asked, his tone more clipped than he intended. If Poppy thought for a second they could work together, she was cracked in the head.

Poppy's gaze remained cool as she answered, "Two people who can blend into the typical Miami scene. One male, one female. Someone who looks younger than they are."

Hobbs's gruff voice cut in. "Let's get to the point. The deputy chief inspector has chosen agents Jones and West from the DEA and I've chosen agents Kelly and Stapp. Agent Stapp, you will be Agent Kelly's tech support behind the scenes, and Agent West will do the same for his partner. Once in Miami, we will have two contacts within the Miami Police Department. These officers have been thoroughly vetted through private means to ensure that they are not on the payroll of El Escorpion."

Ah, hell.

Shaine chose to ignore Poppy so he could get his thoughts on the right track. This case was the kind that made or broke careers.

It was also the kind that put agents in the ground.

"For the sake of security," West said, "our contact in Miami will not meet with us until we land. Agent Stapp and I will stay at an undisclosed and newly acquired safe house, while agents Kelly and Jones will be set up in a different location, more central to the college party scene."

Hobbs nodded. "If you'll look in your dossiers, you'll find a comprehensive list of suspected players. We suggest you start there."

Shaine thumbed through the sheaf, his mind humming. Undercover work fed his need for adrenaline and he loved it—but he'd rather chew nails than work side by side with Poppy and her pretty boy, Marcus.

"With all due respect, this isn't my first rodeo. Going deep cover gets risky when there are more players involved. I don't mind the DEA providing support from behind the scenes, but frankly, dealing with a partner just adds to the risk for everyone involved."

Not to mention I work better alone.

Poppy offered a brief but chilly smile. "The DEA appreciates your expertise in deep cover operations, Agent Kelly. Your success rate for apprehensions is impressive. However, you've gained a reputation for being reckless, which makes you unpredictable. El Escorpion has managed to elude capture for years. It will take more than luck to bring him or *her* down."

Shaine held Poppy's stare, amazed at the balls on the woman. "I'm not sure if I should take your comment as a compliment or an insult," he said, toying with the pen in his fingers.

"Your choice." Poppy's smile returned as if daring him to go a round with her.

Hobbs cleared his throat, sensing the brittle tension growing between Shaine and Poppy. "Let's remember, we're all on the same side. El Escorpion is the enemy, not anyone in this room. Private transport has been arranged to Miami at 0600 hours tomorrow. Pack light. A Miami summer is hot, humid and filled with alligators."

"Sounds like fun," Poppy quipped, scooping up her folder. "See you tomorrow morning."

Shaine watched them leave, his one thought being, *Poppy will fit right in with the wildlife*, before turning to Hobbs.

"What's the deal with you and that DEA agent?" Hobbs asked, narrowing his gaze. "Is there something I should know?"

"Nope," he lied.

"Then why are you being so hostile? Those agents are highly trained in their fields and your posturing makes us look bad. This is a high-profile undercover case with a lot of pressure from the higher-ups to get it closed. That means you're going to put on your *good boy pants* and do what you're told." Hobbs put it bluntly. "Whatever bee you've got in your bonnet…squash it."

"You're the boss," Shaine said, mock-saluting Hobbs.

"Try to remember that," Hobbs growled as he headed out the door. "Damn Kellys. Always a pain in the ass."

"You must have me mixed up with my brothers, Sawyer or Silas. I'm the nice one, in case you were confused," Shaine called out, but Hobbs was already gone.

Shaine rubbed at the slick table veneer. Time to focus.

And pretend that the one woman he'd ever loved—and who'd subsequently trashed his heart—wasn't about to be his partner.

"What was that all about?" Marcus asked as soon as they left the FBI building. "You know Agent Dickwad or something?"

"No," Poppy answered quickly, not interested in sharing details. "But I know his type and I don't have time for his games. He thinks because he's some brilliant undercover agent that he gets to call all the shots, and that just rubs me the wrong way."

"I get it, but you have to work with him. We can't let anything get in the way of this case. If you can't be objective, you need to bow out."

Poppy shot Marcus a dark look. "Not going to happen. I worked my ass off to qualify for this case. I'm not about to give it up over some FBI agent with a bloated ego. I'll be fine."

She knew Marcus was right and that, unlike her, he was being honest, but there was no way in hell she was walking away from this case, not even if she had to work with the devil himself.

Which in this case, was nearly true.

Shaine Kelly.

Why him?

Because he was, simply, damn good at his job.

Of course, the brass wanted him working this case.

Shaine Kelly closes cases.

Shaine Kelly doesn't get shot.

A phantom pain pierced her chest at the exact spot where a bullet had ripped through her flesh two years ago, narrowly missing her heart.

She tried not to think about how close she'd come to dying that night. Fear clouded judgment.

And she had a lot to prove.

To whom?

Don't say Shaine, an inner voice hissed as a familiar hurt threatened to boil to the surface.

Marcus, seemingly satisfied with her answer, moved on. That was what she liked about him—he didn't dwell or dig. Best quality in a man as far as she could tell.

Too bad he was gay.

"Ever think of transferring to the main headquarters here in Washington?" Marcus asked as they climbed into the rental car to head to their hotel. "The weather is a bitch, but it would be nice to be so close to the movers and shakers, you know?"

"I like Los Angeles," she answered, which wasn't entirely true. She hated the frivolous culture and the self-absorbed people that seemed to flock to Hollywood trying to find their big break, but there was no shortage of action in the LA office, which had enabled her to make her own reputation.

Marcus, a transplant from the Seattle division, had his eyes on the chain of command. He made no bones about wanting to move up the ladder. "Closing this case will look damn good on our résumés," he pointed out with a grin. "I heard there's a potential opening in the New York field office. It's not headquarters but it's a step closer, right?"

"You planning to hop, skip and jump right into the chief deputy's position?" she joked.

Marcus grinned. "Not saying it isn't on my radar. Gotta have big dreams, Jones. If your dreams don't scare you, they ain't big enough."

"Such a philosopher. Let's focus on closing this case first."

Marcus chuckled, his gray eyes bright with the big dreams in his head, content to let the subject go.

Poppy knew all about big dreams—and their cost.

They say to aim for the moon, for even if you miss you'll land among the stars. But what they don't tell you is that what goes up, must come down, and the landing was a bitch.

Leaving Shaine was necessary, but it'd hurt more than taking that bullet.

But she couldn't stay with someone who wouldn't treat her as an equal.

She'd spent her life being treated as arm candy.

When she'd announced her intention to join the FBI, her family hadn't supported her decision, saying she was too pretty to take on a job like that.

Her father, an old-school type with decidedly archaic beliefs, had been dismissive.

That's not the future for you. God blessed you with a beautiful face. Find a good man to take care of you. Treat you right.

She hated saying that being considered beautiful was a burden because people tended to think she was being falsely modest, but it was true.

The irony was that she'd fought to be seen as a good agent because of her skills, but the biggest case of her career thus far would hinge upon her ability to use her looks to her advantage.

Time to put that pretty face to work for more than being someone's trophy.

No one was going to take this opportunity from her.

Especially not Shaine Kelly.

Chapter 2

The plane touched down in Miami and they were immediately whisked away in a nondescript black SUV to the debriefing at a secure location.

The small room, located in a government building disguised as an insurance office, was cramped with everyone inside.

Introductions were brief and to the point, with Chief Hobbs doing the introducing via video call.

"I'll call your names, you raise your hands. This ain't no tea party and there's no time for a meet and greet. Miami police officers Richard York and Ben Rocha, DEA agents Marcus West and Poppy Jones, FBI special agents Shaine Kelly and Victoria Stapp, Miami DEA contact Rosa Ramirez." Murmured greetings were exchanged and Hobbs continued, "From here out, Ramirez will be your primary on-scene superior. Ramirez will be in constant contact with me via videoconference. She will handle all immediate concerns regarding the investigation. Any questions?"

No one ventured a comment and Hobbs took that as a cue to turn the meeting over to Rosa.

"Thank you, Chief Hobbs," Rosa began, a no-nonsense woman with slicked back dark hair pulled into a tight bun. "This is the biggest covert operation in recent history, and we're anxious for a successful end to this El Escorpion character."

Rosa gestured to the packets on the table. "For the agents going undercover, you'll find IDs, cash and backstories for your covers. Officers York and Rocha will be your only contacts inside the Miami PD for obvious reasons. We know there are cops on the take, but we haven't figured out who. York and Rocha have been determined to be trustworthy."

"And who vetted them?" Shaine asked. When his life was on the line, he didn't care about being nice.

Rosa smiled. "Ahh, Special Agent Shaine Kelly. I've heard about you. Smart, fearless…a chameleon in the field."

"Guilty as charged," Shaine said with a grin.

But Rosa wasn't finished. "Also known for having an issue with authority. Let's be frank, Agent Kelly… the reason you're here is that your ability to close cases outweighs your undesirable qualities. But make no mistake, eyes are on you, so watch yourself."

Shaine caught the tiny, infinitesimal twitch of Poppy's lips and his own thinned, though he chose to remain quiet.

So Rosa Ramirez wasn't a fan.

Great.

Nothing like your direct superior looking for reasons to toss you out.

Rosa moved on briskly. "The Scorpion has been a thorn in Miami's side for years, but until now the product of choice was always the usual, heroin or meth. This new drug is lethal, cheap and moving quickly. It's the new cash crop, and unless we put a stop to it here, it will spread. We could have an epidemic within months. That's not going to happen. We're counting on this team to bring The Scorpion to justice. Please open your packets."

Paper rustling was the only sound in the room as they quickly read through the details.

Shaine and Poppy would pose as twentysomething college kids. Shaine would bartend at a popular upscale bar and strip club, Lit, while Poppy would be a dancer.

A strip club? Poppy didn't outwardly react, but he suspected her gut was churning. He knew Poppy didn't have hang-ups about her body, but she wasn't an exhibitionist, either.

Poppy's attention was focused on the paper in front of her, but the absent way she chewed her bottom lip told him her thoughts were elsewhere.

"The idea is to blend into the scene where Bliss is commonly found. The dealers are like sharks circling the chum. It's your job to seek out the higher level dealers to get close to anyone who knows El Escorpion's identity. Once we discover a name, phase two will start, which is why we need a male and a female undercover agent. You must be willing to do whatever it takes to get this information. Are you up to that challenge?"

"Not a problem for me," Shaine answered, looking pointedly at Poppy.

"Nor is it for me," Poppy replied coolly, adding, "Looks

like all those dancing classes in my childhood are going to finally pay off."

"You're sure about that?" Shaine asked, not buying her answer.

"Why wouldn't I be?" Poppy returned with a dispassionate expression. "Do you feel you can handle being a bartender?"

"All right, all right, settle down. We're all on the same team. Like I said, the bar is upscale, so it's not going to be some seedy place with sticky tables. Full nudity is not required, though many of the girls finish with a topless number."

"Again, I'm fine with it," Poppy assured Ramirez, dismissing Shaine's comment.

"Good." Rosa seemed pleased. "You are dismissed to settle in. Tomorrow is your first day of work. Remember, you're college kids looking for a good time. Leave your law enforcement persona behind. These people are pros. They can smell a cop from a mile away."

Shaine smirked. "Like I said…not my first rodeo. This is the fun part."

Rosa said, "Both Kelly and Jones will have separate cars, but a rental is outside to take you to the location where your cars will be assigned. It may seem as though these are extraneous precautions, but we can't take the chance of an overlooked loophole."

He went to grab the keys to the rental car, but Poppy beat him to it.

"I'll drive," Poppy said, snatching the keys. "Being a passenger makes me carsick."

Since when?

The little liar.

He always used to drive.

But someone was proving a point.

"Be my guest," he said, following her out the door.

Yeah, this was going to suck.

Thanks a lot for ruining what could've been a cool undercover gig, Poppy Jones.

Having Shaine in the car was unnerving. Her plan had been to treat him like any other undercover agent.

Dispassionate.

Professional.

But the humid air lifted the scent of his skin straight to her nose and she was awash with memories.

Her breath caught.

No. She wasn't going to do that—no going backward.

Do the job. Stay focused. Be chill.

As it turned out, Shaine broke the unbearable silence first.

"How'd you get this gig?" he asked.

"The usual way. Working harder than everyone else. Harder than every other man in my way."

"Still the ballbuster. Glad to see some things never change."

"That's where you're wrong. I've changed plenty. I no longer care what small-minded people think of me."

"Whoa, right out the barrel, an insult. I was trying to make polite conversation."

"Right. You forget I know you, Shaine. You don't do polite and you certainly don't do idle conversation. Your question was a dig at me. A bit passive-aggressive for my taste, but you got your point across."

"Since you seem to know the inner workings of my mind, why don't you enlighten me with what I was thinking when I *passive-aggressively* asked you a polite question," he suggested, his tone laced with sarcasm. "Personally, I thought I was being nice to a person who certainly didn't deserve my niceness."

Why was she arguing with him? Two seconds into an enclosed space alone and they were ripping into each other. She was not about to let her personal feelings about Shaine ruin the biggest case of her life.

"Just stop. We need to get into character. We are not Poppy Jones and Shaine Kelly, former lovers. We are two college kids without a care in the world, ready for a good time. Let's keep to the script, shall we?"

"And what if I don't think you're up for this part?"

"Oh, that old argument again? Please, get some new material—that bit is tired."

"I'm not kidding around. You're not ready to take on a case like this. You can't even be around me without switching to bitch-mode. How are you supposed to pull off melting into someone else's skin when you can't even handle your own?"

Poppy's cheeks heated with embarrassment. Swallowing the bile that'd risen in her throat, she said stiffly, "I didn't expect you to be on this case. It's just taken me a minute to adjust. I worked my ass off to get on to this detail and nothing is going to keep me from closing it. Not even you. So if that means I have to pretend that there's no history between us, I'll find a way to do it."

"You sure you can?"

This time she had the wherewithal to send him a withering glance. "Yes," she answered. "I've managed to put you in my past before, I can do it again."

"Good," Shaine said. "Maybe that'll keep you from getting shot this time."

"Now who can't let go of the past?" she retorted, freshly

irritated even though she knew she needed to put a cap on it. "I'm not the only agent who's been shot in the line of duty."

"No. But you were the only one I was in love with," Shaine said.

"That was a long time ago."

"Yeah, it was."

"So don't bring it up again. I'm a better agent today than I was then. Leave it at that."

Shaine accepted her answer with a short nod and did, indeed, leave it, which was surprising. To her memory, Shaine rarely let anyone else have the final word—on that topic.

Only because he had another bone to pick.

"You really think you can pull off being a stripper?" he asked.

"And why is that so hard to believe?"

"Because you're more modest than most. You wore a one-piece to the beach."

"I also wore a hat. Skin cancer is no joke. It had nothing to do with my comfort level. If the ozone layer wasn't an issue, I'd run around naked if I could."

"Oh, c'mon, who are you trying to convince? Me or yourself? This is dangerous, Poppy."

His condescension scraped against her nerves. "It kills you that I'm on this team, not because of my qualifications, but because of our history. If anyone can't let go of the past, it's you," Poppy said.

"Honey, I let go a long time ago," he disagreed. "I just don't feel like dying because you don't know what you're doing. There's an art to going deep cover and I don't think you have what it takes."

Poppy resisted the urge to snap back. He was baiting her purposefully.

What an ass.

"Well, thankfully, you're not in charge and it wasn't your call. I'm here… Get used to it."

Shaine shook his head as if he wasn't going to waste more time arguing and she was glad. She didn't know how much longer she could keep her cool and the last thing she wanted to do was give Shaine any kind of valid reason to have her tossed from the case.

They arrived at the apartment fourplex, a gray building with nothing charming or exciting about it, and walked around to the back where the two apartments they were to occupy were situated.

From a defensive standpoint, the place was deceptively secure, which was why it was owned by the Miami DEA office as the newest safe house used for informants needing a place to hide before their testimony.

There were also hidden cameras in the narrow alleyway that fed into the four apartments so no one could sneak up on anyone inside.

No more words were exchanged as they each disappeared into their apartments.

Poppy set her suitcase down and took a minute to compose herself.

Damn it.

Around Shaine she devolved into someone she swore she'd never be.

Surveying her new living environment, she saw it'd already been decorated to reflect the tastes of someone much younger, which was the part she was playing.

Shabby chic, repurposed furniture, a thrift-store sofa

and a few picture frames featuring people she didn't know were placed here and there.

This operation was costing a pretty penny.

Everyone expected results.

"So failure isn't an option," she murmured to herself as a reminder. "Time to get your game face on."

Suddenly a door, which she'd assumed was a closet, opened and Shaine walked in.

"What the hell?" she exclaimed, not expecting Shaine to walk into her living room.

"Adjoining rooms," he explained, surprised himself.

"Is there a lock?" she asked. The last thing she wanted was Shaine Kelly traipsing through her living room as if he had the right.

"Looks similar to a hotel room door." He showed her how to lock it and then exited again. The sound of him locking the door from his side made her exhale. Had she actually been holding her breath?

Okay, so it made sense to have an adjoining room, for safety purposes if the DEA was housing someone who needed protection, but she could take care of herself.

Poppy grabbed her suitcase and went to the bedroom, finding more shabby chic, girly stuff—stuff for someone who was stuck between wanting to be an adult and still wanting to be a kid.

But she supposed that was pretty much what some college girls felt like.

Not that she had.

She'd been more than happy to leave behind all that crap.

Opening her closet she saw clothes already chosen to match her cover story.

Poppy lifted a skimpy shirt from the rack and frowned at how barely there it was.

Sure, she could pull it off, but it'd been a long time since she'd purposefully worn something so revealing.

Shaine's earlier comment about the one-piece bathing suit came back to poke at her. Okay, so she preferred tailored suits to string bikinis and microminis. *Sue me.*

Poppy liked to leave something to the imagination, but there was no hiding the goods in these outfits.

"Good Lord," Poppy murmured in faint distress as she pulled a tiny dress from the closet. A tight, formfitting number with a cutout where her cleavage would show, she wondered how she was supposed to wear a bra with this thing.

Or underwear for that matter.

Even a damn panty line would show.

Oh, well.

Her new motto was, "When in Miami…do as the party girls do."

Time to make some friends.

Chapter 3

Rosa Ramirez was Miami born and bred and she'd made it her business to clean up her beautiful city.

When the opportunity came around to take down El Escorpion, she didn't hesitate, but in truth, this operation had been a long time coming.

And she wasn't blind to the fact that if a certain senator's daughter hadn't gotten herself doped up on Bliss and put on life support from her last party, taking down that piece of shit drug dealer wouldn't have gotten so much attention.

But Rosa never looked a gift horse in the mouth.

The operation was in play and she was going to see it succeed.

But she had a bad feeling in her gut about some of the people involved.

Mainly Agent Kelly and DEA agent Jones.

Now, she hated to think one of her own might be dirty, but El Escorpion had a long reach and a deep pocket.

Times are hard, people slip.
All it takes is once.

One agreement to look the other way for a handful of cash and you were hooked.

Cash was a persuasive bargaining tool.

Rosa had seen too many good agents get caught up in bad shit because the allure of quick cash was too hard to ignore.

She poured herself two fingers of scotch and nursed it while reading the personnel files of both Kelly and Jones.

Both were exceptionally nice to look at—something Rosa hadn't been graced with—not that it mattered to her.

Rosa was the job and the job was her.

And she was good with that.

But even Rosa had to admit Shaine Kelly had that enigmatic quality of a bad boy wearing a badge, with a devil-may-care attitude that instantly drew women like a flower bathed in pollen drew bees.

Dark, wavy hair, deep blue eyes—shit, this guy was sex on a stick.

Rosa flicked away Kelly's file and picked up Jones's.

White-blond hair like a fairy-tale princess, long, lean body and cornflower blue eyes. California prom queen material.

It should be a cosmic law that if graced with physical perfection, they couldn't also be smart and well accomplished.

Hell, bitter much?

Rosa sighed at her own thoughts, ready to call it a night when something in Jones's file caught her eye.

Shot on the job.

Now, that's interesting. Rosa sat a little straighter.

Bullet to the chest; missed the heart by inches.

"You've got a guardian angel, kid," Rosa murmured before sipping her scotch.

Savoring the burn in her throat, she leaned back in her chair to read the details of the operation that'd gotten Jones shot.

First undercover gig with the FBI.

Rough start.

Then she left the FBI to work for the DEA in Los Angeles.

Rosa double-checked which FBI office she worked for—Washington.

Same as Kelly.

Coincidence?

True, the FBI headquarters was huge. It was possible to work in the same office and never know every employee there.

But two highly skilled undercover agents?

What were the odds of that?

Rosa didn't believe in coincidences.

Her hunch had been that Jones and Kelly were hiding something.

And her hunches were rarely wrong.

Was Hobbs aware that Jones was from Washington?

Likely not.

Hobbs was relatively new—transferred in from the New York office when the previous chief retired.

And clearly, neither Kelly nor Jones had been eager to cough up the information.

Which meant, they had history they were trying to hide.

Rosa finished her scotch.

That wasn't going to work.

No secrets. No hiding.

The stakes were too high to mess around with unknown variables.

She wasn't one to knee-jerk react, but she was very good at watching and waiting. In her experience, people revealed their biases, prejudices and their dirty laundry if you were patient. All she had to do was watch and wait.

And if it turned out that Kelly and Jones were hiding something, they'd be on the first plane back to where they came from.

Rosa Ramirez didn't mess around.

Shaine finger combed his hair, grabbed his wallet and fake ID and headed out.

There was no way he was going to sit in that apartment all night, stewing about the fact that he couldn't shake the certainty that Poppy was in over her head in some lame attempt to prove something.

She was an adult.

And capable of making her own decisions—she'd made that abundantly clear when she'd walked out on him.

If she got herself shot again, why should he worry about her welfare? All he owed her was the same amount of professional courtesy that he would give any agent.

Undercover work was risky business.

Not everyone was cut out for it.

It wasn't that Poppy was weak or afraid. She lacked that certain something—intuition—that guided an undercover agent and kept them from getting killed.

A good undercover agent knew when to cut bait and run and when to bluff.

Shaine could take things to the edge and stare down into the abyss without fearing a fall.

Poppy just had crazy determination and a thirst for adventure.

Hell, he'd liked that about her.

Until she'd started going undercover.

Then, he'd hated it.

Because that didn't keep you alive.

"I can do this," Poppy had insisted. "Lachlan doesn't know I'm wearing a wire and he has no reason to suspect it, either."

"The intel is bad," Shaine had nearly shouted, wanting to grab her by the shoulders and shake her stubborn head off. "Can't you tell that you've been made? Why else would Lachlan invite you back to his place even after someone recognized you?"

"I'll slip in, grab the file and be gone. It'll be quick. Lachlan is having a huge party. He'll be too busy to even think about me."

"You're naive, Poppy. Don't go. My gut is saying he's luring you into a trap."

Poppy's gaze narrowed. "You don't believe I have what it takes to be a hotshot like you. Well, I do. I can do this and I'm going to do it."

The events of that night were etched in his memory, but Poppy bore the scars.

He'd thought taking a bullet would've cooled her jets about undercover work, but it'd only made her more determined than ever.

That'd been the beginning of the end for them.

Now it was happening all over again and he was supposed to just let it happen because now it wasn't any of his business?

Talk about a messed up déjà vu.

But it is what it is.

They weren't dating. They hadn't even spoken to each other since the night she bailed.

Up until yesterday when Poppy walked into the debriefing, she'd faded like mist from his life.

So...whatever.

Shaine hailed a cab, telling the driver, "Take me to the hottest nightclub in Miami," and leaned back to get his head on straight.

Time for a little research.

Game play level: professional.

Chapter 4

Poppy heard the door on the other side of the apartment close and she briefly perked up, wondering where Shaine was going.

They weren't scheduled to start until tomorrow but that was the thing about Shaine, he did as he pleased and went where his gut told him to.

Which then also made her wonder why he was stepping out on his own.

Did he know something? Was he trying to get the jump on the investigation so he didn't have to work with her?

Stop panicking, she told herself. Second-guessing every move was a rookie mistake, and if it weren't Shaine, she wouldn't think twice about her partner acting as he should undercover.

Forcing herself to relax, Poppy grabbed her file and started reading, committing her identity to heart.

Name: Laci Langford, 22, from Connecticut. Moved
to Miami to escape the cold East Coast winters.
Major: Marketing.
Parents: Sara and John Langford, deceased. No
siblings.

She perused the rest of the file, closing it as she tried
to envision herself as the person described in the file.

Laci Langford…definitely sounded like a stripper
name.

She'd have to remember to answer to Laci, not Poppy.
Getting tripped up by a simple detail was usually the way
rookies got made.

The phantom ache pierced her chest again and she
rubbed at the small scar beneath her blouse.

Would she always feel as if she were running from
that one event in her life?

She'd made a mistake—screwed up and paid the price.

The upside of getting shot? Poppy worked hard to make
sure it wouldn't happen again.

Unlike her persona, Laci, Poppy's parents were still
alive and well.

And they'd been as unsupportive as Shaine about her
decision to remain in her line of work.

"Your father is worried," her mother had said after her
father had stormed from Poppy's house during her re-
covery, trying to soften the blow. "You know he doesn't
understand this job of yours."

"He doesn't have to understand the job. He just has
to understand me."

"Well, you know that's always been a challenge," her
mother, Dottie, admitted, her hands fluttering as she
straightened everything she could get her fingers on.

"Frankly, sweetheart, we're all a little surprised that after this incident you're not ready to get into a less dangerous line of work. I mean, Poppy…in all the years I've been a nurse, I've never been shot at."

Yes, but Dottie had been shit on, spit on, yelled at and otherwise abused by her patients, and Poppy had never wanted any piece of that.

"I love my job," Poppy said firmly, holding back the wince as she shifted her weight, trying not to agitate her healing wound. The doctor said it would be weeks before she could even think about returning to work, which sounded like an interminable amount of time to her ears, but she couldn't exactly go against the doctor's orders.

Of course, that left her to suffer the opinions of her parents and friends who didn't understand her job, nor did they appreciate that Poppy absolutely loved what she did.

She tried to tell herself that they meant well, but after gritting her teeth through the same conversation for the *umpteenth* time, she'd practically worn her teeth down to nubs.

"Of course you do, sweetheart," Dottie said with open distress. "But some people aren't cut out for these types of jobs. You've always been a delicate thing… Surely the Bureau could find a suitable desk job? Maybe a secretary position?"

Poppy glared. "Do you realize how offensive that is to me? I didn't work my ass off to sit behind a desk." When her mother's eyes started to water, Poppy bit back the rest of the hot words dancing on her tongue. Her parents would never understand—and honestly, she never expected them to—so their opinion wasn't a huge shock. But the one person she'd thought would understand…

Unwelcome tears crowded her sinuses and she sniffed them back.

Dottie seemed to understand where the tears were coming from and tried to comfort her. "You two can work things out," she assured Poppy, but Dottie didn't know that there was absolutely zero chance of that happening. "It was probably very scary to see the woman he loves almost die. You really need to think of how this situation has affected those who love you."

"Damn it, Mom," she muttered, pulling away with a curse. "Just stop."

"What did I say?"

"You always turn it around back on me. As if I should be thinking of everyone else when no one seems to give a damn about how I feel about the situation. Shaine is just as bad as you, demanding that I give up a career I love without considering how doing so would kill me faster than any bullet. If you can't support me, then stop pretending that you care. I'm done with all of you."

"Poppy Jones, what has gotten into you? You were never this aggressive, or so rude. This job has changed you and not for the better." Dottie gathered her purse, her upper lip stiff. "I hope you come to your senses soon. Otherwise, I just don't think my heart can take it. I didn't raise my daughter to want a career she's so ill-suited for."

Ill-suited? she'd wanted to scream. *I was top of my class in Quantico, ranked in the top five in intelligence training and broke the record for fastest time running the eight-mile Hell Run.*

But none of that mattered to her parents, which was why Poppy hadn't bothered.

A sigh escaped her parted lips as she roused herself from that terrible memory. Moving away from DC, leaving behind everything she'd ever known, had been her only choice.

Facing Shaine after their breakup would've been a torture she wasn't up to and having to listen to her parents berate her for her choices would've been the straw that broke her.

Since moving to LA, her relationship with her parents remained stilted. She made obligatory phone calls now and then just to check in, but for the most part Poppy had cut ties.

It'd been easier that way.

She liked to think that it was easier for her parents, too. A kindness.

Now they no longer had to lament the fact that their only daughter had become a "ballbusting man-hater" as her father liked to put it, and her mother didn't have to hide her head in shame when her nosy, gossipy nurse friends pestered her for why Poppy hadn't married or had kids by now.

For cripes' sake, they weren't living in the '50s.

But you'd never know it from the way her parents were acting.

The truth was, she could probably forgive her parents for their ignorant thinking, but she could never forgive Shaine for his.

Up until this moment, Poppy had managed to shove Shaine and everything that came with the memory of their time together into the deepest, darkest, most remote part of her brain.

But that all changed the minute he was assigned to her case.

And yes, it was *her* case.

El Escorpion was a DEA target and the FBI was assisting, as far as Poppy was concerned.

Maybe she did have something to prove, but one thing she knew for certain—Poppy wasn't going to let anything, or anyone, get in her way of closing this case.

Not even Shaine Kelly.

Shaine walked into the slick, upscale strip bar Lit, where he and Poppy were supposed to be embedded, and observed the crowd, his body loose but his observation skills sharp.

The blast of cool air was a welcome respite from the sticky Miami heat, but the place was crowded with half-dressed people with banging bodies. The bar should've been named Sin because that's what oozed from the walls.

He grinned suggestively at hot women, allowing his gaze to linger as if he wanted to imagine what it would be like to run his hands up and down those smoking curves, but actually, he was simply taking in the scene, gauging who may or may not be someone he needed to put on his radar.

Shaine's gaze snagged on the raised platform where the dancers were dominating the floor, and he realized with a grim start that some of the girls were topless. And while he enjoyed the view, he knew that Poppy was going to be up on that stage and he didn't like that idea at all.

Suck it up.

Poppy wasn't anything to him. Just another agent undercover.

He shouldn't care if she was gyrating on a pole as naked as the day she was born, as long as she was doing her job.

He'd have to forget about all the times that lithe body

had been pressed against his, her high breasts pushed into his face as they did things that were probably illegal in some states.

Sweat popped along his hairline and he swore under his breath at how easily he was breaking character the moment something involving Poppy entered into his brain.

Nice way to get yourself killed, hotshot.

Get over it. Poppy was old news.

This case could catapult his career and he aimed to make that happen.

Plus, on a personal note, he hated drug dealers.

Scum of the earth getting fat on the misery of others.

Shaine approached the bar, needing a drink for multiple reasons, but the biggest being his need to scope out Angelo Costa.

Angelo, the man in charge of the bar, looked as slick as everything else in the place. Dark hair, darker eyes, and if it weren't for the hard glint in his eyes, one could almost call him pretty.

Shaine knew right away that if he was going to get into the inner circle, getting tight with Angelo was going to be the key.

Depositing himself casually at the bar, he ordered a beer and then swiveled back around to survey the crowd.

Angelo delivered the beer with a comment. "You new to the area? I haven't seen you around."

He was assessing Shaine as much as Shaine was assessing Angelo. It was a game—a game Shaine knew well.

A thrill raced his spine.

This was the exciting part. And it was the most dangerous.

If everything was going to fall to shit, it would fall to shit right then and there.

Shaine grinned as he swept up his beer for a swig. "You could say that. But you're going to see a lot more of me. I'm your new bartender." He extended his hand for a quick shake. "The name's Rocco Pacheco. This place always jumping?"

Angelo shrugged. "What can I say, it's a smokin' club. So you're the new hire. Gotta say we don't usually hire sight unseen. But you come with a hot résumé. Not many people leave Grind. What gives?"

"Let's just say the owner and I had a difference in opinion."

"Yeah?"

"Yeah. He thought I should stop banging his wife. I disagreed."

Angelo laughed, shaking his head. "Ohh, you brave. Or stupid. Was she worth it?"

"I don't do anything that's not worth my time."

"All right, yeah, yeah, I feel you. But the question is, do you learn from your mistakes?"

"Are you asking am I going to sleep with the boss's wife? Then, yeah, I've learned my lesson."

Angelo seemed amused. "Sounds like you'll fit right in. So before you left Grind, what brought you to Miami?"

"You're looking at it. I like my women fast, my liquor expensive and a beautiful beach on which to nurse my hangover. Miami seemed the perfect place."

"Then you did come to the right place. But if you have a taste for expensive liquor, what's with the cheap beer?"

"I said I liked expensive liquor, I didn't say I could afford it. At least not yet."

"I like your style, kid. I think you'll fit in real well."

So far so good. But it could all be smoke and mirrors. If Lit was, in fact, the hub where El Escorpion was peddling Bliss, chances were Angelo was involved. And if that was the case, it was imperative that Shaine get in tight with the man.

"So where's the action?" Shaine asked, appearing hungry and horny. "I'm ready for a good time."

"I doubt you need my help. Just flash those pearly whites and you'll be glommed by women looking to put their stamp on you," Angelo said with an enigmatic smile.

"Yeah sure, but you seem the kind of guy who would know the real scene."

"Maybe. What did you have in mind?"

"Anyone I should steer clear of? Not looking for a wife, just a good time, if you know what I mean."

"In that case—" Angelo leaned forward with a conspiratorial glance toward a sexy redhead who'd just taken the stage "—you might want to give Raquel a pass. She's trouble, if you know what I mean."

"Yeah?"

"Screw her once and she'll start picking out rings."

"Damn, thanks for that." He pretended to shudder, then added, "That's a shame. She looks like a hot piece of ass."

"Oh, she is, for sure," Angelo remarked as if he knew from experience just how she could set the sheets on fire. "But you play, you pay. Takes weeks to brush that Stage 3 clinger off your junk."

"Good to know."

Just then, a sassy brunette, wearing not much more than a thong sliding up her near perfect ass and a matching bikini top that was barely two tiny triangles covering her nipples, sidled up to the bar with a blinding smile for Angelo.

"Hey, baby, I need a drink, I'm parched. That last set was brutal." Then she slid her gaze over to Shaine, bold and interested. "And who are you?"

Angelo answered for him. "Down, girl. Brandi, this is Rocco Pacheco, our new bartender."

"So you're replacing Tommy?" Brandi asked. Shaine just shrugged as if he couldn't care less who he was replacing. "Hmm, big shoes to fill. Everyone liked Tommy. Well, everyone except Angelo."

"The guy was a prick," Angelo said with a small smirk. "And he didn't seem to know his place."

"You were just jealous," Brandi replied, still watching Shaine, her gaze as probing as Angelo's, except Brandi's stare lingered just a little too long on the areas that interested her more.

Angelo pushed a blue drink Brandi's way and she snatched it up, tossing an inviting smile at Shaine before walking away.

"Watch out, she'll eat your heart for breakfast," Angelo warned with a chuckle, but his gaze never left Brandi's swaying ass as she disappeared backstage. "But she's a wild ride."

"So what's the story with that one?" Shaine asked.

Angelo poured a shot of premium vodka and set it in front of Shaine. "The story is, that one is mine."

Shaine chuckled and downed the vodka shot. "Duly noted. Anyone else you got dibs on?"

"Just that one. The rest are fair game."

"Thanks for the info." Shaine pushed away from the bar with his beer in hand. "Until tomorrow night, then."

"Happy hunting," Angelo called out as Shaine melted into the crowd.

Chapter 5

Poppy walked backstage at Lit, taking a quick note how every eye was on her, openly judging with barely restrained mistrust and hostility.

For a stripper, a new girl was competition.

Poppy saw an empty dressing table and began to drop her duffel, but a redhead jumped in front of her with a dirty look.

"Keep walking, scrub."

"Sorry, I didn't realize it was taken."

"You don't know sorry yet but you will."

Poppy could break this redhead, but could Laci Langford, a small-town Connecticut girl?

Probably not.

Poppy refrained from engaging the hostile redhead and kept walking, finding a dresser in the corner of the brightly lit, slightly alcohol-soaked dressing room and plopped down her bag.

She didn't have to wait long before someone Poppy assumed was the manager came up, a woman who looked impossibly perfect with a tight, honed body, long dark hair and big, perky breasts that looked too amazing to be real but too soft to be fake.

"You're the new girl, I'm assuming?"

"And who are you?"

"Your only friend so lose the attitude," the brunette returned. "Look, it's real simple. You might've been hired by the boss or maybe you're blowing the owner and you think that you've got some kind of safety net, but the fact is we run this bar and if you piss us off, you're out of here. Get it?"

Poppy knew there was a hierarchy in strip clubs, and judging by this woman's stance she was looking at the ringleader, or at the very least the one the other dancers respected. So it would behoove her to be nice.

"Sorry, I didn't mean to be rude. I could use a friend," Poppy said, trying to make amends. "My name's Laci."

"Brandi," she replied, sliding her behind on Poppy's dressing table, eyeing Poppy openly. "So, you have that fresh-off-the-bus look. Guys love that. Some will even try to *save* you. If you play it right, you could make a mint off those ones."

Poppy nodded as if she appreciated the advice. "So how does this work? How much does the house take?"

"You pay thirty dollars to the house for the privilege of dancing, and then whatever tips you make the house mom takes 20 percent. The rest is yours."

"And who is the house mom?"

"That would be Big Jane," Brandi said, pointing to the older lady, who was maybe forty, talking to a short busty blonde. "She's a bitch but she keeps the really insistent guys off us because no one messes with Big Jane."

"Is that a problem here?"

Brandi leveled a cynical look Poppy's way. "Honey, you dance topless for a bunch of men with too much money and a sense of entitlement. What do you think?"

"So I should maybe be real nice to Big Jane?"

"If you're smart."

"Thanks for the tip."

Finished with the blonde, Big Jane found her way to them and Brandi took that as her cue to leave.

"Brandi tell you how things work around here?"

"Yes," Poppy answered, taking in every detail about the older woman. Probably a former stripper, but hard living had taken its toll. Little pockets of jiggly flesh softened her middle and her jowls, but otherwise she seemed in decent shape.

Not dancing shape, though.

Big Jane tossed a tiny sequined outfit to Poppy and said, "The sides have Velcro so it'll come apart easily enough. But make them work for it before you show off your goods. Depending on your performance, we'll see if you're good enough to become a Lit regular."

Unlike Shaine, who had a secure position as a bartender, she had to work to keep hers. Why should this be any different than anything else in her life?

Poppy smiled with feigned confidence. "Don't give away my spot. I'm coming back."

"We'll see."

Big Jane walked off, leaving Poppy to figure out how she was going to wow a crowd that was accustomed to seasoned exotic dancers when her talent had been in classical training.

Somehow she doubted the patrons were interested in seeing her arabesque.

Poppy managed to shimmy into the tiny dress, the sharp sequins scraping her skin as she pulled it up over her hips and over her breasts. It clung like a second skin but the Velcro held.

A bubbly blonde bounced over to her, bright smiles and brilliant blue eyes, looking all of sixteen, which immediately made Poppy want to run a background check to ensure a fake ID wasn't in play, but she squelched the concern.

"You're so pretty," the girl gushed with unabashed honesty. "I mean, your skin is like perfect. What's your secret?"

"Good genes I guess," she answered. "What's your name?"

"I'm Capri. Nice to meet you," she chirped with a sweet smile. "And you are?"

"Laci."

"I love that name. I knew a Laci when I was in high school and she was the prettiest girl in school. I wonder if all girls named Laci are just naturally destined to be gorgeous."

"Oh, God, shut up already," the redhead muttered, rolling her eyes as she stalked past them. "Your set is next and if you get in my way, I'll shove you off the stage."

Capri scowled but otherwise didn't retaliate, waiting until the redhead had left to talk again. "Ugh, that's Raquel. She's a bitch. Try to ignore her, though. She's mean to everyone. Well, everyone except Big Jane, 'cause Big Jane would knock her head off."

Capri was silly and seemed completely oblivious to anything beyond the sparkle on her sequins, which made her a safe harbor for Poppy. Maybe the witless Capri could unwittingly give her information.

"You're so sweet," Poppy said, smiling. "Thank you. New city, new job, I'm a little out of my element. I came to Miami for school but you know how that goes… Money is tight so I heard dancing at the right club could solve my tuition problem."

"You can make a ton of money if you know what you're doing," Capri answered, adding with a giggle, "But I'd never spend all that hard-earned cash on school when there are so many other things you can spend it on like nice clothes, sparkly things and fast cars, you know?"

"Tempting," Poppy said, smiling. "But for now, I'd just like to graduate college without a ton of debt."

Capri shrugged, bored. "To each his own."

Poppy realized talking about aspirations wasn't going to draw the girl to her, so she switched tracks.

"This place is amazing. So cutting-edge. I can't believe I got in."

Capri's eyes lit up, happy to talk about something she cared about.

"Lit is one of the best clubs I've ever worked for."

"Yeah? How many clubs have you worked for?" Poppy couldn't help her curiosity. "I mean, you look so young."

"Age is just a number, right?" Capri giggled. "I mean, it's experience that matters."

Poppy withheld the cringe. "Yeah, I guess so."

"Anyway, yeah, Lit is the best. I worked my butt off to get into Lit. You don't even want to know what I had to do to earn a spot."

Poppy ignored the little voice in her head that told her to dig deeper into Capri's backstory. She couldn't stand the thought of a young girl selling herself because she didn't know any better, but she wasn't here to save anyone. Not even exploited teens who didn't have the sense God gave a goose to know they were headed down a dark path.

"I'm so nervous," Poppy admitted. That part wasn't acting. Her hands were shaking. "I wish I had a drink before hitting the stage."

"If you're real nice to Angelo, he'll take care of you," Capri said. "He's a sweetie. And so cute. But watch out because Brandi is a jealous bitch if she thinks you're moving in on her man. Geesh, you'd think she owns the guy or something."

"So Brandi and Angelo have a thing?"

"Yeah, I guess so. But can you keep a secret?" Capri leaned forward with an excited gleam in her eye. When Poppy nodded, Capri shared, "Angelo likes me, too. He says he's going to take care of me, introduce me to the right people."

"And how exactly would he do that?"

"By introducing me to a sugar daddy, of course, silly," Capri said with a giggle. "The amount of money that comes through these doors is obscene. You'll see. Maybe if you're lucky, you'll catch your own sugar daddy."

Good lord, she hoped not.

"I mean, I have my regular and he's pretty nice," Capri continued, playing with a sequin on her tight body suit. "But a girl needs to spread her wings, see what else is out there, you know?"

"Is he your boyfriend?" Poppy asked.

"God no. He's not the boyfriend type," Capri answered with a laugh as if the idea were absurd. "Actually, he's... let's just say, he likes what he likes and he doesn't mind paying for it. But he's superrich. I'm talking loaded and he's very generous when he's pleased."

The girl had just admitted to prostituting herself. Poppy tried not to fixate on that point. Busting people for underage prostitution was not their focus.

"Are you sure that's safe?" Poppy couldn't help but ask.

"You sound like an old lady," Capri said, giggling. "Besides, he doesn't ask for too kinky of stuff. It's like a date but instead of dinner and a movie…you get a fat wad of cash. Can't beat that, right?"

Poppy nodded as if she agreed, but inside she was horrified. Capri was too young for this.

"Hey, maybe after we get to know each other, I can introduce you. My friend is always looking for new playmates."

"Thanks," Poppy said, forcing a bright smile for Capri's benefit, but inside she was stunned at how cavalier Capri was about selling her body.

This was a foreign world and Poppy was feeling the cultural differences.

"No problem," Capri said with a sweet smile as if she'd just offered to swap banana bread recipes instead of sharing sexual contacts. "There's something about you that I like. I hope you stick around. Good luck with your set."

Poppy murmured her thanks and watched as Capri returned to her vanity to touch up her makeup.

Heaven help her. When this was all finished, Poppy was going to find a way to help Capri see that there was a different life out there waiting for her to grab on to it.

Of course, Poppy knew that people who didn't want help didn't appreciate the effort others took on their behalf, but Poppy didn't care. Capri needed something better than what she was doing.

Whether she knew it or not.

Poppy swallowed as Big Jane hollered for Capri, who then hurried off to start her set, leaving Poppy to try to figure out how she was going to hold on to her position when she didn't have a clue as to what she was doing.

You're in over your head, Shaine's voice intruded in her thoughts, and her gaze narrowed.

Like hell she was.

Moving backstage, she watched Raquel as she finished her set and then Capri danced onto the platform. The girl could move and she could work a crowd.

Pushing aside the concern that Capri might be younger than she let on, Poppy took mental notes, memorizing every move and grind that seemed to garner more attention from the patrons so that by the time it was her turn, she'd have an idea of what to do.

And now taking the stage, a sweet treat, a country girl from Connecticut, Lovely Laci!

Poppy emerged from the curtain, her eyes blinded by the neon lights until they adjusted, and then, of all people, the first person to make eye contact was Shaine.

For a moment she froze, her lungs squeezing with panic, but her desire to win this case was bigger than her fear.

Stop being a pussy. Get the job done.

Any way possible.

Deliberately holding Shaine's gaze, she slowly gyrated onto the pole, remembering a time when being sexy for Shaine Kelly had been natural.

The rest of the crowd disappeared and it was just Shaine and her.

And when she ripped her tiny dress off, she could've sworn Shaine stopped breathing.

Just like that…Poppy was back on track.

* * *

"Hot damn," Angelo murmured as he rested his elbows on the bar during Poppy's set. "The new girl is a smoke bomb."

Shaine forced a casual grin but shrugged. "Not bad. I've seen better."

The words actually felt stuck in his mouth, but Angelo didn't seem to notice as he was too busy staring at Poppy.

Close your damn mouth, you prick.

Horny patrons were throwing their paychecks at Poppy and she was eating it up, dancing as if she'd been born to it.

A tiny blonde with giant breasts popped up to the bar, practically purring at Angelo. "Can I get something to drink?"

"Sure, babe. What do you want?" Angelo asked, distracted, still watching Poppy.

The girl tracked Angelo's gaze and then giggled. "That's Laci. Isn't she pretty? I think she's really nice, too."

Shaine nudged Angelo as if fishing for an introduction, but actually he needed to know all the players coming and going through Lit, and at this point all the dancers were suspect. "Who's your cute friend?"

"Oh, sorry man, this is my girl, Capri. Capri, meet the new bartender, Rocco."

Capri exaggerated the hard *C* with a suggestive look. "Rocco? That's a hot name." Then she giggled again before returning to Angelo with a soft pout. "Brandi is being a royal bitch again. Can you please tell her to be nice?"

"I'll see what I can do," Angelo said, his gaze dipping to Capri's breasts as he grinned. "I liked your set. Good job, sweetheart."

"Thank you, baby."

Angelo looked to Shaine. "Hey, can you hold down the bar for a minute? I've got some business to take care of."

Shaine nodded and watched as Angelo draped his arm around Capri and led her off to the back office.

I wonder if Brandi knows that her guy is shagging Capri, too?

He made a mental note to poke around and ask some questions, maybe even play some head games to see what got put into motion.

Sometimes stirring the pot uncovered interesting ingredients.

Poppy's set ended and Shaine refused to let his stare gravitate toward her. But damn it, his eyes didn't seem to want to obey. Against his better judgment, he caught an eyeful of Poppy's strong body and succulent breasts, immediately hating that men were practically drooling on the stage, calling out her name and catcalling.

Poppy scooped up the cash being thrown at her and then walked with sass off the stage.

The redhead, Raquel, approached the bar. "Whiskey sour," she said, watching him with interest as Shaine made her drink. "What's your name?"

"Rocco."

"Nice to meet you Rocco… I'm Raquel."

"Pleasure."

"We'll see."

He arched his brow with feigned interest. "Oh?"

She smiled, revealing slightly crooked teeth. "Only if you're lucky."

Shaine chuckled. "If I were a smart man I'd stop right now, but I've never been accused of being overly smart."

"Dumb and cute…just the way I like them."

Shaine pushed her whiskey sour toward her, then leaned forward, using every bit of his charm to get what he wanted.

"So, you seem like a woman who knows what's going on… Tell me, who really runs this joint? Do the owners ever pop in?"

"Stick around and you'll find out," Raquel said, grabbing her drink and sauntering off, leaving him with an unobstructed view of her generous ass and the tramp stamp etched along her lower back of a scorpion.

Chapter 6

Poppy's legs ached from the workout on the dance platform, but the fat wad of cash in her purse felt pretty good, even if she was required to log the cash into evidence.

She was loath to admit it, but knowing Shaine had been watching her dance had given her that boost of adrenaline that'd put her back into character.

Thank God her realization was between her and the Almighty.

Shaine was already insufferable; knowing she'd needed him would make him unbearable.

She kicked off her shoes and clicked on the light, going to check her perimeter cameras. The sound of Shaine entering his own apartment made her painfully aware of how close they were, but still so apart.

A few moments later, the adjoining door opened and she had to bite back sharp words, reminding herself that they were on a case together.

"I have some intel that might be useful," Shaine said without preamble. "That young girl, Capri, is either sleeping with Angelo or she's moving product for him. And Raquel has a scorpion tattoo on her lower back, which doesn't seem like a coincidence."

"She's probably sleeping with him," Poppy said, worrying her bottom lip. She hated the idea, still troubled by how young Capri seemed. "But I'll check it out. What do you think about Angelo?"

"I think he's smart. He's not going to slip up easily."

"So you think he's involved with our target?"

"My gut says so."

"Too bad we can't use your gut to get a search warrant."

"What did you learn backstage?"

Shaine was all business. His gaze didn't flicker or falter at the topic of her stripping, but her cheeks felt unaccountably warm as she began to share her intel.

"Big Jane runs the girls backstage. She seems to keep the girls safe from overeager patrons, and she takes a cut of their earnings," Poppy said. "Raquel is an angry person with a chip on her shoulder. I don't know if there's drama between Raquel and the rest of the girls or if she's just like that naturally, but she's not very friendly. So I doubt it's going to be easy to get any information out of her. Capri is sweet and doesn't seem to realize when she should keep her mouth shut."

"You ought to friend her. She's your ticket in."

"I know that," Poppy retorted, irritated that Shaine was telling her how to run her end of the investigation. "I'm already working on that angle."

"Good."

"What about you? How are you doing getting tight with Angelo?"

"It's a work in progress. He's not just going to let me in after a few 'bro' moments. I have to earn his trust."

"And how do you plan to do that?"

"I'll play it by ear."

"Don't you think it's a good idea to share your game plan with the people who are involved?"

"You stick to your plan, I'll stick to mine. We're not supposed to know each other so it doesn't make sense to share every detail with you. If by some chance someone starts to get suspicious, plausible deniability is your friend."

He was schooling her and she hated it. "Of course, I realize that. I'm just saying, I didn't want to inadvertently step on your plan while making my own."

"Don't worry about me."

"I'm not," she replied coolly. "My concern is for the investigation. You're not the only one thinking of their résumé with this case."

"Of that I have no doubt," he said wryly. "Ambition is your middle name."

Poppy paused, wondering where that came from. "Which means?"

"You're so damn sensitive," Shaine said, shaking his head as if he realized nothing that came out of his mouth wouldn't set her off. "It doesn't mean anything. It was never a secret that you wanted to climb the ladder—and judging by how quickly you managed to put yourself on a major undercover case, I'd say you're well on your way."

It was true. She'd been tireless in her pursuit up the chain. She'd taken every case she could get her hands on, just to prove that she had what it took to close cases.

Her superior had remarked often that if the DEA had ten more agents like Poppy, they could take down every major drug dealer exporting illegal substances out of the country.

"Thanks," Poppy allowed, loosening up just a little. She supposed she could drop the chip on her shoulder for now. But that chip kept her focused, kept her mindful of the past and mistakes she didn't want to repeat.

So hold on to that chip for now, you'll need it to work beside Shaine.

"Look," Shaine started, as if needing to get something off his chest. "I know I didn't take it so well that you were on this case, but we have to put our differences aside to focus on the job."

"I don't have a problem with that. I have no interest in dredging up the past."

"Good. I won't lie to you and say that I didn't have reservations, but I trust that you know what you're doing and that you've learned a lot since your first case."

Poppy stiffened, hating that he'd brought up the case with Lachlan. But she supposed she couldn't expect him not to reference it when she'd nearly died because of a rookie mistake. "I always make it a point to learn from my mistakes," she said pointedly, leaving it at that. "But I appreciate your professionalism."

Shaine jerked a short nod. "Now that we've gotten that out of the way... I'm done for the night."

Poppy watched as Shaine let himself out, locking the door behind him on the other side, and she exhaled a shaky breath.

Would she always feel so uncentered around Shaine? Although leaving the FBI had been an act of self-preservation, it'd also allowed her to spread her wings without fearing the opinions of those who'd known her.

Such as her family.

And Shaine.

Their judgment weighed on her like a sack of boulders and it'd been a relief to walk away.

But her love for Shaine had been fierce—nearly as fierce as her drive.

Leaving him had been like ripping an arm off and tossing it into the grinder.

It wasn't just Shaine; it'd been losing his whole family that'd stung, as well. Shaine and his brothers, Sawyer and Silas, had become closer than her actual family. Unlike her own, Shaine's family had supported her career goals.

The phantom pain of her bullet wound always reminded her of what she'd given up for her ambitions.

Working with Shaine was going to be the biggest challenge of her life.

Not because he wasn't professional or a good agent… but because seeing him again ignited that tiny spark that refused to die no matter how much she smothered it under layers of denial and hurt.

And she couldn't chance that spark turning into something bigger.

Not again.

She'd rather take another bullet—it'd hurt a lot less.

Sprawled naked on the pristine sheets, Angelo lit a cigarette and drew on it with a lazy, sated inhale as Raquel pulled her clothes back on, her agitation raining on his good mood.

"What's your problem, baby-girl?" he asked, more curious than concerned. "You're ruining an otherwise good night with your 'tude."

Raquel, a hot number with a sizzling body, turned to glare at him with open accusation. "Did you hire her?"

she demanded, momentarily confusing Angelo. "The new girl. Did you hire her?"

"No," he answered, enjoying the flash of jealousy in her eyes. "But even if I did, what of it? She's hot and she dances well enough."

"I don't like her."

He chuckled. "Big surprise. You don't like anyone."

Raquel pulled her long red hair up into a messy ponytail with a sound of disgust as she walked into the adjoining bathroom. "There's something about her that rubs me the wrong way."

"You're paranoid." He stubbed out his cigarette and rose from the bed, admiring Raquel's body as he joined her in the bathroom, walking past her to piss. "And stop being such a bitch to Brandi. You make more problems when you mess with her and then I have to clean it up."

"Screw Brandi," Raquel shouted back, leaving the bathroom. "You said you were leaving her and yet, here you are, still meeting with me in secret. What gives? I'm tired of that bitch thinking she's got you wrapped around her finger."

"Baby, patience. I told you, there's a lot going on that you aren't aware of," he said, dropping back onto the bed. Did they have time for a quick bounce? Maybe he'd make time. Raquel was a wildcat in bed, but he'd have a helluva time explaining the scratches to Brandi.

Raquel returned to the bed, sullen and still unhappy. "I don't understand why you keep playing her like that. If you want to be with me, you ought to just man up and tell that bitch to get off your dick."

"What if I like the idea of two hot women fighting over me?" Angelo asked with a smart-ass smirk that was entirely genuine.

Raquel straddled him, nestling herself right up against his junk, but she twisted his nipple so hard he yelped. "I don't play well with others," she said sweetly as she released his nipple and kissed him hard before issuing an ultimatum. "Lose the bitch, or you lose me."

Angelo didn't like ultimatums. "Careful, baby-doll. Don't forget who you're dealing with."

"And the same goes to you," Raquel said, moving off him to grab her purse. "You're not the only one with options."

And then she left, closing the door with a hard slam that made Angelo want to jump up and jerk her back by her long hair to teach her some manners.

But that would have to wait. He had better plans.

He checked his watch and quickly cleaned up. Brandi was due to show up any minute.

The sound of a car pulling into the drive made him peer out the curtained window.

Brandi's silver Mercedes.

Damn, he liked to live dangerously. Chances were Brandi and Raquel had passed each other in the dark without even knowing it. He chuckled and returned to his bed, waiting for Brandi to bound up the stairs to his bedroom.

"Hey, baby," she said, kissing him as she began to strip. "Are you ready for me?"

"Always."

After sharing a deep kiss, he stopped to ask, "Baby, did you get that package for me?"

"Yes," she answered dutifully, rolling away to grab her purse. She withdrew a large manila package and handed it to him.

"Good girl," he said, pleased. He'd get a fat bonus for

delivering without incident. He reached over and grabbed Brandi by the back of the neck to kiss her roughly. Brandi liked to be dominated, and he didn't mind muscling her around. He tossed the package onto his dresser, then barked an order, "Now get your ass naked and get over here, woman."

Brandi laughed and did as she was told, stripping slowly, teasing him in the way he liked.

Whereas Raquel was all fire and brimstone, Brandi was classier, more refined.

He liked the differences in the two women.

And, in spite of what he told Raquel, he had no plans to turn either of them loose.

Playing both sides against the middle assured him a never-ending supply of quality ass in his bed.

At least for now.

But after a quick romp, something Raquel said came back to him and he thought to question Brandi.

"What do you think of the new girl?"

Brandi shrugged. "She's all right. Nothing special as far as I can tell. Just your basic small-town country girl who thought it would be cool to go to the big city."

"You think that's all there is to her?"

"Yeah? Why?"

He shrugged. "No reason. Just trying to get a feel for her."

"And why is that?"

He chucked her chin gently. "Hey, you know it's my job to make sure that everyone is playing nicely," he said, brushing a brief kiss across her lips. "So don't be getting something in your head that it's anything more than professional interest."

Brandi nodded but she said, "Are you sure? You wouldn't be messing around on me, right?"

"Of course not, baby. You're my number one girl." The lie tripped easily from his tongue, but there was a certain amount of truth to it, too. Brandi was the kind of girl he could potentially see a future with, whereas Raquel was just an exciting diversion.

Satisfied, Brandi settled against his chest. "She seems like a cool person. I mean, she has this slight edge to her, like she's holding back something, but when she went out on stage, she really went all out. I was kind of impressed."

"A natural," he mused. "How did the other girls take to her?"

"The usual. Raquel was a bitch and Capri was a chattering twit, fawning all over her with that little bubble-gum voice of hers, and Big Jane was no-nonsense. I didn't pay attention to anyone else." Brandi looked him in the eye. "And what about you? How's the new guy? He any good?"

"Yeah, he's decent. He said he worked for Grind. That's pretty impressive cred."

"I know someone who goes to Grind all the time. Want me to ask around if they know about him?"

"Yeah, baby, that's real smart."

Brandi snuggled in tighter and yawned, but before she could fall asleep, Angelo nudged her. "Time to go home, baby-girl. You know I can't sleep with anyone else in the bed."

Brandi groaned and sleepily rose to a sitting position with a pout. "But I'm so tired," she complained, rubbing her eyes. "Why can't I just stay?"

"Because I want our time together to be special and

something I look forward to. If we start living together…
that's a death sentence, baby."

She knew this wasn't an argument she would win and
she knew better than to push it. He slapped her ass as she
climbed from the bed and grudgingly dressed.

"That's my girl. Make sure you lock up when you leave."

"Sure," she mumbled and made her way downstairs.

He listened as she exited the house and then drove
away.

Grabbing his cell, he sent a quick text.

Product in hand. Party set.

Extremely satisfied with how the day had ended, he
fell asleep within minutes.

Chapter 7

Shaine tossed back the shot purchased for him and grinned with a wink directed at the cute coed who was trying to get his number.

Miami was a happening place with everything from drag queens to supermodels milling around. Everyone had the same agenda, and Shaine's goal was to circulate, so he happily flirted, charmed and lied his way around every female that came within two feet of him.

And he'd just hit the jackpot.

"There's a party over at the warehouse. Wanna come?"

"I don't know… What kind of party is it?" Shaine said with a shrug, playing hard to get. He knew just how to twist women into doing exactly what he wanted. Poppy had once called it a diabolical skill and he hadn't disagreed.

However, the one time he'd needed it to work, it'd blown up in his face.

Yeah, don't go there. Not now.

He pushed that particular memory away and refocused on the blonde in front of him.

"It's going to be epic. DJ Raven is spinning tracks. It's going to be off the hook."

"Yeah?"

"And who knows…you might get lucky," she said suggestively, leaning over the bar, giving Shaine a good, unobstructed view of her ample breasts.

"Tempting." He pushed a pen and napkin her way. "Write down the address."

She grabbed the pen and his hand, scribbling an address on his palm with girly loops and swirls before pressing a kiss to the center of his hand with a tiny dart of her tongue. "I hope to see you there. I'm Carly, by the way."

"Nice to meet you, Carly." He waited a beat, then said, "I'm Rocco."

"Yeah, I know."

That was interesting. "Have we met before?"

"No, but I've heard about you. Capri is a friend of mine. She said you're supercute."

"Did she?"

"But I have dibs," Carly said with a wink before melting into the crowd.

Angelo appeared from the back and Shaine asked if he knew about the warehouse.

"Yeah, it's a place where the college kids end up when they want to rave. It's usually an abandoned warehouse in the industrial district. Pretty wild. Usually everyone's high on Bliss or Molly. Great place to go if you want to get laid. Nearly everyone is down for some action."

He tried not to react, but asked with natural curiosity, "Bliss? What's that?"

"You've never tried Bliss? Oh, buddy, you're in for a treat. It's the best high there is. No pain, only gain."

"Sounds too good to be true. Does my dick fall off or something?"

"Only from overuse," Angelo wisecracked and Shaine grinned. "You in? I was planning to make a pit stop. See who's kicking it."

"Sounds like a cool place. You sure the cops ain't gonna bust it up? I can't afford a run-in. I already have a strike."

"Naw, you're good. Nothing to worry about."

Angelo didn't elaborate, nor did he share how he knew that the cops would leave them alone, but that made Shaine believe that whoever was on the take within the police department was probably on shift to help divert any calls.

"You in, brother?"

"Hell yes. I need to blow off some steam. Am I supposed to bring anything?"

"Just cash and your appetite for destruction and mayhem."

"Sounds like my kind of party."

Angelo grinned and drifted toward the end of the bar, leaving Shaine to process what'd just happened.

He knew Victoria and Marcus were listening on the other end, thanks to the discreet wire that looked like a diamond stud earring in his left ear.

Capri appeared with Poppy in tow, her perennially bubbly personality almost too sweet to handle.

"Laci, you have to meet Rocco. He's the cutest bartender ever," Capri gushed, winking at Shaine. "I've been telling Laci all about you."

"Flattered," Shaine replied with a casual flick of his gaze toward Poppy. It was imperative that no one suspected that they knew each other. He returned to Capri. "What kind of trouble are you up to tonight?"

"I don't find trouble, trouble finds me," Capri returned with a little-girl playfulness that was entirely too convincing. He shared Poppy's belief that Capri was younger than she claimed to be. "But tonight I'm heading to the warehouse. You coming? It's going to be epic."

"So I heard."

"What's the warehouse?" Poppy asked. "Is it another bar?"

"Nope. Invitation only, hottest party in town. And the best part is, the location changes to keep out the people who don't belong," Capri said.

That tidbit of information seemed useful. "Sounds like a bitch to coordinate," Shaine said.

Capri shrugged as if she never thought about the logistics, nor did she care. Curling her arm around Poppy's she begged, "Please say you'll come. It's so much fun."

"Yeah, why don't you come?" Shaine added with a predatory grin as if he liked what he saw.

Capri giggled. "See? Even the new guy thinks you ought to come."

Poppy laughed, playing along. "And if I do…"

Shaine's smile curved with promise. "You'll just have to show up and find out."

An undercurrent of something real flickered dangerously between them. Shaine's pulse raced as his breathing quickened.

"If you two hook up, can I watch? You guys are hot," Capri said, laughing. "Okay, it's settled. You're coming, right?"

"Sure," Poppy said with a flirty smile at Shaine. "I'm down."

"Perfect," Capri exclaimed, bouncing on her toes a little. "Okay, I have to get ready for my set. I'll see you after. We can ride together."

Shaine shared a final look with Poppy and then walked away with a small wave, as if he were hooked.

Of course, he didn't like the idea of Poppy going with him to the party, but he'd have to get over it.

Moreover, playing up a flirtation with Poppy could work in their favor. Angelo seemed to enjoy certain privileges with the strippers. He would follow Angelo's playbook.

He knew Poppy would do whatever it took to solidify her cover, even if it meant pretending that they were attracted to each other.

Was it an act?

Yeah, that was sort of the problem.

It wasn't an act. At least not on his part.

Poppy was still in his blood and his dreams.

Perhaps now wasn't the time to admit that when he fantasized, Poppy was the one stroking him, getting him off, not some porn star or supermodel.

That was his own shameful secret. One that he couldn't quite shake loose.

What could he say? Sex with Poppy had always been pretty hot. Why wouldn't he fantasize about hot sex?

Will you friggin' focus, already? Get your head out of the damn gutter.

Shaine wiped the bead of sweat dotting his hairline and forced a chuckle at his own ridiculous detour.

Detours like that could get a man killed.

Rookie mistake.

It'd only been a few days since becoming embedded in

the scene, but he was already catching the ebb and flow of the clientele through Lit.

Upscale, trendy and flashy, the clientele were millennials with plenty of cash, no sense of how precious life was and a general belief that they would live forever.

A perfect breeding ground for a drug dealer to peddle something dangerous such as Bliss.

And tonight he'd get a chance to see firsthand how the drug was being moved around.

Marcus, Victoria, Shaine and Poppy met at Poppy's apartment to debrief before heading out to the party.

"You're both equipped with state-of-the-art wires disguised as a necklace for Poppy and the earring for Shaine. These are undetectable and used by the CIA for clandestine operations, so they are the best money can buy," Victoria said, handing the necklace to Poppy so she could put it on.

"It's pretty, too," Poppy said as Marcus clasped it. "Added bonus."

"Only the best for this operation," Victoria said with a wry twist of her lips. "See what happens when a senator's daughter gets caught in the cross fire? The stranglehold on the budget suddenly loosens."

"True," Shaine agreed, and then he returned to business. "All right, so we're going to focus on the Bliss trail, find out who's distributing it and then follow the chain. Sooner or later, someone is going to slip up and we're going to be able to find out who El Escorpion is."

"Don't be overconfident," Poppy warned. "I've been doing my own snooping around and whoever this person is has layers of protection, which means they are serious about hiding their identity."

"Of course, but human nature is generally predictable. Someone is going to slip."

"They haven't yet."

She knew Shaine was being Shaine—confident, cocky, self-assured—but this case was bigger than either had ever worked, and Poppy didn't think those "Shaine" qualities were going to be helpful this time.

"All right, you two, settle down," Victoria said, flashing Shaine an irritated look, which could've been referencing either of them. But she left it a mystery by continuing, "Marcus and I will be monitoring the situation via our coms. If anything goes sidewise, we'll send in the cops to break it up."

"That's not going to work," Poppy said. "If the cops show up, they're going to know someone is planted on the inside." She shook her head, adamant. "No, we are going to have to be on our own for this one. We can't blow this opportunity to see how this operation works."

Shaine agreed, saying, "Poppy is right. We'll be fine. This is just a fact-seeking operation. There's no need to get twitchy."

Victoria and Marcus seemed to share a private concern. Poppy frowned. "What was that look?"

Marcus took point. "Look, we're a little worried that you two were invited too quickly to this ultrasecret party. Something doesn't feel right. I think you ought to sit this one out, make some excuse to see how they react."

"And if we never get another invite?" Shaine returned, echoing Poppy's fear.

"It could be a trap," Victoria said, shaking her head. "Think about it. You've been on the scene for three days and suddenly you've been invited to this inner circle party? Doesn't that smell like something rotten?"

Shaine tightened his lips as if unwilling to admit that maybe they were right but couldn't ignore what everyone was saying.

But Poppy didn't want to back down. This could be their only chance. "What are you doing? We're supposed to be elite agents and you're all acting like rookies."

"They have a point," Shaine said, freshly irritating Poppy. "Let's take a step back and see what happens."

"I can't believe this. A minute ago, you were all cocked ready to go and now you're backing down. What's going on?" An ugly thought came to her. She narrowed her gaze at Shaine. "Is this about me? You think I can't handle the heat? That's bullshit, Kelly. Utter bullshit."

"I didn't say that," Shaine returned hotly, but Poppy wasn't buying it now.

Marcus and Victoria didn't know about the history between Shaine and herself, and neither of them wanted to enlighten their partners, but damn, Shaine was making it difficult to handle things professionally.

"Nobody is saying that," Marcus said. "Stop wearing your feelings on your shirtsleeve and listen to reason. If you stop and think for just a minute, you'll agree that it was too easy. It was a test and you're about to blow it."

Poppy couldn't believe this. Everyone was turning on her. Her chest tightened with the urge to scream, but she held it back. Instead, turning to Shaine she said stiffly, "I disagree with the consensus, but since you have more experience in the field, I'll defer to your judgment."

God, the words felt like glass leaving her mouth, but at least she managed to get them out.

Shaine held her gaze for a moment and a shock of awareness coursed through her—an electrical current that sizzled down her nerve endings and jolted awake a fitfully sleeping giant—and she had to break contact to preserve the illusion that they had no history.

"Poppy is right," Shaine finally said, shocking her. "We might not get another chance to get into the inner circle. We have to take the risk that it's a trap and go for it."

Poppy blinked back the sudden wash of emotion and managed to jerk a short nod of gratitude, then turned to Victoria and Marcus who were shaking their heads, resigned to going through with it.

"Fine," Marcus said. "Good luck. Don't get your ass killed trying to be a hero."

Victoria said to Shaine, "Same goes for you."

Poppy's cell jangled to life. "It's Capri. We're riding together."

Shaine nodded. "Stay sharp. Capri may look young, but she's got something going on with Angelo, which makes her a suspect."

Poppy accepted that advice, though she hated to think that Capri was bad. She knew that was dangerous thinking, but she had a soft spot for the kid and desperately wanted to put her on the right path when this was all said and done.

Grabbing her purse, Poppy exited the apartment, leaving behind the team.

Shaine would follow fifteen minutes later in his own car.

Capri honked and waved from a sleek convertible Mercedes and Poppy cringed internally. The kid was in deep if she was buying sports cars for herself or, worse, allowing someone else to buy her expensive cars.

"Hot ride," Poppy said with appropriate envy, admiring the black leather interior. "Damn, girl, that's a lot of lap dances."

Capri giggled as Poppy buckled up, saying, "Only if you're giving the right people private shows."

Poppy swallowed her trepidation and smiled encouragingly. "You go, girl."

Time to put on the game face.

Chapter 8

It was difficult to listen to your gut when your heart was saying something different. He knew Poppy had something to prove.

And if he were on his own, he would have ignored the warning in his gut saying that it could be a trap, because when he was on his own he only had to worry about himself.

The fact that he hesitated meant that he was thinking of Poppy in ways that he shouldn't, which was why he decided to go through with attending the party.

If they were willing to back down at the slightest hint of danger, they had no business going undercover.

That was what the logical side of his brain told him.

But logic wasn't running the show right now.

He knew this because all he could think about was that Poppy was fifteen minutes ahead of him, possibly driving straight into a trap.

How was he supposed to be okay with that?

The part that was trying to create distance was quick to remind him that they were no longer dating, and it wasn't his responsibility to care about her on a personal level. But the other part of him argued that he would care about any agent's safety.

Regardless of any prior history between them.

It wasn't as if he would willingly watch another agent walk into a trap.

And this was why his head was all messed up.

Was he concerned because she was a fellow agent or was he concerned because he and Poppy had shared time together?

Okay, let's be honest. It wasn't just time—he'd loved her.

Loved her with every ounce of his being. There was no one else he'd ever felt that way about and letting her go had been the hardest thing he'd ever done.

Damn it, just focus on the case.

The growing frustration made it hard to think straight.

Maybe he should've backed out of this assignment. Maybe he was the one who should've known better.

Maybe he was worried that if he had backed off, a less experienced agent would've taken his place, there-fore putting Poppy in more danger.

As much as he wanted to put the past where it be-longed, their history remained between them, unresolved.

No closure.

And how could they have closure? She'd just split. One big fight and the next day she was gone.

Personally, he thought that'd been pretty chickenshit. And he'd never had the opportunity to tell her exactly that.

What was the point? It wasn't as if she would come back.

Besides, he'd been so angry and hurt, he probably would've made things worse.

That was the thing about relationships ending, they were filled with crappy situations, where there was no winning, only losing.

But most people didn't end up having to work with their ex-partners.

Victoria walked him to the door, apprehension in her expression. "Why are you going against your instincts? I've never known you to ignore your gut."

"This isn't only my case. Agent Jones is an experienced agent in her own right. I was told to play nice, to listen to others. I'm trying to do that."

"There's a time and a place. Don't go getting yourself killed just to prove a point."

"I have no intentions of doing that," he assured his partner. "Like I said, this is me playing nice."

"Yeah, well, screw that if the other agent is TSTL."

"Jones isn't Too Stupid To Live." Shaine laughed to cover his discomfort. He shouldn't be the least bit tweaked over Victoria throwing shade on Poppy. If it were anyone else, he'd laugh and trade barbs.

"Oh, c'mon. You and I both know she's not cut out for this kind of work. Frankly, I'd worry that her dumb ass would end up getting me killed."

He had to stuff down the overwhelming urge to continue to defend Poppy and that meant he needed to split.

"Stay sharp," he said as he walked out the door, ending the conversation.

"Stay smart," Victoria called out, and he waved in the air to indicate he'd heard her.

That's all he had to say.

His mouth was clearly at odds with his brain.

Time to find out how the kids were partying these days.

Poppy tried not to grip the seat with clawed fingers, but Capri drove like a bat out of hell.

"I love to drive fast," Capri chirped as she took a turn nearly on two wheels. "Makes me feel alive."

"Yeah, well, I'd like to arrive alive, so can you slow down before I crap myself?" Poppy said, trying to sound only mildly alarmed instead of truly terrified. Kids suffered from an overblown belief in their own immortality, but Poppy had seen one too many dead kids on the morgue slab to drive the point home that humans were unbelievably fragile.

"Sorry." Capri giggled, easing up on the throttle. "I didn't mean to freak you out."

"It's okay. My mom always said I was an old woman in a young person's body," she lied. "My sense of adventure isn't quite as wild as yours."

"That's okay, I like you, anyway."

"Thanks, I like you, too," Poppy said with an easy smile, but she was taking note of every turn they made. "So, nice ride. I'm so jealous."

"I just got it. I'm still getting used to it," Capri shared. "I mean, it drives so different than my last car that I keep screeching tires now and then."

"Yeah? What was your last car?"

"A Lexus."

Oh. She'd been hoping that Capri was going to say something sensible like a Honda or Toyota, like most kids her age.

"Okay, I have to ask… How'd you afford a car like this? Dancing at the club doesn't pay that good, does it?"

"For the right people, it does," Capri answered but didn't elaborate. The kid was young and seemingly airheaded, but she knew enough to keep some cards close to her vest. That in and of itself sent a warning bell ringing in Poppy's head.

Please don't be involved, Poppy thought to herself almost desperately. She didn't want to be the one who had to put Capri away.

"Let me guess…your regular?"

"Bingo."

"What's his name?"

"I can't tell you that, silly," Capri admonished. "But I can tell you he's very important."

"Politician?"

Capri laughed. "Good try. I'm not saying nothing."

"Is it safe?"

Capri sent Poppy a quizzical look. "You sure worry a lot."

"Sorry. Can't help it. It's in my DNA."

"Can I give you some advice?" Capri said, flipping the switch. Poppy nodded slowly, curious. "Stay away from Raquel. She's a terrible person. If she even thinks you're trying to move in on her territory, she'll cut you faster than you can blink."

Poppy hid her revulsion with a smile.

"Speaking from experience?"

"Let's just say that I know someone who crossed Raquel and came out the loser."

"Yeah? Who?"

"It doesn't matter now. Just trust me when I say she's dangerous."

Capri's normally sunny disposition dimmed as if she were recalling something painful, but she broke the moment with a bright smile. "Enough about sad things. Time to party!"

Poppy knew she wasn't going to get more out of Capri at that point because her head was already elsewhere.

They headed into an industrial park that looked abandoned, but it could've just been the darkness that made everything look creepy, and the hairs on her neck began to prickle.

Had Marcus and Victoria been right? Was this a trap and sweet Capri was a duplicitous killer?

She snuck a glance at Capri as she sang loudly at the top of her lungs to some rap song, totally in her own world, and Poppy had a hard time believing that Capri was anything but a dumb kid playing an adult's game.

But that could just be wishful thinking, too. She couldn't afford to go soft on anyone. Not even the cute and bubbly Capri.

"We're here," Capri announced, shutting off the car and climbing out. "C'mon, the party has already started. We're not sleeping tonight!"

Poppy had no choice but to follow after Capri as she bounded toward a looming building. The faint sound of music became louder as they got closer.

Capri knocked on a solid metal door toward the back of the building and a large, criminal type opened up. The handlebar mustache was disturbing enough, but the freakish muscles roping his arms weren't natural in the least.

"Hi, Bear," Capri said with a sunny smile. "We're here to party!"

"Who's she?"

"A friend," Capri answered, lifting up on her toes to whisper something in the man's ear. Judging by the way the man allowed them to pass, whatever Capri said must've been the magic words. Capri slipped her hand through Poppy's and led her inside the cavernous building.

"What was that all about?" Poppy asked. "What did you say to him?"

"Don't worry about it. Bear is a softy deep down. He just looks scary."

"That's for sure," Poppy murmured, glancing back at the hulking guard. "Does he eat small kids for breakfast?"

"You're funny." Capri laughed, shaking her head as if Poppy said the weirdest things. "Okay, let's find DJ Raven and get this party started."

Poppy followed Capri through the thick crowd of people wearing neon paint that glowed in the black light streaming in from the high ceilings as they danced to the throbbing music.

Capri waved at the DJ, lost in his own world, one ear covered with the headphones while the other ear was free, his fingers working in time to the beat. "That's Raven," she said to Poppy with a happy squeal. "He's so cool."

Although Capri identified him as male, DJ Raven could've been male or female. He had that androgynous look that was pretty and handsome at the same time. Plus, the name? Raven? Maybe his name should've been Peacock judging by the wild array of bright colors in his long hair.

"Hi, Raven," Capri said, waving again to catch his attention. Raven looked up and Poppy startled at the pale contact lens bleaching out the natural color of the irises.

"This is my friend Laci. I want to show her a good time. Got anything that could help?"

Poppy perked up, tensing imperceptibly while holding the easy smile. So DJ Raven was one of the suppliers. Capri lifted on her toes to accept a tiny package from Raven and then bounced away in time to the music.

"C'mon," Capri shouted above the din, pointing as she said, "Bathroom."

Poppy nodded and followed Capri, taking a quick sweep of the room, hoping to catch a glimpse of Shaine. But it was too dark and the writhing knot of people was too dense.

She had no choice but to follow Capri and hope for the best.

Chapter 9

Shaine knocked on the metal door and when he was greeted by a giant, stone-faced man, he wondered if he was about to get his ass stomped into the concrete.

"Private party."

"I was invited."

"By who?"

Technically, he was invited by the hot chick at the bar but he used Angelo instead.

"Angelo."

The man slowly stepped aside, but continued to stare Shaine down as if hoping Shaine would do something stupid just so he could wipe the floor with him.

But Shaine wasn't stupid. He slipped past the man and into the party, immediately assaulted by a kaleidoscope of neon colors as people walked by in glow-in-the-dark body paint illuminated by the black lights.

Music—if you could call it that—was nearly a wall of sound that vibrated his insides, and he wondered if kids nowadays were deaf.

He scanned the crowd and caught a glimpse of Poppy being led into the bathroom by Capri, and he headed that way. He wanted to have eyes on Poppy in this place.

His instincts told him to stay sharp; anything could go south at any point and they had zero backup.

But before he could get too far, he was clapped around the shoulders and spun around to face Angelo, who was wearing a big-ass grin, and Brandi draped on his arm.

"You made it," Angelo exclaimed. "I'd almost given up hope that you were coming."

"I never miss a good time," Shaine responded with an easy smile. "Where's the bar?"

Angelo pointed. "That way, my friend. However," he added with a wink, "it's time for you to graduate to the big kid table."

"Yeah? Intrigued. Tell me more."

Angelo's wide grin was as much an invitation as a warning. "Come. I'll show you," he said, pulling away from Brandi to lead the way.

Shaine gave one final glance toward the bathroom where Poppy supposedly was, but had to trust that she could handle herself.

They walked up a short flight of stairs to what appeared to be an old office from when the building had once been occupied, and stepped inside.

Angelo closed the door and the prickles danced on the back of his neck when he saw Poppy standing there with Capri, waiting for them.

"Private party?" he drawled, trying to sound casu-

ally interested when he had a bad feeling about this little get-together.

Angelo dragged a metal chair over and straddled it,
resting his forearms on the back with a grin. "We haven't
had the opportunity to properly welcome you into the Lit
family and we're about to rectify that right now."

"Why does this sound like a hazing about to happen?"

"No worries," Angelo assured him. "You're going to
like this hazing."

Poppy cast an uncertain look toward Capri. "What's
going on?"

"We like you," Capri said as if that answered all questions. "And if you go through with this…we'll like you
even more because we'll know that we can trust you."

"What is this? High school. C'mon, I came for a good
time, not stupid games," Shaine retorted, hoping to put
an end to whatever was about to happen. True, if he was
alone, he'd go feetfirst into whatever shit was about to
go down, but he could practically feel Poppy's apprehension even though she was doing a decent job of hiding it.
"This is starting to feel like a drag."

But Poppy surprised him by stepping forward with a
shrug, saying, "Let's do this. I came for a good time. I'm
down for whatever. Just get on with it already."

Capri giggled. "I told you she was fun." Then she
popped from her perch on the cluttered table and disappeared for a moment, only to reappear with something
clenched in her fists. "Hands out," she instructed with an
impish smile that was half adult and half kid but all sorts
of messed up.

Poppy thrust her palm out, her chin set. Shaine had
no choice but to follow suit. If Poppy was going for it,
he would, too.

Capri dropped a tiny pink pill into each of their palms.

"Bottoms up," Angelo said with a grin.

Poppy didn't hesitate and threw the tiny pill back and washed it down with a swallow of beer. She looked to Shaine. "Your turn, big guy."

Ah, hell. He knew it was Bliss. Things were about to get sidewise.

"Let the good times roll," he murmured as he tossed it back.

Capri cheered while Brandi smirked, her dark eyes watching their every move.

She's the one to watch out for.

"So what was the point of all that?" Shaine asked, effecting a bored expression. "I'm no virgin to Molly."

"It's not Molly." Capri giggled. "Welcome to Bliss."

Confirmation.

"It's going to hit you fast," Angelo said, rising to bring Shaine and Poppy close. "You're our newest family members and we look out for our own. But we have to know you can hang. So this is your official job interview."

"Funny, I thought I already had the job," Shaine quipped.

"Naww, that was just the preliminary. This is the real deal. We're a special group here at Lit. It takes a special kind of person to fit in."

Poppy teased Shaine, "Afraid you might fail the job interview?"

"I never was one for tests," Shaine said, but he was already starting to feel different. His mouth began to taste like the Sahara. Well, that much was similar to Molly.

Shaine shoved his hand through his hair, impatient. "I need a beer. This shit's going to dry me out."

"First...we have to seal the deal," Capri said, looking to Poppy and Shaine with expectation.

"There's more?" Poppy asked.

Brandi stood by Angelo's side, her arms sliding around his waist. Angelo opened his arm for Capri to move in on the other side. He looked like a sheikh with his harem.

Shaine reacted with instinct and grabbed Poppy, pulling her straight to his mouth, kissing her deeply. Poppy's little startled moan was like sweet poison and he drank it up.

Their tongues tangled and Shaine squeezed her behind, drawing her tight and snug against his hardening length.

An onslaught of memories assaulted him as he fought to remain in control, but the drug was loosening his ability to think in a straight line, and he was bombarded with sensory pleasure.

It took Herculean strength to keep from bending Poppy over the nearest surface and burying himself inside her, no matter that they were in full view of an audience.

Hell, that made it even hotter.

Somehow Shaine managed to get a grip and slow his sensual attack, but they were both breathless when they broke apart.

He came to his senses to the sound of applause and squeals of laughter.

"That was so hot," Capri gushed, hooking her arm around Poppy's. "Now, let's party!"

Capri and Poppy were gone in a flash, and Shaine didn't have time to chase after them. It was all he could do to keep on his feet. A euphoric grin found his lips and he couldn't quite stop it from stretching his lips.

"This shit is legit," Shaine admitted, shaking his head like a dog. But he remained muddled in a fairy cloud of pink rainbows and happiness. No wonder this drug was quickly climbing the party scene.

"Brother, you have no idea," Angelo said, laughing. "Now, let's see if we can get you laid tonight. There's nothing like sex on Bliss!"

Shaine grinned as if he was down for that, but there was only one person he wanted naked in his bed and that was Poppy.

Poppy. All day, every day.

And he was rapidly forgetting why that was a terrible idea.

In fact, the more he thought about it, the more he was certain it needed to happen.

Poppy drifted on a cloud of sensation, moving her body in time to the beat that seemed to vibrate her bones. Everything felt amazing, everything was wonderful.

"This drug is incredible," she said, mostly to herself, but Capri caught it.

"Bliss will change your life," Capri said with great authority. "It's the new biggest thing. Bliss is going to change the world."

"It'll change the party scene, for sure," Poppy returned with a dreamy sigh. No wonder it was so addictive. Feeling this good shouldn't be a crime—it should be a right.

Snap out of it, a faint voice intruded on her happy thoughts, and she actually frowned as if she were responding to someone.

Capri tapped Poppy's forehead. "No frowning allowed. Frowning causes wrinkles and wrinkles make you look old and no one wants to pamper an old lady."

Ah, Capri and her endless quest of finding that perfect sugar daddy.

"Capri, you need bigger goals," Poppy said. "A rich man isn't going to solve all your problems."

"What problems? I love my life. But I love to shop, too."

"Yeah, but wouldn't you rather be in charge of your own money, instead of having to suck up to some old guy with lots of money?"

"Old guys with lots of money are my favorite and they're the easiest to catch. Perverted old men love girls like me."

Poppy would've winced but she didn't have the where-withal to summon the effort to be worried about that telling statement. Instead, Poppy shrugged and said, "To each her own. Just make sure you use protection, kid. None of those sugar daddies are looking to be a real daddy."

"Ha! As if I'd ruin this moneymaker by popping out kids," Capri scoffed as if Poppy was the one being naive. "Besides, I do have goals. And right now, my goal is to take home that cutie by the bar. Toodles."

And then she was gone, leaving Poppy all by herself amongst a crowd of doped up, highly primed, twenty-somethings who had a hive mind-set to *GET LAID*.

The worst part…she was tuned in to that message as well and she was struggling with her urge to get wild with the first person she saw or seek out Shaine.

Either decision seemed awesome and terrible at the same time.

As if summoned by her drug-addled secret thoughts, Shaine grabbed her hand and pulled her to him, moving those hips in a way that intensified the urge to get naked—with him.

"This stuff is amazing," she admitted, looping her arms around his neck as he nuzzled the soft skin where her shoulders met her collarbone. "I can understand why it's so popular. This is better than Xanax."

She hadn't meant to let that slip.

For six months Xanax had been her saving grace after leaving the Bureau and taking the DEA job.

Not because she'd suffered anxiety over a new job— hell, that'd been exciting.

No, the Xanax had been to help with the pain in her heart.

Shaine had really done a number on her.

"You're such an asshole," Poppy said with a dreamy smile. "You really know how to drive a knife straight to the bone."

"What are you talking about?" Shaine said, drawing her closer. "You're the one who left."

"You're the one who treated me like I wasn't good enough."

"Shut up," he growled, sealing his mouth to hers. His kiss ignited a firestorm of need made ferocious due to the drug. Her skin was on fire. Her brain was melting. She wanted to be naked against Shaine and forget all the crap that was still jagged between them.

Get a grip. It's the drug. You've trained for this. Get it together!

Poppy pulled away reluctantly, so hungry for his touch, that tiny, insistent voice becoming an irritant in her head. "Why'd they pick us?" she wondered out loud. "Do you think there's something to that?"

"We're just players in their game," Shaine answered, his arms still anchored around her waist as if he didn't want to let go. It would be so easy to just lean into his touch and stay there. "They set us up. Now we have to see it through."

"What do you mean?"

Shaine grabbed her hand and led her off the dance floor. He found Brandi and Angelo tucked into a dark corner, kissing and groping.

"We're taking off," Shaine announced, still clasping Poppy's hand.

"Have fun," Angelo said with a knowing smile. "I'll let Capri know Laci is in good hands."

Shaine didn't wait to chitchat and simply walked away with Poppy in tow.

She thought of protesting, to pull away, but she didn't want to.

Maybe it was a better idea to let them think that they were going home together to seal the deal and that way, she and Shaine could focus on other things without suspicion.

But that wasn't the reason she was eagerly following Shaine.

She wanted to feel him against her. She wanted to remember what it was like to climax in his arms.

It hadn't been purposeful, but since leaving Shaine, she hadn't been with anyone else.

She hadn't been able to bring herself to think of getting that personal with another person.

Each time she'd gone out on a date, Shaine had been in her head, intruding on an otherwise nice evening.

Unfortunately, by the end of the night, Poppy had always sent them home with a peck on the cheek, placing them firmly in the friend zone.

She told herself that it was simply her dedication to the job that'd kept her love life on the back burner, but with her hand clasped firmly in Shaine's, it was wildly apparent that she'd been lying to herself.

"I think this is a bad idea," she said, managing to get

the words out as they approached his car. "We have to realize it's the drug making us feel this way."

"Don't worry about me. I'm fine," Shaine replied, though his teeth seemed gritted as he added, "But we need to get out of here."

The fact that he was downplaying that he was affected, too, pissed her off.

"Why are you lying?" She shook off the hazy spiderwebs of arousal clouding her brain to focus on how much of an arrogant ass Shaine was and probably always would be. "I know you're affected by the drug as much as I am. Stop trying to be Super Agent and just admit it."

"Do you ever shut up? We need to get ourselves out of this situation and you need to stop throwing those words around. You never know who is listening," he hissed a reminder at her, and she zipped her lip, knowing he was right.

But that pissed her off, too.

What was it about Shaine that removed every filter, made her act in a way that wasn't natural and seemed to strip her ability to do her job?

She was tired of the merry-go-round of her own making.

"Why do you do this to me?" she asked, tears blinding her. "You make me act in a way that I wouldn't. You make me do and say things that I would never think of doing when you're not around. I'm a good agent but somehow I regress when I'm around you."

Shaine shook his head as if he wasn't about to have this conversation right now, and she couldn't blame him. This was not the time or place. But why couldn't she get herself to shut up?

"Just get in the damn car," Shaine said, climbing in. "It's just the drug. We'll get through this."

And she knew it was the drug. She was experienced enough to know that she wasn't going to be able to think clearly with an illegal substance in her body. But somehow everything that she had been repressing, everything that she had shoved to the deepest, darkest place of her soul was bubbling up like a geyser and she couldn't seem to stop it.

"You didn't have to take it with me. You could've walked away."

"Yeah right, like I was going to let that happen."

She frowned. "And why not? You think I can't handle myself?"

"You're the one who keeps protesting that fact. I've never said anything. Get over your own insecurities or you're going to kill this case. And possibly yourself at the same time."

"There you go again, bringing up the fact that I was shot in the line of duty. Let it go already."

"It's hard to let something go that actually happened. You were inexperienced and you got yourself shot. End of story. How else am I supposed to frame that situation? Before you answer that, you need to start realizing that this shit is real and we could both be killed because you're so intent on proving a point. Get it together or I'll have you replaced."

"You don't have that authority. This is a DEA case. And I'm the lead agent. So suck it, Kelly."

"Well, that was mature, wasn't it?"

"Are we seriously fighting right now? We are probably the only two people who can take a euphoric party drug and end up bickering."

At that he actually smiled. "Some habits die hard."

They rode in silence away from the party, enabling Poppy to settle down. Was she overreacting? Yeah, probably. But she did have a lot to prove. Maybe mostly to herself. This case meant a lot. It meant never having to prove that she had what it took to take on the big cases, the dangerous ones.

She also hated that Shaine was right. She'd been careless; the drug had loosened her tongue too much.

Poppy swore under her breath, realizing something else too late.

They were still wired. Marcus and Victoria had probably heard everything.

So much for hiding the fact that they had history.

She removed her necklace and buried it in her purse to muffle the reception.

Shaine caught her action and realized, too late, that they'd screwed up. He pulled his earring out and tossed it out the window.

"What'd you just do?"

"Giving us some privacy."

"A little late," she grumbled, pissed that neither remembered that they were being monitored.

"We'll figure it out," Shaine said, seeming unconcerned.

Hell, Shaine didn't seem bothered by anything.

"Why aren't you affected by the drug like I am?" she asked. "It's not fair that you seem unaffected and I'm losing my mind."

"What makes you think I'm unaffected?" he asked. "I just handle it differently. I will say this, this drug has a kick."

"So did you kiss me because of the drug? Or were you playing to your cover?"

His hesitation sent her mind spinning. Did she really think the answer to that question was going to make her feel better either way?

"Never mind, forget I asked."

But he wasn't going to let it go. "It's the drug," he finally answered. "Lines blur when you're undercover. Sometimes you have to go with the flow, do as the Romans do. This isn't the first time I've had to take something to keep up appearances."

"So it's just the drug that made you want to kiss me?"

"My inclination is to say yes because before that moment I didn't feel like kissing you. But right now I've decided it's best not to jump to any conclusions about anything."

Smart. "I guess you're right," she allowed, trying to hide her disappointment. What had she expected? For him to admit that he hadn't gotten over her and that she'd always have a special place in his heart?

Did she even want that?

No, she told herself firmly. She couldn't—and wouldn't—be with someone who couldn't respect her as an equal.

Another wave of euphoria hit her out of nowhere and she had to grit her teeth from moaning as her insides tingled with awareness. How was it possible that she could feel everything in her body?

"I can feel the rush of blood through my veins," she murmured in amazement. "I think I can see color and taste sound."

"There must be a time release to sustain the high," Shaine guessed, pressing his foot down harder on the gas pedal. "We need to get off the streets and into our apartments before something terrible happens."

"Such as?" she asked in a breathy whisper as she closed her eyes, trying to keep herself from rubbing up against Shaine like a cat in heat.

"Such as me pulling over this car and taking you on the hood."

It's just the drug talking, she thought feverishly, trying desperately to keep her hands to herself. The second wave was worse than the first.

How was she going to resist?

And what if her insides were melting and she was actually dying?

Honestly, if it felt this good…she wouldn't care.

Chapter 10

Good God, this was a special kind of hell.

If hell was sprinkled with aphrodisiacs and clouds that rained glitter.

How much longer could he hold out with Poppy moaning and twisting in her seat as if she couldn't stop herself from rubbing sensitive places?

Sweat popped along his hairline, and he tried not to wreck as his every muscle tensed with the urge to slam the brakes and bury himself inside that tight body.

Poppy wanted to know how he wasn't affected? Was she blind? He'd practically stuck his tongue down her throat and he was ready to do it again.

"Stop moaning, will you?" he practically begged.

"I can't," Poppy cried, her gaze heated as she turned to him, hungry and doped at the same time. "I can't stop myself. Pull over. Now. I'm going insane."

"If I pull over, you know what's going to happen," he told her, determined to drive faster, and yet his foot was letting off the pedal. "Hold on, Poppy. We're almost there."

"Let's screw like rabbits," Poppy said, laughing like a drunk. "Remember? Like we used to do. Do you remember, Shaine?"

"Yes, I remember," he rasped, rubbing his eyes. "Let's talk about something else."

"Remember that time we went camping up at Hillard Lake?" she purred, knowing full well he remembered.

The heat of the summer had nothing on how hot Poppy had been.

Poppy leaned in to whisper in his ear. "Nothing but wilderness all around us. We made love beneath the stars…in the water…on the beach…everywhere…"

He closed his eyes briefly, trying to shut out the images that'd begun to bombard him. But it was no use. He had a pornographic movie playing in his head featuring the highlight reel of their healthy sex life.

Wrenching the wheel, he chewed up the shoulder, spewing gravel as the car came to an abrupt stop. He reached over and pulled Poppy roughly to him, kissing her hard.

"I told you to stop," he said against her lips with a silky growl. "But then you never did listen to good advice."

Darkness blanketed them, the only light coming from the glowing dashboard as he pulled Poppy on top of him.

Straddling Shaine, her core fit snugly against his aching length and he nearly lost control at the feminine heat cradling his groin.

Too many memories of doing exactly this together was a sensory overload. Too much, not enough, all sorts of wrong—the messages crashing into his brain were short-circuiting his ability to think straight.

In his fevered state he didn't even notice that somehow Poppy's shirt was off and his hands were filled with her breasts. All he cared about was the taste of her perfection in his mouth.

Words may have been exchanged—hard to tell—but soon enough all either cared about was being skin on skin.

And it happened quickly.

Shaine leaned back in the seat, giving Poppy better access, and she wasted no time in sinking down on his erection.

There was no sense of time or place, just pleasure.

Shaine loved sex, but he had to admit, sex on Bliss was something on another planet.

He had just enough sense to realize that getting this drug off the streets was paramount because nothing this good came without a cost.

Right now, he was all about the hot, dirty car sex with a former lover. But eventually, the drug would wear off and he would be left with the consequences.

Poppy groaned and shuddered, finding her release quickly as she fell forward, breathing hard.

Shaine anchored her hips with his hands and pumped hard and fast into her sheath, nearly blacking out when he came.

It took a long moment before either could speak, but slowly, Poppy lifted herself off him and returned to her seat to curl up with a drowsy "That was incredible," before passing out.

Shaine shook off the building lethargy and quickly drove back to the apartment. He helped Poppy out of the car and into his place, planning to use the adjoining door to get her into her own bed.

But sometimes plans just don't work out.

Instead, he detoured to his own bedroom and deposited Poppy there. He didn't waste time grabbing a blanket to hit the couch; he climbed in beside her. The damage was already done. What difference would it make if they were sleeping beside each other?

And besides…he was exhausted and ready to pass out himself.

Poppy awoke to a pounding headache and a mouth full of sand. Even though she felt more like herself, the memory of last night was still a little foggy. More dreamlike than anything else.

For a second she actually had to think through the events to determine if they were real or not.

However, the moment she realized there was someone else in bed with her, she knew everything had been real and she wanted to vomit.

She shifted in the bed. Her cheeks burned as she recognized the scent of sex, sweat and bad choices.

The smell of each other still clung to their bodies.

A wave of inappropriate longing caused her to nudge Shaine a little more forcefully than she needed to.

"Wake up," Poppy said, becoming rapidly pissed that she was in his bed and not her own.

Wasn't it bad enough that they'd had sex? Why hadn't he taken the couch? "Wake up, Shaine. We have to talk."

Shaine slowly awoke and rolled to his back, throwing an arm across his eyes. "It's nice to see some things haven't changed. You're still not a morning person."

"We are not playing that game," she muttered, kicking the covers free as she climbed from the bed. She yanked on the covers when it seemed Shaine was more interested in going back to sleep than talking things out. "I mean it, get up."

"Or what?"

"Or I'm going to dump an entire glass of ice water on your head."

That seemed to get his attention.

"Fine," he grumbled, throwing the blankets free, revealing his naked body. She quickly averted her eyes, but it was like closing the barn gate after the horses had fled.

"What we did…" she started, searching for the right words. Guilt and anger were present but so was amazement. It was hard to shake the memory of how incredible it'd been, which was in direct opposition to what she knew was right. "I mean, I realize it was the drug, but this is going to create a ripple effect that we're going to have to deal with."

"Calm down," Shaine responded, sliding his jeans on while Poppy glared. "What?"

"Never tell a woman to calm down when she is clearly upset about something," she warned as she began to pace. "Here's the situation as I see it. We have to figure out what our stories are going to be when we debrief. When they find out we have history and we withheld that information, that's grounds to have us removed."

"You worry too much," Shaine said, cracking a yawn as he went to the bathroom. The sound of him urinating made her want to shout at him to at least close the damn door.

"And you don't worry enough," she shouted back. "We screwed up. It's bad enough that we didn't remember that we were wired. If they find out that we slept together last night… I don't even want to know how quickly our careers will go down the drain. We have to keep this little mishap to ourselves if we want to remain on this case."

The sound of the toilet flushing followed and Shaine reappeared.

"Relax. No one is going to find out. You think I want everyone knowing that I slept with a partner? I have my reputation to protect."

She sent him a withering stare. "Nice to know you're more concerned about your rep than the case."

"Stop. It's too early to deal with your freak-out. Has anyone ever told you you have a tendency to overreact?"

Poppy stiffened. "Only you."

"Yeah, well, I would know best."

Low blow. And it actually stung. "Can we stick on topic, please?"

Shaine seemed to realize he was veering and nodded. "All right, let's go over the important details."

"Details?" she repeated, a little stricken. "What kind of details?"

"Not those details. I remember what happened quite clearly. And judging by the way your cheeks flared up, you do, too."

Poppy rubbed her cheeks but didn't deny it. However, she did have questions. "I don't understand how this happened. You seemed in more control than me. Why didn't you just resist?"

At that he became irritated. "I'm not going to sit here and debate with you over who was more messed up. Let's just deal with facts. Are you on birth control?"

She balked. "That's a little personal, don't you think?"

"We had unprotected sex last night. I need to know if that's going to be a problem."

Poppy was immediately grateful that she hadn't stopped her birth control even though she'd had no action. The hormones kept her skin clear and that was enough of a reason to keep popping those little pills. "You can stop stressing that you're going to be a dad. I'm protected."

His relief was evident. "At least that's one thing we don't have to worry about."

Now it was her turn. "And what about you? Do I have to worry about an STD of some sort?"

"I was checked out a month ago. All clean."

"Well, now that we've covered those bases, what's next? Aside from the awkward silences and potential disaster to our careers hanging over our heads?"

"What's next is coffee. I've reached the end of my ability to function without it. Either follow me or don't, doesn't matter to me either way."

Poppy wanted to put an end to this conversation, but questions remained that she couldn't quite let go of, so she followed him to the kitchen.

"I don't understand why you didn't walk a couple extra steps to put me in my own bed. It seems unnecessary that you put me in your bed."

Shaine didn't even bother to hide his annoyance. "I know you think I have superhuman strength and I can overcome the effects of an illicit drug if I just put my mind to it, but the fact was I was dealing with my own shit and barely holding on. I put you in the bed, I got in and went to sleep. The damage was already done. Sleeping beside each other wasn't the problem and even messed up on Bliss I could rationalize that out. What's so difficult for you to comprehend?"

Once again, he was right. She was out of sorts. Sitting abruptly in the chair at the kitchen table, she cradled her head in her arms. "I can't believe this happened. I'm so embarrassed. This is incredibly unprofessional. And of course it would be with you. So how do we handle this?"

"These things happen. You roll with it. If Angelo, Brandi or Capri ask, be honest with them. We had sex. Play it off. That's what they're looking for. We're just playing into the undercover story. Our superiors don't care how the job gets done, just that the job gets done. You feel me?"

"Somehow I doubt that being with each other was what they had in mind."

"They just want results. If we bring in El Escorpion, all will be forgiven. Trust me. I've seen this movie and I know how it ends."

Why did it drive her nuts every time he brought up his past experience? Was she so insecure that she couldn't handle Shaine's obvious expertise in the field?

Get a grip! Stop being so damn sensitive.

She drew a deep breath. "You're right. I'm sorry. But just to be clear, we know that's not happening again, right?"

"Of course not."

"Good. I just want to make sure that's very clear."

"Yeah, I get it. You don't have to pound it into the ground."

"Hey, don't snap at me just for wanting clarification on a difficult situation. I'm just trying to avoid complications later."

He grunted some kind of agreement but didn't comment further.

"So what's our story? We did the dirty, and moving on?"

Shaine nodded. "Sounds good to me. And plausible. None of these kids are looking to hook up for meaningful relationships. Most of their encounters are one and done. Especially sex on Bliss."

"Okay about that. What are we supposed to put in our report about our experience? We have to share that we know what it's like but how can we do that without admitting that we had sex with each other?"

"We don't have to share who we had sex with. They don't care about that."

"I disagree. Whoever we come into contact with has to be noted. We never know who might be integral to the case."

Shaine sighed as if he knew she was right but didn't want to admit it. "We'll have to fill out a shit ton of paperwork. I hate paperwork."

"Yeah, well, it's part of the job. I don't know how you've gotten away this long without the obligatory report filing like most of us."

Shaine briefly flashed one of his infamous grins that made women melt—including Poppy back in the day—and said, "That's what friends are for."

Yeah, friends with benefits, she wanted to grumble, but held back.

They were saved from any more awkward conversations by simultaneous text messages.

Another body found. Report to HQ ASAP.

And just like that, it was time to drop everything and move.

Chapter 11

"Do you recognize her?"

Victoria and Marcus were both looking at Shaine and Poppy as they awaited an answer.

Poppy stared, nodding slowly, her voice choked as she answered, "I knew her as Capri. I was with her last night."

The coroner pulled the preliminary toxicology report. "She tested positive for a full host of street drugs, including one that the computer didn't recognize. I'll have more information when the full tox screen comes back."

But Shaine already knew what that mystery drug was.

Bliss.

How many times had Capri done the drug before it'd done her in?

"Do you have an ID on her?"

"Yeah, she was actually in the system." The coroner

rolled away on his small stool to a computer covered with a plastic protector and pulled up the ID.

"According to her record, her name was MaryBeth Johnson, aged sixteen, from Orlando, Florida. Listed as a runaway from foster care a year ago. She fell off the grid and no one cared to look for her."

"I knew she looked too young," Poppy murmured with distress. "I should've done something."

"You can't save them all," Victoria said, trying to soften the blow, but Poppy didn't seem to appreciate the sentiment.

"This one was different. She was a kid who didn't understand what she was getting into."

"They never do," Shaine said quietly, knowing Poppy was taking this one hard. For whatever reason, Poppy had been attached to Capri, even though she might've been a suspect. It happened sometimes, even as much as they tried to prevent it. He looked to the coroner. "Any family listed?"

"A mother, but it's doubtful she cares. She hasn't looked for her daughter since she ran away from foster care."

Poppy excused herself and Shaine let Marcus go after her, even though he wanted to.

"Official cause of death?" he asked.

The coroner looked at Shaine and shook his head. "In all my years of doing this job...I don't think I've ever seen something like this. When I opened her up, her heart was a pulpy mess. It was as if a bomb went off inside."

"That's disgusting," Victoria murmured, looking a little green. "I think I might need some air, too."

Shaine let her go, leaving him with the coroner. "Anything else we might need to know? Any sign of physical trauma? Sexual trauma?"

"She was definitely sexually active the night she died, but whoever she was with must've worn a condom because there was no evidence of sperm, but there was a residue of spermicide."

"So are you listing the death as drug overdose?"

"I've never seen a drug do this, but I don't know what else could cause this. Technically, she died because her heart exploded."

How much Bliss had the kid taken? The previous users had died of heart attacks, but Capri's heart had practically disintegrated.

Something felt off about Capri's death, more so than the other users.

Dumb kid, he thought sadly, understanding Poppy's distress. Capri had grown on them both.

And now she was dead because she chose her friends poorly.

"Thank you," Shaine said, and the coroner covered Capri's face with the sheet. "Call me when the official toxicology report comes in."

Shaine left the coroner building and climbed into his car. No one could be seen leaving together. They were all scheduled to meet back at headquarters to discuss the events over videoconference with the brass.

He wasn't looking forward to that meeting. Not only because of what'd happened with Poppy, but Capri's death was sitting wrong on his shoulders.

Maybe it was because Poppy was taking it so hard, but Shaine understood Poppy's distress over the young girl's death.

Sixteen was too young to die.

Shaine walked into the insurance building front and

immediately went to the debriefing room where DEA director Rosa Ramirez was waiting.

None of the other agents had arrived yet, which left him to field questions alone.

Rosa leaned back in the leather chair, watching him intently. "Exciting twenty-four hours," was all she said and left it to him to elaborate.

But seeing as he was wise to the games people played when they were fishing, he just nodded as if agreeing, but to what specifically, he wasn't sharing.

"Tell me about the dead girl."

"She went by the name Capri. Her real name was MaryBeth Johnson. She was only sixteen."

"Was she a suspect?"

"Not sure she was dealing but definitely using. But even if she wasn't dealing, she was connected to who was. We were exploring leads. Hard to say now that she's dead."

Rosa considered that, then asked, "Do you think someone killed her to shut her up?"

"Again, hard to say. It's way too early. All we know is that she most definitely died from a Bliss overdose. The coroner said her heart exploded. However, we have no idea how many times she'd actually taken Bliss."

"She must've had one hell of a fake ID in order to dance at Lit."

Shaine shrugged. "Or maybe nobody checked. I know she drove a sports car, but I don't even know if she had a license."

Rosa nodded, saying, "Fake ID operations are getting more and more complex. That's a whole other problem for another day."

Shaine wasn't going to argue that point. Luckily, the

need for small talk was done as the rest of the team filed in. It didn't escape his notice that Poppy's eyes were red, giving away that she had probably privately cried in her car on the drive over.

The videoconference started up and Patrick Hobbs appeared on the small screen.

"Hey, boss," Shaine said with a short wave. "How's DC?"

"Still standing, still filled with stupid bureaucrats."

"Glad to see it's business as usual."

Rosa started talking first. "Agent Kelly has already filled me in on the dead girl. MaryBeth Johnson, stage name Capri, died last night between the hours of 3 and 5 a.m. from what we assume is a Bliss overdose. What else do we know so far?"

Victoria jumped in. "Agents Kelly and Jones were invited to a party last night that we suspect was a test of their loyalty. Capri was at that same party."

Shaine caught Victoria's look and held his breath. When she didn't seem interested in elaborating Shaine breathed a little easier.

"And how'd that go?"

"They seemed to buy the act," Shaine replied.

Poppy wiped her nose. "I don't sense that our cover's been blown."

Rosa's sharp eyes noted Poppy's red eyes and queried, "Is there a problem, Agent Jones?"

Poppy shook her head, denying any problem. "I'm fine. It was just a shock to see Capri on the slab. I didn't expect that to happen."

"Are you going to be able to go forward with this case objectively?"

"Of course I am. I'm just sad because she was a kid.

She should've been doing kid stuff, not pandering to old men and ultimately dying without anyone ever caring about who she was."

Rosa dismissed Poppy's comment. "Well, throwaway kids are a dime a dozen. You can't attach to one or you'll be heartbroken by the end of the day. What more do we know about Angelo?"

Shaine could tell Poppy was upset at Rosa's cold attitude. He understood the director's stance but also understood that Poppy was struggling. Capri had been a cute kid playing an adult game.

Collateral damage was a bitch.

Shaine cleared his throat, bringing the topic back on point. "By now everyone's heard that Capri is dead. How are we supposed to play this?"

"Act natural. The kid is dead, so some appropriate sadness wouldn't be out of line. The idea is to earn their trust. Maybe ask around and find out why she died. Find out what the official story is on the street. Chances are nobody wants word to get out that Bliss ultimately is a one-way ticket to dead. Not a good way to get repeat business. It's likely they haven't perfected the formulary yet, which means we're going to end up with a lot more dead kids showing up until they get it right. It's our job to get Bliss off the streets before they get that chance."

"One of the things they said to us last night was they wanted to know if they could trust us," Shaine shared. "We had to take Bliss."

Rosa's brow arched. "Make sure you log that in your report. You're going to need to get checked out with the doctor, check your vitals. We don't need agents with exploding hearts."

Shaine nodded, accepting her directive. What choice

did he have? He didn't want his heart exploding. And he certainly didn't want Poppy to be in danger, either. "We've only scratched the surface of the inner circle. It's my guess that Angelo is the closest to whoever El Escorpion, is but he's not sharing, and we haven't found anyone else who's willing to talk. It's a very tight circle. There is a dancer by the name of Raquel with a scorpion tattoo on her lower back who might be worth checking out. I think she's jealous of Brandi. I'm gonna work that angle and see if I can get anything out of her."

Rosa nodded with approval, then turned her attention back to Poppy. "In the meantime, you need to get closer to Angelo. Seems with Capri gone, there is room for a new girl on his arm. Get close to the man. Use that pretty face."

Shaine tried not to growl. He knew Poppy must hate that aspect of her undercover story. She tried so desperately to be seen as more than a pretty face, but to her credit, Poppy nodded firmly as if ready to do whatever it took to get the job done.

Which was probably true.

The idea of Poppy sleeping with Angelo made Shaine want to break something.

He drew a short breath, trying to calm his reaction. "And what if it was Angelo who did this to Capri?"

"Then there's no better person than Agent Jones to figure that out and bring him in."

Shaine didn't dare look to Poppy to gauge her reaction. Things were already tenuous between them; he didn't need to make it worse.

Dismissed, they left the building, scattering in different directions. But he knew at some point he was going to have to talk to Victoria about what was said last night.

He had a few hours to get his head on straight before his shift at Lit, and he knew exactly what he was going to do.

Taking a friggin' nap.

He needed his A game tonight.

Rosa waited a beat before addressing Patrick Hobbs, extending a professional courtesy.

"I told you I had a bad feeling about those two. They're hiding something. The tension between them was almost palpable. Would you like me to handle this or would you?"

"Shaine Kelly is one of my best agents. He closes cases. I'm not sure what you're seeing, but I'm not seeing it. Cut them some slack. A kid just died unexpectedly. I know you're supposed to have a heart of stone, but sometimes the human element does get in the way."

"I think you may be blind to your agent. I know he's made you look really good these last two years, but this is my case and I'm not going to allow anything to fall to chance."

"Is this an official inquiry?"

Rosa paused. An official inquiry would require paperwork—a paper trail if you will. She wasn't entirely ready to go that far. Not until she had proof. "I don't think that's necessary just yet. Let me see if they'll be honest when I talk to them."

"Honest about what exactly?" he asked, annoyed that she wouldn't let it go. "Just what exactly are you getting at?"

"My gut instinct is telling me they're hiding something. This case is too big, and I can't afford that kind of misgiving. Whatever it is they're trying to conceal, I will find it. When I do, I will decide whether or not it's worth filing for an official inquiry."

Patrick blew out a short breath before grousing, "Fine. You do what you have to do. In the meantime, just let them do their jobs."

"Of course."

Patrick Hobbs clicked off, leaving Rosa to her thoughts.

Maybe she was jaded, but the death of a street kid/baby hooker barely merited on her empathy meter. As far as she was concerned, the girl got herself in a mess and ended up dead because she'd made bad choices.

Agent Jones better keep sight of that fact if she wanted to make it in this field.

Rosa was packing up when she was surprised by Agent Jones.

"Is there something you forgot?" she asked.

"I overheard your conversation with Bureau Director Hobbs," Poppy said, going straight to the point.

"Eavesdropping isn't polite," Rosa said with a small smile. "And you want to enlighten me?"

"Yes, actually," Poppy said. "This case is important to me, too. More so now that Capri is dead. And before you say anything, I know that I'm not supposed to get attached, but when you're working deep undercover, it's bound to happen a time or two. It would never interfere with my ability to stay objective, but I won't deny if it happens."

"That's smart of you," Rosa said, returning to her chair, intrigued by Jones's desire to be a straight shooter. That was a point in her favor, depending on what she chose to share. "So tell me about you and Agent Kelly."

"There's nothing between me and Agent Kelly now, but there used to be. We dated when I was in the DC Bureau."

"I don't recall seeing that in your personnel file," Rosa said.

"Because it wasn't there."

Rosa wagged her finger. "Naughty, naughty. I suppose you think you have a justifiable reason for breaking protocol?"

"No, we just didn't file the necessary paperwork and when it ended, I left, therefore negating any need to follow through."

"The paperwork is not for your closure, it's a departmental requirement, which is supposed to remain with your personnel file in the event that future assignment decisions can be made with full disclosure."

"I know," Poppy answered, accepting Rosa's rebuke. "We made a mistake. I thought by leaving it wouldn't become an issue. I never could've imagined that we'd end up on the same undercover operation."

"But you did," Rosa pointed out. "So where does that leave my investigation? If you're not willing to be honest about your past, how am I supposed to trust you with such a sensitive operation?"

"To be frank, ma'am, the issue isn't whether or not we're trustworthy, it's whether or not we can work together successfully to bring down one of the most dangerous drug lords in Miami. Or am I mistaken?"

Clever. "No, you are not," Rosa agreed, grudgingly impressed with how Agent Jones was shooting from the hip without apology. "And was this dating situation serious? Or a fling?"

She swallowed. "It was serious."

"Marriage, kids, the whole enchilada?"

Again, Poppy seemed to have something stuck in her

throat but her eyes remained clear. "I mistakenly thought we were headed in that direction."

"Ah, I see." Rosa didn't feel the need to dig any further aside from one small detail. "And now? How do you feel about him now? Any residual feelings?"

Without blinking, Poppy said in a firm voice, "Absolutely not. Today, he is just my coworker. And I'm happy to keep it that way."

"Good. I won't act on this information for the time being. We have bigger fish to fry and your messy love life isn't my concern. But don't let me regret this decision, Agent Jones. Bad choices can end up derailing an otherwise promising career."

"Yes, ma'am," Poppy said with a short nod, and Rosa dismissed her.

A long moment after Poppy had left, Rosa churned the conversation over in her mind. Did she believe Agent Jones that a clandestine romance was the only skeleton dancing in their closet?

Rosa was a straightforward person and she appreciated Poppy's bold choice to come to her instead of waiting for Rosa to question her.

That said something about Poppy's integrity.

Kudos for her honesty…but would she really be able to put the past behind her so that it didn't affect the case?

Rosa would keep an eye on those two. If there was any hint that they were losing their objectivity…they'd both be out of here.

This case was too important to lose.

Chapter 12

Shaine walked into Lit, deciding to act as if he hadn't heard about Capri. He wanted to take his cue from those around him. If no one mentioned Capri's death, Shaine would remark on her absence, as if he were interested in hooking up with the girl.

He didn't have a chance to pass on his plan to Poppy before work, but that was okay, as it would be more organic if they had separate reactions, anyway.

Angelo was already behind the bar, wiping down a glass. He looked up when Shaine walked in and gestured for him to follow him into the back.

Showtime.

"I don't know if you've heard but there's been a terrible tragedy," Angelo said somberly. He waited a beat then added, "Capri is gone."

"What do you mean?"

"She kicked it last night. It was a horrible thing. Brandi is a wreck about it. We're all pretty broken up. Capri was our girl. She had a special place in all our hearts."

"Holy crap, what happened? She seemed fine at the party last night. What went wrong?"

"Capri was a wild child, man. There was no stopping her when she was on a quest to party. Bad juju to mix your cocktails, you know?"

"You mean she took more than Bliss?"

"Raquel was with her when she croaked. She just died. Like fell over and was no more. I don't know…it's pretty wild."

Yeah, pretty wild when a kid's heart disintegrates, asshole. "Anyone tell her family?" Shaine asked.

"We were her only family," Angelo said with a sigh. "We're going to have a little get-together after work, say a few words in her honor. You in?"

"Yeah, sure, of course," he murmured. "I just can't believe it. It's hard to take it all in. I mean, Capri was fine at the party. And now she's just gone?"

"Yeah, it's a shit-bag of messed up proportion. Grieve with us, man. She'll be missed. No one could reel in those old moneybags like Capri. It was like watching a bee make honey."

Bile rose in Shaine's throat, but he nodded as if he agreed. "She was talented."

"For sure," Angelo said, then exhaled as if he were finished with that topic and he was ready to move on. "So tell me about you and that hottie, Laci. Did you seal the deal? I want details, my friend."

Shaine forced a cavalier grin. "I don't kiss and tell."

"Bullshit. Family doesn't keep secrets, man."

Angelo's tone was joking but there seemed an edge, making Shaine wonder if this was all part of the test.

"All right, if you must know, let's just say someone did the walk of shame this morning and it wasn't me."

"That's my man." Angelo laughed, clapping him on the shoulder. "Am I right that Bliss is out of this world?"

"It's wild. What the hell is in that shit? I've never even heard of it."

"Miami special, baby. Nowhere in the world are you going to find a high like Bliss, at least not yet, but we're working on that. Are you a businessman, Rocco?"

A jump of adrenaline made his palms sweat. "I don't own stocks or anything," he said with a shrug. "But I can manage to pay my own bills. Why?"

"Let's talk later. I have something you might be interested in getting in on that could end up being very lucrative."

"I like the sounds of that," Shaine said, nodding. "Let's talk now."

"Patience, brother. All good things come to those who wait, right?"

"Naw, I heard good things come to those who chase after it," Shaine countered boldly, which seemed the right thing to say, as Angelo's approving grin widened.

"I like your style." He pointed. "Now get to work. There are tips to be made and bills to be paid."

Shaine didn't have a choice but to do as he was told. He couldn't seem overeager or else it might come off as strange, but he was humming with the urge to press harder.

This was where experience trumped youth. He tamped down his urge to go balls to the wall and returned to the bar, ready to sling drinks.

That's when he saw Poppy enter. He only caught a

flash of her long blond hair before she disappeared behind the stage, but he could tell it was her from the way she walked.

The memory of her riding him in the front seat of his car blasted his brain and he poured himself a shot of whiskey to blot it out.

It wasn't healthy to dwell on a situation that'd been out of their hands.

They both accepted that they'd acted outside their realm of what they'd normally do because of the drug.

Neither was blaming the other.

And they were both on the same page about making sure it didn't happen again.

So why was he fixating on last night?

It'd just been sex.

Okay, sex on Bliss had been something extraordinarily amazing—if the general public caught wind of what it could do, there'd be an epidemic worse than the meth wave.

But he couldn't help but wonder, just a tiny bit, if the reason the sex had been out of this world wasn't so much about the drug but because he still missed Poppy.

Shaine chewed on that for a minute. They'd had no closure. She'd just bailed, leaving him behind with a broken heart and no explanations.

And now they were working together.

It was as if they were never apart.

That worried him.

He still loved the smell of her hair.

Somehow she always managed to smell like summer rain on a hot day.

Should he admit that he'd buried his face in the pillow she'd slept on last night and inhaled so deeply, he could've sucked up the whole damn thing?

Knock it off, already.

Shaine wondered what kind of words Angelo would share about Capri.

It was too much to hope that Angelo would admit that he was somehow responsible for Capri's death so Shaine could nail him for it.

Solving a throwaway kid's murder wasn't the priority, but he wanted justice for Capri and he knew Poppy wanted it, too.

Maybe with some luck, something would go their way and they'd manage to take down their target and find some kind of peace for Capri.

Poppy paused, catching Shaine behind the bar as she entered Lit and, knowing that Angelo was watching, sent Shaine a sizzling smile before heading to the dressing room.

Big Jane was comforting a girl Poppy didn't recognize, but she immediately saw Raquel and Brandi squaring off in a corner, whispering furiously to one another.

She decided to mind her own business and went straight to her vanity, dropping her bag and beginning her makeup. Her gamble paid off. Whatever Raquel and Brandi were discussing had ended because Raquel grabbed her bag and split, leaving Brandi to stare daggers in her direction.

Poppy took that as a cue to ask questions.

"Are you okay? What was that about?"

"Bitch, doesn't know her place," Brandi growled, still pissed. "She's lucky she still has a job. As far as I'm concerned she can go peddle her fat ass over at Tank, that's about her speed, anyway."

"What were you arguing about?" Poppy asked.

"Don't worry about it," Brandi told her, flicking her

gaze to Big Jane. "Now's not the time to talk about it, anyway. We're grieving."

"Grieving?"

Brandi shot her an incredulous look, and then she remembered. "Ah, that's right, you went home with Rocco last night. You missed all the excitement."

"Sounds like I'm glad I did?"

"Capri is dead," Brandi said without softening it. Poppy covered her mouth as a tiny sound popped out. "Yeah, it was awful."

But judging by Brandi's flat response, Poppy wasn't entirely sure that Brandi was truly sad to see Capri gone.

For crying out loud, the kid was only sixteen. Had Brandi known that? Would she have cared?

"What happened?" Poppy asked, stricken. "Oh, my God…this is terrible. She was such a great kid."

"She was no angel," Brandi retorted, going to the costume rack and thumbing through it idly. She selected a sparkly number and admired it. "Capri won't be needing this any longer. It always looked better on me, anyway."

"Criminy, Brandi," Poppy murmured with a frown. "A little empathy wouldn't be out of order."

"Look, am I sad that the kid bit it? Sure. I didn't have a beef with her but she was a pain in my ass most times and that's the truth. I didn't have time to constantly babysit her. She was a handful. Always getting herself into trouble. You know that car she drove? Do you know what she did to get it?"

Poppy shook her head, not wanting to know. "I can imagine."

"No, you can't. Anyway, the kid had something wrong with the wiring in her head. I hate to say it, but she was living on borrowed time. Sooner or later someone was going to punch her clock. It just so happened that she brought it on herself this time."

"How so?" Poppy asked, offended for Capri. "No one deserves to die. Especially not one so young."

Brandi eyed her with interest. "And just how young do you think she was?"

"I mean, she looked twelve, but I'm assuming she had to be eighteen to dance at Lit, right?"

Brandi shrugged. "Well, that's what her ID said, anyway."

"Do you think she was younger than she let on?"

"What do I care?" Brandi replied as if Poppy's question was stupid. "I'm not her mother. That's what Big Jane is for."

"I thought you and Capri were close."

She sighed and replaced the costume. "Yeah, I guess. One screwed up family. Birds of a feather, right?"

The sound of sobs reached a crescendo and Brandi rolled her eyes with disgust as she hollered at Missy even as the girl continued to sob on Big Jane's shoulder. "Get it together, you hag. You're supposed to go on in five minutes. Like anyone is interested in a weepy stripper."

"Did she know Capri?"

Brandi sank into her vanity chair with a smirk. "Does anyone truly know anyone?"

"I mean, she seems pretty upset."

Brandi waved away Poppy's observation. "Missy cries at the drop of a hat. Hell, I think she cries over YouTube videos of cats. She's a hormonal mess. Ever since she gave that kid up for adoption, all she does is cry whenever she gets the chance. Get over it, already. I say she's better off, anyway. Who needs a brat hanging on your tits when you can have some rich old man buying you everything you need for the price of a little show?"

Poppy hid her distaste and left Brandi to get ready.

Brandi might very well be a borderline personality. She was definitely walking a fine line toward narcissism.

But was she involved with the Bliss operation?

Brandi seemed more put out that everyone was mourning Capri's death rather than concerned that Bliss had been what killed her.

And someone who was in the inner circle would care about the product killing customers.

Big Jane came over to Poppy, a concerned smile wreathing her weathered face. "How ya doin' honey?"

"Okay, I guess," Poppy answered. "I'm still in shock."

"We all are, sweetie. We all are. It's such a tragedy when a brilliant, vibrant beauty goes much too soon. Capri was a special girl."

"I didn't know her very well but I wish I'd had the chance to know her better."

"Oh, honey, she was a good egg. Hard to find in this business, but she really was."

Brandi overhead Big Jane and snorted in disgust, muttering, "Good grief. By the end of the evening, the kid will have a halo and angel wings."

"Shut your bitter mouth," Big Jane snapped. "Just because she was sweet where you are sour, doesn't mean you get to run her over in death. You did enough of that while the poor girl was alive."

Poppy took quiet note of that statement. Maybe it was time to have a private chat with Big Jane, away from the club.

"I'm just saying, she wasn't perfect. I don't know why everyone is trying to make her out to be now that she's dead," Brandi said, but she looked away from Big Jane and returned to her makeup. "Hell, just last week you were bitching about how she was a little whore because she moved in on your target and got him to buy her that flashy new diamond around her neck. Remember that?"

Big Jane sniffed. "It's bad luck to speak ill of the dead. Didn't your mama ever teach you that?"

"My mama was a crack addict whore, so no, she didn't teach me much more than how to get her fix."

"Figures. You're broken to the core, child."

Big Jane left with a final look of disgust toward Brandi and then ambled off, leaving Poppy with more questions and no one to ask.

She couldn't explain it, but Poppy felt certain that Capri didn't intentionally overdose.

And if that was true…was El Escorpion involved or was it just a case of jealousy?

Chapter 13

Selena Hernandez sipped at her caramel skim milk latte, smiling faintly at the delicate foam art swirled at the top. She savored the full-bodied flavor of the hearty roast, enjoying the simple pleasure of an excellent cup of coffee.

If only life's problems were so easily solved with a hot beverage.

Her lunch date was officially late.

She abhorred tardiness. Being unable to manage one's time was a sign of a messy mind.

If only it weren't her twin brother holding her up.

Mateo walked into the café and found her immediately. He pressed a kiss to her cheek and took his seat.

"You're late," she said unnecessarily. Mateo didn't care about being punctual, but Selena enjoyed pointing out that she knew he was purposefully needling her. "Please tell me you have a good reason for wasting my time, brother dear."

"Charming as always," Mateo said with an engaging smile. Mateo was quite handsome—*debonair* might even be the word—but he was a smug asshole when it suited him. "Did you order my latte, as well?"

"Of course," she answered, moving to pull a spreadsheet free from her satchel. She settled her glasses on top of her nose and started reading. "A shipment from our friends in China was waylaid in Customs. We will not be able to get the necessary help to make the scheduled timeline, which puts us in a significant bind, as you can imagine."

"Straight to the point, sister? Do you ever take a moment to enjoy a fine day? Breathe the salty air and let it invigorate your soul?"

"I don't have time for that nonsense," Selena answered with a short smile. "Besides, you do enough of that for the two of us."

"A workaholic to the core. How did we share the same womb for nine months?"

"I'm sure I did all the work then, too," Selena retorted, returning to the subject. "We're going to need to find a new distributor if we cannot get our product out of Customs."

"I've already told you I have a new distributor lined up. I know you think I do nothing all day but comb my hair and get facials, but I actually had a meeting with a particularly eager new potential partner who already has an established pipeline."

Impressed, Selena said, "Is that so? And when did this happen?"

"When you were off in the Caribbean last week, entertaining those dreadful women you insist on calling friends."

Selena waved off Mateo's comment. "Friend is a loose interpretation. I like to think of them as useful and potentially profitable acquaintances."

"However you choose to classify them."

Selena chuckled, but it was time to speak of serious things.

"We do have a problem. Something that requires immediate attention."

"A bigger problem than our distribution issue?"

"The latest batch is not promising."

Mateo appeared shocked. "What happened?"

"The chemists aren't sure. All we know is that it's dangerous."

Selena knew she didn't have to say much more. Mateo swore under his breath. "This new batch was supposed to correct that problem."

"Well, it didn't. And now we have a mess to clean up."

"Just dump the evidence in a drum and drop it off as chemical by-product. We pay for the service. No one will ask questions."

"You are too cavalier and it's going to end up biting us both in the ass."

"And you worry too much. Thank God for all the Botox you put in your face otherwise you'd be Wrinkle City. You need to relax. Everything will work out."

Bless his heart, the idiot. Mateo didn't understand the full implications of what was happening. "We've already attracted attention."

Becoming serious, Mateo said, "I'll find out who is on this task force and make them go away."

"If you'd been more careful with the shipment manifest, this wouldn't have happened."

Mateo scowled. "Careful, sister. I am not to blame for this latest development. But I'll handle it."

"No. I will handle it."

Selena had always been the stronger of the two, a fact their father used to lament, saying it wasn't natural for a female to be so headstrong.

But Selena had inherited her father's sharp mind and cutthroat disposition, whereas Mateo had inherited their mother's love for fine things and fun parties.

"You don't think I will succeed?"

"I love you, brother, but some things you are not cut out for."

"Now you sound like Father."

Selena reached over and patted her brother's hand. "My apologies, *mijo*. I did not mean to bring up bad memories. However, too much lies in the balance. I will not trust that it is done properly unless I do it myself. That is my flaw, not yours."

Mateo sighed. "Sister, you're ever, as always, the smarter of the two of us. What can I say? Whatever you have in mind I am sure will work."

Selena smiled, satisfied. "In the meantime, I need you to follow up with the new distributor. We have a timeline to keep and investors to keep happy." She grabbed her purse and prepared to leave, surprising Mateo.

"Aren't we having lunch?"

"Sorry, my schedule is packed. Perhaps if you'd arrived on time…"

Selena rose and tossed a few bills onto the table before pressing a kiss on her brother's cheek and exiting the small café.

A woman's work was never done.

* * *

Shaine, Marcus, Poppy and Victoria all gathered at headquarters to compare notes. Victoria was the first to start the conversation.

"Since Ramirez isn't coming, we need to clear the air," she said, shocking Shaine. "The elephant in the room is that you left your mics on and we heard everything between you two that night."

But Poppy surprised him more when she said, "Yes, it's true. Shaine and I withheld that we had history because we didn't feel it was relevant to the case. I've already informed Ramirez and now it's no longer a secret we need to hide. As long as we remain professional, everything should be fine."

"Why'd you tell her?" Shaine asked, irritated that Poppy took matters in her own hands. "You could've discussed this with me first. It affects me, too."

"I overheard a conversation Ramirez was having with Hobbs about her misgivings about us as a team and I decided to put her fears to rest."

"You could've let me handle it," Shaine growled. "Your gamble could've cost us the case."

"And how were you going to handle it? Lie? That would've made things worse," Poppy returned coolly. "I took action. It worked out. Deal with it."

Shaine knew now was not the time to hash this out. Poppy was right in that since things had worked out, it was best to leave it be, but he was still pissed.

He turned to Victoria and Marcus. "So the question remains, do either of you have a problem with the fact that Jones and I have history?"

"If it doesn't affect your ability to close this case, I

couldn't give a crap," Victoria answered, looking to Marcus. "Your turn."

Marcus shared a look with Poppy. "I trust you. If you say there's nothing to worry about, I'll go with that."

"Thank you, Marcus," Poppy murmured, nodding to Victoria, as well. "I promise we can be professional."

"Glad that's over with," Shaine grumbled. "Can we get back on point?"

"Happily," Poppy said.

"Good," Shaine said. "Since Capri didn't have any family who was interested in her well-being, I think we should ask the people she hung around with. Someone has to know what Capri was into. The other night, I was actually invited to the warehouse by a friend of Capri's. Her name was Carly but I didn't get her last name. Unfortunately, she wrote her name and number on my palm and that's already gone."

Poppy jumped in. "I might be able to help with that. Maybe Big Jane knows who Carly is. She seemed soft on Capri."

"Good idea," Marcus agreed, and Poppy added another tidbit.

"Another thing, Capri had said something to me on the drive over to the party about Raquel. Something had gone down between Raquel and another dancer, but Capri wouldn't elaborate. She just said that I should stay away from her, saying that Raquel was dangerous."

"Dangerous how?" Shaine asked.

Poppy wasn't sure. "I don't know. She wouldn't say. But I've had dealings with Raquel and the woman is a nightmare. Not that Brandi is much better, but at least Brandi isn't so openly hostile. Raquel has a permanent chip on her shoulder."

Poppy looked to Marcus. "I want you to run a background on Raquel and see what you can come up with. I want to know why she has a scorpion tattoo on her back. It might be related to our target or could be completely coincidental. But we won't know unless we dig."

Shaine approved of the plan, liking Poppy's direction. "And I'll try to find Carly. Hopefully Big Jane knows who she is. Something tells me that there's a tight circle surrounding the Bliss operation. Someone has to know something."

Poppy remembered something else. "Another thing, Big Jane mentioned something about Brandi and Capri's relationship that seemed worth digging into. Big Jane implied that Brandi bullied Capri frequently."

"Do you think it's more jealousy?" Victoria asked.

Poppy wasn't sure. "I've seen jealousy between these girls but this seemed deeper."

"I'll run a check on Big Jane and see what comes out on her."

Both Shaine and Poppy nodded in agreement.

Shaine recapped, "So here's the deal, we're still no closer to finding out who El Escorpion is and we have a dead girl. We need to broaden our search beyond Lit because I really don't believe they wouldn't be so stupid as to mess where they eat."

Shaine added, "Angelo had mentioned bringing me into a business proposition but he hasn't said anything since. I don't know if he's gotten cold feet or he's just distracted. I don't know the guy well enough to know if this is normal or if I should be concerned."

"Maybe bring it up?" Victoria suggested, but Shaine shook his head.

"I don't want to seem overeager. Besides, if he is our

guy then I don't want to do anything to spook him. Right now, I think he trusts me and I want to keep it that way."

"We can check out Grind and Tank but I think Lit is our best chance," Marcus said, shaking his head. "I believe Angelo's our guy. He fits the profile. Slick, smart and hungry. The guy has ambition. See if there's anything we can pull out of his background to use as leverage. We'll have Miami PD run his prints and see if anything shakes out. Even if we can get him into custody to shake him up, that might be enough to make him make a mistake. Right now he's too comfortable, too secure in his own safety. Whoever El Escorpion is, they must be pretty damn powerful."

Victoria pulled some documentation. "I did some research on my own, widening the search. I came across something in a customs report that flagged my interest."

"What is it?" Shaine asked, reading the document. "It looks like a bunch of pharmaceutical chemicals."

"Exactly. And they were headed to a pharmaceutical company right here in Miami—Amerine Labs. However, none of those drugs listed are on the manifest for that company. All companies dealing with this type of chemical compound must report what they're using it for."

"And what happened to the shipment?" Marcus asked.

Victoria shrugged. "Nothing. No one has come forward to claim it. The name on the packaging is a dummy name. The address doesn't exist. Whoever was coming for that shipment disappeared with the wind."

"Then I guess it's time to make a trip to Amerine Labs to talk with whoever may have ordered the chemicals."

Poppy frowned. "Don't you think it's a little stupid of whoever ordered the shipment to put it in the name of the pharmaceutical company? That's way too easy to track down."

"What if they've been doing this for quite a while and it always passed under the radar? They'd have no reason to feel insecure or nervous until now."

"True. If that's the case it could mean that the pharmaceutical company itself is dirty."

"Or, it could mean that someone within the company is dirty and is using the company as a front."

So many variables. So many alternate and completely viable conclusions.

Shaine mused quietly, "I can't shake the feeling that Capri was killed for a reason. The girl wasn't afraid of anything. She was too young and too dumb to realize that she was in danger. But I think she knew too much and whoever did this to her knew that one slip on Capri's part could bring everything tumbling down. Basically, she was a liability."

Poppy agreed, saying, "That makes sense. Capri brought me to the party and secured the Bliss."

Victoria said, "And what if that was done purposefully? So that if any questions arose there was plausible deniability. And now she's dead, so no one can be asking her any questions about where the Bliss came from."

But Poppy didn't agree. "But I know where the Bliss came from. It came from DJ Raven. I saw him give it to her."

"DJ Raven is likely a lower level dealer. Chances are he has no idea who he's getting his product from. However, let's bring him in and shake him up. Maybe if we squeeze hard enough something interesting will pop out," Marcus suggested, seeming as if he would enjoy that interrogation.

Shaine nodded. Maybe there weren't so many dead ends, after all. "So while you're chasing down the Raven angle, I'm going to find Carly. Poppy is going to talk with Big Jane and Victoria is going to find more information on where that customs shipment originated from."

Victoria and Marcus nodded and scooped up their paperwork, leaving Shaine and Poppy behind. It was important that none of them left at the same time, so Poppy and Shaine agreed to hang back.

But that also meant that they were alone together, which was intensely uncomfortable.

"How are Sawyer and Silas?" Poppy asked, making conversation.

Ah, his favorite. Small talk. "They're good. Sawyer is in the white-collar crime division chasing down identity thieves and Silas is working in the child abduction division. But I haven't seen either since Christmas. Things have been pretty busy for all of us." He waited a beat then asked, "How are your parents?"

"Same judgmental pair. Still colossally disappointed in my choices. Good times."

Shaine could genuinely say, "I'm sorry, Poppy. That sucks. They ought to be proud of a daughter who can kick ass like you." He'd never understood how Poppy's parents could be so hurtful to their only daughter. "You deserve better."

Maybe he hadn't meant to be so honest, but that sentiment flowed from his mouth with ease. Poppy was a good agent. If he hadn't been in love with her, he would've been wildly impressed with her ability to jump into any situation without hesitation.

Funny how things change when the heart is involved.

Was it ironic that the very thing he loved about her was the thing that had torn them apart?

Poppy accepted his condolences, her eyes suddenly glassy. "It is what it is."

True words.

Nothing could change from the past, whether they wanted to change things or not.

"Look, I know you're really broken up about Capri. I don't blame you. She seemed like a nice kid. I know sometimes we get into this business and we run across people we want to try to save but that's not our job. We can't save them all. Just try to remember that it wasn't your fault what happened to Capri."

"I know," Poppy said, rubbing at her nose. "I don't know why it's hitting me so hard. I've seen countless kids fall through the cracks. She's just one of many."

"It doesn't get any easier," Shaine said. "One of my first cases involved a kid who was being used as a mule to move drugs from one place to the other. His own parents had offered him up in exchange for a steady flow of product. Before I could get him out, he died of an overdose. A balloon of heroin broke inside him, killing him instantly. The kid was fourteen."

"That's terrible," Poppy murmured. "Do you remember his name?"

"I can't seem to forget. His name was Walter. Sweet kid. Loved school. Just wanted to learn. He drew the short straw and ended up with shitty, drug addict parents."

"Did you manage to arrest his parents?"

"Yeah," he answered, dissatisfied with how that case had ended. "They got off with probation because the defense attorney argued that Walter had been old enough to make his own decisions and they'd claimed they had no knowledge of his drug running. It was all bullshit but the jury bought it. They walked."

"That is, indeed, bullshit," Poppy agreed. "I'm sorry."

He drew a deep breath. "My point being, there will always be a Walter or Capri out there needing to be saved, but who will be ultimately crushed beneath the wheels of the machine they're riding. That's what I meant by 'we can't save them all.' You just have to let that go."

Poppy nodded, accepting his advice, which surprised him. He half expected her to reject anything that came out his mouth on principle, but to her credit, she didn't.

She shouldered her purse and headed for the door, pausing to offer a soft, "Thanks for the pep talk. I needed that," before leaving.

Why did that feel like a victory?

Maybe because even though he talked a good game, he never wanted to be at odds with Poppy.

They couldn't be together, but they didn't have to be enemies.

Certainly something to work on.

Chapter 14

Poppy managed to talk Big Jane into a lunch date. It was important that Poppy got Big Jane away from the other girls, particularly Raquel and Brandi.

Although Poppy had suggested a café, she was surprised when Big Jane invited her over to her apartment, saying she wanted to make her famous BLTs.

"I don't get to cook much for anyone anymore. And it's not the same cooking for myself. Capri used to love my BLTs. That girl would eat anything. Surprising that she kept that cute little figure."

"Did you know her well?"

Big Jane fluttered around her kitchen. "As well as anyone can know a person, I suppose. Girls in our profession tend to keep things close to the vest, if you know what I mean."

"I have to ask, was she really eighteen?"

Poppy needed to know if Big Jane had known all along that Capri had been a minor.

To her credit, Big Jane looked troubled as she shared, "I had my suspicions, but she had an ID that said she was. It's not my job to be the social services, Lord knows I'm in no position, but I did have my suspicions. I think that's why I tried to keep her out of trouble as much as possible. I like to think I was sort of a mother figure to her."

"She seemed like a nice kid. I really miss her."

Big Jane sniffed back a tear, which was probably the most genuine emotion Poppy had seen out of any of the girls thus far. "I remember when she first came to Lit, all big eyes and pouty lips and absolutely no fear. She just walked straight up to Angelo and asked for a job. I think he respected that gumption. Angelo likes people with ambition. It's something he can understand."

"He didn't think she looked a little young? He didn't think to check to see if her ID was legit?"

"You know how it is in this business—the less questions the better. We all try to mind our own business. Poking around is dangerous and, most times, unwelcome."

Poppy couldn't resist. "Do you think Capri got caught poking around where she wasn't supposed to?" It was a bold question; maybe she was even taking a risk posing such an obvious question to Big Jane, but the older woman didn't seem to notice.

"Oh, honey, it's hard to say. Capri had a knack for finding trouble. She was never satisfied, always wanting more. The girl had a hole inside her heart and she kept trying to fill it with all sorts of sparkly things. I'm not saying we haven't all done it. But I think it got her in trouble."

Poppy didn't disagree on that point. "I gotta ask some-

thing. I saw Angelo and Capri go in the back room together… Were they sleeping together?" Poppy tried not
to cringe, hoping against hope that Angelo had not been
sleeping with a sixteen-year-old child. Not because she
had any kind of faith in Angelo, but because she didn't
want to think of Capri lowering herself in that way.

Big Jane remained silent while she cut the lettuce, then
said, "Here's the thing, and listen well, women in this
business have to do all sorts of things to stay on top.
You're only as useful as you are able to be used. Capri
had a young face and a young body. That was a huge
commodity. And she used it well. Whether or not she was
sleeping with Angelo… I hope for her sake she wasn't.
Brandi doesn't share."

"What about Raquel? She seemed to have a beef with
Capri."

Big Jane snorted in disgust. "That whore? She'd have
a problem with Mother Teresa. She doesn't know how to
be anything but a bitch. Frankly, I'm surprised she gets
any business. If I were a man, I'd be afraid to have my
tender parts around her sharp teeth."

"Big Jane, what if I told you that the word on the
street was that Capri died from taking Bliss. Would you
believe it?"

Big Jane chewed her bottom lip, plainly troubled. "I
tell the girls not to mess with that shit. But they don't
listen. I've seen too many go down that road and never
come back. Capri is just one of many."

Curious, Poppy asked, "Have you ever taken Bliss?"

"Of course not," Big Jane retorted as she sliced toma-
toes. "I have enough problems. When you reach my age
you realize when it's wise to walk the other way."

Was that what'd happened? Had Big Jane walked the

other way when it came to Capri? Had she known that Capri was in danger and known she couldn't do anything to save the girl without putting herself in danger?

"You seem like you really cared about Capri. I appreciate you talking to me about this. I didn't feel like I could talk to anyone else," she said, creating a bubble of intimacy between she and Big Jane. "I really liked Capri. She seemed like the little sister I never had. I'm just trying to understand what happened."

"What happened was she died," Big Jane said flatly, sniffing back a tear. "And we can't bring her back. And that's that. Now let's just enjoy these wonderful BLTs and try to remember the good times we shared."

Poppy nodded as if she agreed, but her mind was racing. There was something Big Jane wasn't talking about, something she was holding back. Did she know more than she wanted to share or was she afraid to share? Maybe she was deliberately being ignorant to protect herself. Either way, all signs pointed to Poppy needing to dig around in Brandi's and Raquel's background.

"Hey, I noticed that Brandi and Raquel were arguing the other night. Is everything okay between them?"

Big Jane laughed as she served up the sandwiches. "Those two are ridiculous. They fight all the time about everything. You'd think that they were related."

"Is Angelo sleeping with both of them?" she asked boldly.

Big Jane paused as if irritated by Poppy's insistence to return to the same subject. "Now, don't let your sandwich get cold. I worked hard on this."

Forget the fact that it was just lettuce, two slices of bread, a tomato and some bacon. Poppy dug into the sandwich as if it was the best thing she'd ever eaten. "Amazing. I can tell why Capri loved them so much."

Big Jane smiled, immediately forgiving Poppy. "My girl did know her way around a sandwich. I'm going to miss that kid."

And that was the extent of the conversation. The fact was, Big Jane didn't want to talk about Capri too much, which was a huge red flag for Poppy. There was something going on in that bar, something everyone was hiding. The more she dug, the more people seemed to clam up. That was always a sign to dig a little deeper.

Finished with her sandwich, she patted her stomach and groaned, "If I'm not careful you're going to fatten me up and I'll have to dance at Tank," she teased, referencing the club that Brandi had used disparagingly. "I hear they like bigger girls."

"They like *dirty* girls. Dancers at Tank aren't very discerning, if you know what I mean. That's why Lit is special. Only the top clientele get to spend time with our girls."

Poppy chuckled. "Is that so? So tell me about the sugar daddies. Are there any I should look out for? Actually, why don't you tell me who Capri managed to get a Mercedes out of," she teased. "I could use a new set of wheels."

Big Jane shook her head ruefully. "Oh, honey, I don't think you're ready for that one. Capri had a way of twisting people around her little finger to get what she wanted, but she toyed with dangerous men. To be honest, it could've been a client who took care of Capri. But since we know it was a drug overdose, at least we know it wasn't that way."

"Just out of curiosity, who were her biggest clients?" she asked, feigning benign interest.

"Well, I'd say her favorite was Mr. Pennington. She

sure had a thing for him. She'd leave with him for hours on end and come back with a wad of cash. I have no idea what she did for that cash but it seemed worth it. She bought that Mercedes with cash."

Poppy smiled as if impressed, but inside she was feeling sick. "Good for her. That's pretty impressive. Well, not to be insensitive, but now that Capri's gone, maybe he's looking for someone new to hang out with."

"You'd have to fight Raquel for him. Raquel has had her eye on Pennington since the day he walked through those doors. She seems to think she's going to be the next *Mrs. Pennington*."

"Oh? Is that so. And why is that?"

"Raquel seems to think she's high society quality. She's always turning her nose up at everyone at the club. Always putting it in our faces that she's better than all of us and that she's gonna get out of this life. She even went so far as to call Lit a *shit-hole*. Honestly, she's never worked in a shit-hole. Lit is as uptown as they get. She wants to know what it's like to roll around in the mud, she ought to hang out at Tank like Brandi said."

Poppy chuckled as if amused, but her mind was moving in fast circles. "Thank you so much for this wonderful lunch. I like you, Big Jane. You seem like a really nice person."

Big Jane smiled, tickled. "Well, I like you, too, honey. Now, keep your nose clean and don't find yourself poking where it doesn't belong. I want you to stick around. That last girl didn't follow my advice and she didn't last very long."

"Last girl?"

Big Jane seemed to have something stuck in her throat.

"She went by the stage name Tinsel. Very pretty girl. She had a special spark that was hard to ignore."

"What happened to her?"

The older woman paused as if lost in a memory, then smiled briefly and said, "She just wasn't a good fit. She quit coming. I have no idea where she ended up."

"Tinsel? How'd she get that stage name?"

Big Jane laughed. "Because she liked sparkly things. If my memory doesn't fail me, I think her real name was Darcy Lummox. Nice girl."

Poppy finished up, made some small talk and as soon as it was appropriate made her exit.

Had Big Jane just given up something important without even knowing it?

Who the hell was Darcy Lummox? And where was she now?

Shaine walked over to Angelo behind the bar. It was business as usual and Shaine took the opportunity to bring up Carly.

"Hey, the night of the party one of Capri's hot friends invited me but I never got a chance to hook up with her. Do you by any chance know who she is? Her name was Carly."

Angelo grinned. "Carly, that seems to ring a bell. Look at you, you dog. Nothing slows you down, does it?"

"Well, you know the saying, young, dumb and full of *fill in the blank*."

Angelo appreciated the sentiment with a healthy guffaw. "Yeah, yeah, I think I have her number. Let me see if I can hook you up."

Shaine clapped Angelo on the shoulder in a show of

camaraderie. "I knew I could count on you. So, not to be insensitive or anything but when's the next party?"

Angelo made a "slow down" motion even as he grinned. "Soon, soon. These things take coordination. I'll let you know as soon as we have a date. Hey, anything happening between you and Laci?"

"She's hot," Shaine admitted, leaning against the bar. "I wouldn't mind wasting some quality time with her again."

"Don't blame you there. Don't tell Brandi but…she's probably the hottest new dancer we've had in a while."

"She's pretty limber," Shaine said with a sly smile that Angelo appreciated.

Angelo cracked a smile and high-fived Shaine. "That's what I'm talking about."

Shaine figured now was a good time to broach a different subject.

"Hey, man, I gotta admit, I'm a little freaked out about the situation with Capri. Word on the street is that Bliss killed her. What do you think about that?"

Angelo lost his smile and cast a speculative look toward Shaine. "Who is saying that?"

Shaine shrugged, treading cautiously. "You know how people talk. It's just a rumor. But seeing as that rumor could have a basis in reality, it freaked me out. I got plans, man. I don't need to die because I'm messing around with some new drug."

"Calm down, don't freak out. Rumors fly, doesn't mean they mean anything. Bliss is 100 percent safe. It's as safe as smoking a little pot to relax. Except the high is better, stronger and it isn't going to give you the munchies."

"No need to sell me on it, buddy. It was the best high I'd ever had. I just don't want to die if I take it again."

Angelo laughed. "Stop being a pussy. You're fine. Nothing's going to happen to you. Now get back to work. That redhead over there has been giving you 'screw me' eyes since the moment she walked in the building. If you don't at least get her number, I will consider it an insult to my tutelage."

Shaine mock-saluted Angelo and headed in the direction of the hot redhead, but he was just going through the motions. Before long, he'd sent the redhead packing, but not before giving it a good show in case Angelo was still watching.

He'd gotten nowhere on his lead with Carly. He wasn't even sure what he was looking for. But he wanted to find someone who'd known Capri outside the club. Someone had to know what she'd been up to. Someone had to know if she'd been in danger, or scared, or putting herself in a bad spot.

The trick was to find that person before Capri's death sent them running in the opposite direction.

On a break, he managed to sneak backstage and find Poppy before her set.

It was hard to concentrate when Poppy was all dusted up in glitter in a teeny, tiny, sparkling costume that was meant to fall off at the slightest tug.

He hated that she danced topless and men fell all over her, but it was the job and he had to let that go.

Shaine tried—unsuccessfully—to remind himself of that, but the possessive male inside him that had never truly gone dark was awake and growling.

"You got a minute?" he asked, and she pretended to smile and flirt for the sake of anyone watching.

"What did you have in mind?"

"Come with me and find out."

Shaine grabbed her hand and led her into the small bathroom, closing the door behind them. To anyone else it looked like they were disappearing into the bathroom for a quickie. It played nicely into their cover story, seeing as they'd made a point to make sure Angelo had known that they'd left the party together.

The only problem was, they truly were locked in an enclosed space where there was hardly enough room to breathe, much less avoid the other person's bubble.

"Okay you have me, now what? Is everything okay?" she asked.

"I got nowhere with the Carly lead. Angelo said he'd look into it but I don't know that he will. Nor will he do it on our timeline. Did you have any luck with Big Jane?"

"Sort of. I have Marcus running down the lead. He's looking up a woman named Darcy Lummox. Apparently she was a dancer before Capri, who only worked here for about a month and then she left. But it's not clear whether she left or she just disappeared. My gut is telling me that she disappeared."

"I still can't quite fathom why someone would want to take out Capri. She seemed like a harmless kid."

Poppy nodded, agreeing. "Maybe it's shortsighted of me, but I really want justice for her. I don't care if it's unprofessional. I want whoever did this to go down. Even if it's not connected to our target."

Their shared belief in catching Capri's killer bonded them for a second, prompting Shaine to say, "You're doing a good job."

"Thank you."

They both knew that Shaine's compliment was a big deal. But they both had enough sense not to belabor the point. Maybe neither was ready for what it could mean.

"See what you can find out from Raquel and Brandi but be careful. I don't trust either of them."

"Same goes for you about Angelo. When he smiles all I can think of is a snake. He's the kind of person who would stab you right in the gut and smile while your blood drips down his hand."

Shaine couldn't agree more.

But just as Poppy put her hand on the doorknob to leave he stopped her. She looked at him quizzically. "What?"

"If we leave this bathroom without looking like we've at least messed around, suspicions are gonna fly."

Poppy gave a firm nod of understanding. "It's just for our cover story. Go ahead and do it."

"Ready to fall on the sword?" he teased, and she graced him with a patronizing look that he immediately silenced with his kiss.

"Let's make this look convincing," Shaine murmured against her lips, threading his hands through her hair and pulling at the roots to expose the long column of her neck. He traveled down the soft skin, nipping and tasting, until he made his way back to her mouth.

Their tongues tangled and danced. Time stopped for a brief moment, and for a pleasurable blip, all that existed was Shaine and Poppy as they used to be.

No painful past.

No hidden agenda.

No undercover mission.

Just Poppy and Shaine, as his dreams liked to remind him.

He hardened instantly and he ground his length against her, popping a few sequins on her ridiculous costume in the process, but he didn't care.

A loud knock on the door startled them both into awareness as Big Jane's voice on the other side told them Poppy's set was coming up.

"Saved by the bell," he murmured, moving away to adjust the raging erection tenting his jeans. Shaine chuckled when there was no hiding what was happening. "Sorry. A little too convincing, I guess."

But Poppy just gave him a small smile and a coy glance that set his blood on fire before letting herself out of the small bathroom.

Big Jane swatted at Poppy's behind, *tsking* at the popped sequins, sending her to change quickly, before saying to Shaine, "If you weren't Angelo's new favorite, I'd have your ass kicked. No one comes backstage, not even the bartenders. You would do well to remember that, young man, before you find yourself without your favorite part."

"Duly noted," Shaine said with a small shudder before getting out of there.

To Big Jane or anyone else, he was just a horny guy looking to get a little sugar, which could be forgiven.

If anyone suspected anything otherwise…they'd both likely be dead by morning.

Chapter 15

Marcus West stepped into Amerine Labs and went straight to the receptionist with a brief smile.

"DEA agent Marcus West to speak with Mateo Hernandez. I have an appointment."

"Right away, Mr. West. He'll see you in conference room A, straight down the hall and to the left."

Marcus nodded his thanks and entered the conference room, where he found a sharp-looking, impeccably dressed man rising to greet him.

"Agent West, a pleasure, please sit. I must say I am a little intrigued by a visit from the Drug Enforcement Administration. We do our best to ensure all of our paperwork is filled out appropriately. What do I owe this visit? Should I have my lawyer present?" he teased with a wink.

Marcus smiled at the man's charm. "Nothing so dire as that. I think we can accomplish what we need without lawyers. Assuming you have nothing to hide?"

"Nothing at all."

"Excellent."

Mateo leaned back in the leather chair and watched as Marcus pulled the customs report from his briefcase.

"Let's get straight to the point. Your company was listed on the customs manifest for a chemical shipment."

Mateo shrugged, puzzled. "We are a pharmaceutical company. I fail to see why that would be odd or cause for alarm."

"Yes, under normal circumstances that would be true, but a funny thing happened with this particular shipment… The name associated with the pickup was a false identity and the phone number listed went nowhere. The only verifiable identity was that of your company. Do you recognize this name?"

Mateo perused the offered document and after a long moment shook his head but added, "Agent West, I run a multibillion-dollar company and I have hundreds of employees. Of course I don't know each person by name. Perhaps I could run it by our HR department and see if the name pops up?"

"Would you mind? That would be very helpful."

"Anything to be of service. But to be blunt, Agent West, we are a large company and we have enemies as most pharmaceuticals do. It's not unfathomable that someone might've listed my company in an attempt to smear our name in the press."

"Are you familiar with a new drug called Bliss, Mr. Hernandez?"

Mateo shifted in his chair, his disarming smile widening with incredulity. "I deal with legal drugs, Agent West. I profess I don't know what the newest craze on the streets is, nor do I want to know."

"That's good to know. I'll be equally blunt, Mr. Hernandez. Someone with significant capital is shipping chemical compounds to the States through a Chinese pipeline. The fact that this shipment originated from Shenzhen is a red flag."

Mateo's smile thinned. "Maybe I do need my lawyer, after all."

Marcus returned the smile. "Only if you feel it necessary."

"You play an interesting game, Agent West. If I'm reading you correctly, you think that my company is responsible for an illegal shipment of chemicals used to make this street drug, Bliss—is that what you called it? While I have no idea what it actually is, I'm being accused of it nonetheless. Is that about the right of it?"

Marcus chuckled with amusement at Mateo Hernandez's upper-crust indignation. He'd done some checking before coming over. Mateo was a regular on the Miami social scene. He enjoyed fine wine, delicate cuisine and had fluid tastes when it came to his lovers.

On the surface it was difficult to imagine Mateo dirtying his fingers with illicit drug production.

However…with the right connections, a well-oiled production machine could produce a tidy, nontaxable profit, which was something he could see interesting Mateo very much.

"I've taken enough of your time," Marcus said, rising. "Thank you for answering my questions. I'll be in touch."

Mateo rose as well, but he'd lost his pleasant, even flirtatious, smile. "Next time, it won't be without my lawyer present."

Marcus tipped an imaginary hat and let himself out.

Either he'd just rattled the right cage, or he'd just made a huge mistake that could cost him his job.

Go big or go home, West.

Rosa's cell phone buzzed to life just as she was leaving the office. Pausing to answer, she was surprised by the identity of the caller.

"Director Ramirez, this is Mayor Bernardo Ferdinand. We have an issue."

"Good evening, Mayor Ferdinand. What can I do to help you?"

"You can help by keeping your agents from spreading lies about one of our best citizens and the business that employs a large number of people from our community. It's beyond ridiculous to think that Mateo Hernandez and Amerine Labs is guilty of anything. This drug shipment issue is nothing more than a malicious prank aimed at maligning their good character, and I won't have it in my city."

Rosa tried not to take offense, but being dressed down by an elected official with no jurisdiction over her office made her a bit cranky.

"Rest assured our agents are highly trained. If my agent was asking questions of Mr. Hernandez, it's highly likely he had excellent cause."

"Amerine Labs has been nothing but generous to this community and we are lucky to have them here in Miami when they could just as easily move to California with their business."

"I can appreciate that, Mayor Ferdinand—"

"You are Miami born and bred, are you not?" the mayor cut in, overriding her next comment.

"Yes, of course, and very proud of my heritage," Rosa answered.

"Then you should understand how hard Miami must work to retain good citizens determined to make our community family-friendly with enterprise, good jobs and opportunity. This is not the way to encourage businesses like Amerine Labs to stay and make Miami their home."

"Mayor Ferdinand, I assure you, if Amerine Labs has nothing to hide, our business with them will be brief and they can continue operations as they always have. But we have to follow all leads, and this particular lead brought us to Amerine Labs," she explained, wishing she knew more about the reasons her agent had approached a multibillion-dollar company without a warrant. But in the meantime, she would defend her agents against anyone coming at them. Privately, she would kick her agent's ass if he was wrong. "Surely, you can understand how important it is to keep our community safe from the influx of dangerous drugs imported from other countries using Miami as a hub for their operations."

"Of course," huffed the mayor. "But it's absurd to even think that Amerine Labs is anything but as solid as they come."

"I'm sure that's true, but we have to follow all leads, even if it means following them simply to mark them off." She paused for a moment, then said, "Mayor, I am curious, though. How did you hear that a DEA agent was meeting with Amerine Labs?"

"That's no secret and nothing I'm ashamed of admitting. I am good friends with the Hernandez family and I can vouch for them personally that they are above reproach. Good people, truly. Mateo came to me upset and, as his friend, I felt compelled to stand up for him."

"Thank you for sharing your concerns. I will note

your objections and, assuming Amerine Labs is cleared of any alleged wrongdoing, I will personally send a note thanking them for their cooperation."

Mayor Ferdinand grumbled, "This is absolutely absurd. But when you discover you're wrong, you'll need to send more than a note to save face."

"Thank you, Mayor Ferdinand," Rosa said drily, and when he clicked off, she muttered under her breath, "Blowhard," only too happy to be done with that call.

She immediately called Marcus West. Her call went to voice mail.

"Call me," Rosa instructed in a terse tone, then hung up.

Rosa chewed her lip for a moment, digesting the call from the mayor. Either Mateo Hernandez was an entitled jerk and wanted a pound of flesh for his inconvenience, or he was really concerned that the DEA was on to something.

Part of her hoped he was just an entitled jerk because taking on Amerine Labs in court was going to be a real bitch.

They had resources up the wazoo and they kept the best lawyers on retainer.

If the DEA didn't have every *t* crossed and every *i* dotted, the Amerine Labs team would chew up their discoveries like a T. rex running down sheep.

And that wouldn't look good on her résumé at all.

Chapter 16

Ramirez called an emergency debriefing the following morning, and as everyone arrived, Poppy was the first to notice that Marcus wasn't there, which was unlike him.

She swiveled around to check the doorway to see if he was running behind, but he wasn't coming.

Ramirez noticed Marcus's absence, too. "Call Agent West," she told Poppy.

Poppy dialed Marcus's cell. It went straight to voice mail. "Voice mail," she responded with a frown. "He's never late. Ever. Marcus is anal-retentive about punctuality. Something is wrong."

"Let's not jump to conclusions," Ramirez warned, but there was something in her eyes that made Poppy worry more. "He might be in the shower or something."

Poppy shook her head. "No. I've worked with Marcus for a year. He has intractable habits and punctuality is something he prides himself on. You need to send a car over to see if he's okay."

Ramirez nodded, punching in the number for their Miami PD contacts, requesting immediate assistance.

Dispatch sent the information and it took everything in Poppy to sit tight and wait for the police to radio back with information.

But it didn't take long.

Ramirez's cell rang and she answered it on the first ring. Her expression dimmed as she listened. "Thank you. I'll be down in twenty minutes. Secure the scene, please." She clicked off and met the apprehensive gaze of the group.

Poppy felt sick to her stomach as she voiced everyone's question. "What's wrong?"

Ramirez took a moment, then, with a heavy tone, said, "Agent West is dead. There was a sign of a struggle. It appears to be a burglary gone wrong. He was shot at point-blank range."

"No way," Poppy said, not believing that story for a second, rage and grief choking her. "This is El Escorpion, I know it. Marcus was on to something and they took him out by making it look like a mugging."

"We don't know that. This could be a sad coincidence. Miami can be a dangerous place, even to experienced agents."

"Bullshit," Poppy said, her eyes watering as the full import of the situation hit her. Her partner was dead. Someone had killed Marcus. Marcus, the man with his eyes trained on the future, determined to be chief someday. Now none of that would happen. "That's utter bullshit. Marcus was a black belt and a weapons expert. There's no way some punk-ass tweaker looking for something to pawn took him out. No. I'm not buying that."

"That does seem far-fetched," Shaine agreed. "What happened yesterday? Marcus was supposed to be running background on Raquel as well as interrogating Raven."

"Apparently, he went to Amerine Labs and made some inquiries that made some people uncomfortable. I received a call from the mayor telling me that I'd needlessly humiliated an esteemed member of the community."

"I was supposed to chase down the lead at Amerine Labs," Victoria said, frowning. She looked to Poppy. "Did he tell you he was going to the lab?"

"No." She shook her head, but it didn't surprise Poppy. Marcus believed in chasing after opportunity, not waiting for it to land in his lap. If he scented blood on the water, he was like a shark closing in on the kill. "He didn't tell me he was going there."

Poppy pinched the bridge of her nose, trying to keep the tears at bay. "But Marcus didn't believe in hanging back when action was possible. He must've learned something that led him to Amerine Labs. One thing is for certain, if Marcus went there, he was on to something."

"In light of the situation, I want you all to go home. Let's huddle up for now. Kelly and Jones, I want you to call in sick, make some excuse, but don't go into the club tonight."

"You don't think that will look suspicious," Shaine asked.

"No, you're college kids on break. College kids can be notoriously irresponsible, especially when they don't have classes to clock in to. They'll get over it. In the meantime, I will handle arrangements for Marcus's return to Los Angeles."

Blinking back the tears that were suddenly too many to hold back, Poppy rapidly exited the building and headed home, needing air and space.

This case was taking so much and giving back so little.

First Capri and now Marcus.

Someone was playing hardball.

And mowing over anyone in their way.

Poppy pressed the gas pedal down harder and turned up the radio until she no longer heard her own cries, only the sound of rock and roll.

Shaine knew he should leave Poppy to her grief, but he couldn't do it.

He walked through the adjoining door and found Poppy on her bed, sobbing.

On instinct, he gathered her in his arms and held her while she cried. She didn't fight him, only clung to him as she soaked his shirt with her tears.

"Were you…close?" Shaine asked as she pulled away, wiping her nose to stare at him in question. "You and Marcus…"

He didn't want to ask but the question nagged at him.

Poppy wiped her nose, then understanding dawned and she looked irritated. "Marcus was gay, you idiot," she said, rising to rinse her face. Afterward she returned, looking freshly scrubbed but still angry. "Why would you ask me that? I can't feel something for a partner unless I'm sleeping with him?"

"No, not at all," he protested, feeling like a jerk. "I'm sorry. It was inappropriate for me to even ask. I was just…" *Jealous? God, that sounded worse.* "I'm sorry. I was wrong."

The fire went out of Poppy's eyes and she sat heavily on the bed beside Shaine. "It's okay, I'm just…raw."

"I know." He gently clasped her hand. "Tell me about Marcus. I want to get to know him as you knew him."

"Really?"

"Yes."

Poppy sniffed and nodded, taking a moment to regroup. "Well, he was superambitious, even more so than me. He had grand designs to be chief someday. In fact, he was hoping this case was going to help him land a position in the New York field office because it was closer to DC than Los Angeles." The tears started fresh. "But that's not happening now. I can't believe he's gone. I feel like I'm in a fog and I can't wake up."

"He sounds like my kind of agent," Shaine said. "For what it's worth, I believe you. I think you're right… This was no accident."

"I know I'm right." Poppy said, glad to have Shaine on her side. "Marcus was an expert in self-defense, a top marksman and had a black belt. There's just no way it went down the way the cops are saying it did."

"So if he went to Amerine Labs, there must be someone there that felt the heat."

"But how are we supposed to get near Amerine now? It's not as if we can walk in there—it'll blow our covers."

"And if Victoria tries, it'll tip off that the FBI and DEA are working together, which will only put more attention on us as newbies at the club."

Poppy agreed, her eyes welling again. "I can't help but believe that we somehow caused this. Maybe we should've been more cautious, more attentive? I don't know. What made him go off on his own like that?"

Shaine let her vent, knowing that she wasn't exactly looking for answers, just someone to listen.

"I should've checked in more. I knew he was getting

restless. He wasn't cut out for staying behind the scenes and watching the action from afar. He'd put in for the undercover position but he was denied."

"Do you think he could've handled the pressure of undercover work?"

"I don't know," Poppy answered. "He was particular about some things. Very type A. I'm not sure he could bypass that switch in his head to become someone different. But who knows? He was brilliant—he may have found a way. Now he'll never get the chance."

Shaine wasn't going to say something trite such as "everything happens for a reason" because he knew how aggravating it was to hear that when grieving, but he didn't know what else to say.

But Poppy seemed to understand when he remained silent. "Don't worry. It's not the words, but the sentiment. Thank you."

Shaine nodded, relieved. "When Spencer died, I couldn't stand the way people would constantly say that, as if a little kid dying was somehow in God's grand plan. But I was too young to understand that it was just an attempt to make sense of something that didn't make sense at all."

Poppy agreed, murmuring, "I know it's not the same, either. Your brother died before he could really live."

Shaine didn't like to talk about Spencer. The youngest Kelly disappeared when Spencer was ten. His body was found a few days later, dumped in Seminole Creek. Spencer's killer was never found.

Because of Spencer, all the Kelly boys went into the FBI, the thirst for justice their driving need.

Shaine shook off the melancholy that always came when thoughts of Spencer popped up and said, "Marcus sounded like a good man. We'll find whoever did this and make sure they pay."

"How?"

Poppy's plaintive question echoed the concern in his heart. This case was ballooning. No leads, just dead ends. And dead people.

But giving up wasn't an option. "Any way possible," Shaine replied, and meant it.

Poppy leaned against him, resting her head against his shoulder with a small hiccup. "Thank you for coming over," she said.

"You're welcome."

Too bad they couldn't have worked things out before. He missed Poppy and that was evident by the way he craved to be near her, needed to comfort her when she was sad and wanted to rip people's heads off when they stared at her breasts.

Was that missing her? Or was he still in love with her?

Two years should be plenty of time to get over someone.

What if Poppy is the kind of woman you never get over?

Shaine knew it wasn't the time, but he wanted to talk about the past—why she left the way she had; what she'd been up to since leaving.

There were so many questions, so many buried hurts that being around her again had just begun to unearth.

"Are you happy?" he asked instead.

Poppy sighed and shrugged. "I guess. Yeah, I mean, as happy as anyone, I suppose. I have a decent apartment in a good neighborhood and my neighbors aren't jerks."

"That's happiness?"

Poppy pulled away to look at him with a frown. "What's

happiness, Shaine? The definition changes daily. Today, I'm very unhappy, that much I know."

"Of course," he murmured, wondering what he was hoping would happen with that line of questioning. He never threw out random questions. So why was he doing it now?

Talk about passive-aggressive...

"The lines have blurred," Poppy said with a brief smile of understanding. "It's okay. Going two years without even saying hello, to suddenly pairing up undercover, it's bound to confuse things. We shouldn't read too much into it."

He nodded, seaming his lips before he let slip something else that needed to remain buried. "You're right," he agreed, matching her smile. "We're partners. Here to do a job."

"Right," Poppy affirmed. "And we're going to catch this SOB before he or she manages to ruin more lives."

"For what it's worth... I'm glad I'm working with you. You're a good agent," Shaine admitted. "Whatever you've been doing these last two years has been good for you. I'm impressed."

Poppy tried to smile in response, but her eyes were welling. She ducked her head to avoid letting him see, but he'd caught it, anyway. "Oh, man, I can't seem to stop with the waterworks," she said, wiping at her eyes, trying to blink away the moisture.

Shaine knew why she was crying. He'd struck a raw nerve. There was so much left unsaid between them.

For a long time Shaine had refused to admit the reason Poppy had left. It'd been less shameful to say she'd bailed over a fight, instead of the true reason.

It was hard to look yourself in the eye and admit that you'd been a royal dick.

Love was complicated enough as it was, but then add in their career choices and it became downright impossible to figure out.

The bald truth was simple: he hadn't been supportive of her career. Fear had pushed him to squash her ambition.

That wasn't something you could just say "I'm sorry" for and move on. He didn't blame her for splitting. If anyone had tried to do the same to him, it would've been sayonara immediately.

But the time for apologies had passed.

All he could do was respect her as a fellow agent and do his best to work alongside her as he would with anyone else.

And try to forget that they'd slept together.

Again.

Hell, he already knew that would be damn near impossible, but he'd find a way to deal.

That was his job.

Chapter 17

Rosa took a deep breath before starting the videoconference with Patrick Hobbs in DC.

"I heard the news," Patrick said, his expression somber. "Marcus West was a good agent. His record spoke for itself."

"Losing him is a blow to the investigation," she said, pouring herself a scotch from the lower drawer in her desk. "I don't usually drink during the day but I figure this warrants a little latitude."

"Losing a valuable team member is a bitch," Patrick said without judgment.

"Damn straight," she murmured, downing the shot. Rosa savored the burn in her throat and leaned back in her chair with a long exhale. "We know the last person to see West alive was Mateo Hernandez of Amerine Labs. I can't send Kelly or Jones to speak with him or it'll blow their covers and I don't have time to vet another agent to replace West so I'll go myself."

Rosa knew she could send York or Rocha from Miami PD, but she was hungry to close this case and she didn't trust anyone but herself to rattle Mateo and Selena Hernandez.

Patrick seemed to agree that Rosa's idea was the only option. "Sounds like the only play available. Though, I can't help but think that if Hernandez was involved, he's pretty damn bold to do this practically in plain sight. He'd have to know he'd be a primary suspect after their conversation and his buddy Mayor Ferdinand's phone call. Seems either too easy or way too cocky."

"True. But it's the only lead I have right now. The bar isn't revealing much. Angelo isn't stupid. He's not giving up any leads so soon after Capri's death. Everyone is in a holding pattern while the dust settles."

"We knew this case wasn't going to be easy. I just didn't expect the body count to start climbing within weeks of the start."

"Amen to that," Rosa said, pouring another drink as she prepared to share something else. "I had a talk with Agent Jones. I was right about them hiding something… they used to date."

Patrick frowned. "There was no paperwork filed."

"Because they didn't feel it necessary to inform brass, as per protocol, about their relationship." She waited a beat. "How do you feel about that?"

"Honestly, if it's not affecting their job performance, I say live and let live. Shaine Kelly is a hotshot, reckless SOB, but he comes from good stock. All those Kelly boys are solid agents. They get results and I'm not going to argue with that. It's why I picked him for this assignment."

"I'm inclined to feel the same, but I'd be lying if I didn't find their dishonesty troubling. No, that's not entirely true. It's this case… I'm hyperaware of how everything could go wrong and torpedo all our careers as it goes down. I don't want anything coming back to bite us in the ass…even something as seemingly small as a long-past taboo office romance."

"Being able to lie without tipping anyone off is an undercover agent's strongest defense. Besides, so they have history…as long as they can handle leaving the past behind them, let's just let them do their job. Keeping everyone alive is the idea, not policing who they've slept with."

Rosa chuckled, appreciating Hobbs's straight talk. She appreciated facts. It was the gray areas that made her twitchy.

"You're nothing like your predecessor. From what I've heard about him, he liked rules."

"He liked paperwork," Patrick corrected. "Me? Not so much. I like closed cases."

She couldn't argue with that logic, but she had to bring up the obvious. "What happens if they can't keep the past in the past?"

"I say, let's not borrow trouble if we don't have to. Focus on the case."

"You're a smart man."

Patrick chuckled, saying, "Sometimes," and then added before disconnecting, "Keep me in the loop and don't drink yourself stupid."

Rosa smirked as she returned her shot glass to the drawer for another time. If she was going to approach Amerine Labs, she better have her ducks in a row or there was no telling who else was going to be ringing her up for another ass-chewing.

Angelo wiped down the bar, surveying the crowd. Things had been sketchy since Capri's death. As much as he'd tried to stamp out the rumors that Capri's death hadn't been related to Bliss, business had been down.

And that didn't bode well for him.

Raquel walked in and went straight to him, but he wasn't in the mood for her bullshit drama.

Before he had a chance to shut her down, Raquel hit him with both barrels.

"You said you were ending it with Brandi," Raquel hissed, her eyes flashing. "I should've known anything coming out of your mouth is a friggin' lie."

"Calm yourself," Angelo snapped. "Don't try to collar me. It will end badly for you."

"As badly as it did for Capri? Yeah, I know you were banging that little brat, too. But your fun days are over. I'm sick of your shit and I'm done. Brandi can have my scraps. You two belong together."

"Raquel," Angelo growled, moving quickly after her. He grabbed her arm and dragged her into the back, shoving her against the wall. "Who the hell do you think you're talking to? You don't end things with me. If *I'm* tired of your company, I will tell *you*. You hear me? That's how it works."

"Screw you," Raquel hissed, not backing down. "You might have everyone else snowed in this place, but I'm not afraid of you. You're just a two-bit dealer with dreams of grandeur who enjoys playing king. But you're just a boy playing a game and I see that now. So, let go of me before I knock your nuts into your throat."

Angelo wanted to squeeze the life out of Raquel's bitter mouth but he knew meeting Raquel with force wasn't going to work. Raquel needed a softer touch if she was going to be managed.

Switching tactics, he released her arm and gently rubbed where he'd bruised her. "Baby, you know you drive me crazy when you talk like that. I don't know where you get your information, but I wasn't sleeping with Capri. She was like a kid sister, you know that."

"You're lying," Raquel snapped, but her lower lip began to tremble. "I know you were."

"Baby-girl," Angelo said softly, nuzzling her neck. "C'mon, what's really going on? You're all piss and vinegar tonight. Tell me what's happening so we can get through it together."

For a second he thought she'd bought it. That tiny bit of softening in her shoulders tricked him into thinking that he'd said the right things. But suddenly his balls exploded in a rage of pain as she buried her knee into his groin, shoving him away from her.

"Tell it to your whore Brandi. I'm done with your lies."

Angelo gasped, seeing stars as he cupped his abused testicles. Raquel sent a final look of disgust his way and then left.

Rocco appeared, his eyes widening when he saw Angelo hobbling. "You okay, man?"

He jerked a short nod, unable to speak just yet. But he was fantasizing about all the different ways he'd make Raquel pay for that little temper tantrum.

Ways that would inflict major pain and leave permanent marks.

Angelo managed a brief, crooked smile as he said,

"Watch who you spend time with, bro. Sometimes those clingers just don't know how to let go."

Rocco laughed and grabbed a replacement bottle of New Amsterdam gin from the shelf. "You gotta watch where you dip your wick, man. Sometimes, you land in poison."

God knew that was right.

You play, you pay.

Except when people played with Angelo...he always won.

Shaine tried to appear as if he hadn't seen the whole exchange between Raquel and Angelo, acting as if he'd only just walked in as Raquel had stalked out of the storeroom.

But he'd caught an earful.

Raquel was out for blood. She'd found out about Angelo playing both sides against the middle.

Had Capri threatened to say something to Brandi? Did Angelo kill Capri to shut her up?

And if so, why would he care about losing Brandi so much he'd commit murder?

Angelo had only said that Brandi was off-limits, but implied that Raquel was a barnacle once attached. It didn't seem that way when Raquel was ready to add Angelo's nuts to her salad.

Raquel made sure that Angelo knew she meant business. Did that mean Raquel was on Angelo's hit list?

Shaine didn't have time to find Poppy and share what he'd found out. His shift didn't end for another two hours and Poppy's set was starting soon.

He'd just have to sit on it and keep his eyes and ears open.

Once Angelo returned, limping only slightly, Shaine

decided to tease him a bit, just like a regular smart-ass dude would.

"Bit off more than you could chew?"

Angelo's grin was worn around the edges, but his eyes held a dark, angry glint. "Some thrill rides should come with a warning label."

"I thought you said you were done with that one? Something change?"

"What can I say? I'm a sucker for a hot ass and sweet body. Raquel is a firecracker in bed and I'm a weak man."

Shaine laughed. "You dog. So what now? Is she going to make things weird between you and Brandi?"

"Naw, I've got Brandi wrapped around my finger."

"You mean wrapped around something," Shaine supplied with a lecherous grin that Angelo returned, fist-bumping Shaine.

"You know it."

"So what's your secret?" Shaine asked in a conspiratorial tone. "I mean, how do you keep so many hot women chasing after you when they know you're a player? Teach me the ways, master."

Angelo guffawed, plainly amused by Shaine's flattery. "You don't need my help. You seem to have the women flocking around you without any trouble. Whatever happened with you and that hot redhead I sent your way?"

"We exchanged numbers, but ultimately, it wasn't going to happen. Different goals."

"Ah, another Stage 3 clinger?"

"Something like that."

Shaine hated having to throw shade on someone he'd never even spoken to, but he couldn't have Angelo thinking that he wasn't interested in the game.

"How about you and Laci? She's a hot number. I wouldn't

mind putting my stamp on that Grade A Choice, if you know what I mean."

He did, and it took all the strength he had not to throat punch the guy. "We're compatible," Shaine answered with a noncommittal shrug. "And she's down for a good time, so go ahead... That is, if you don't think Brandi would mind."

"Brandi's not my keeper," Angelo scoffed.

"Does she know that?"

"Why?"

"Just wondering. She seems pretty attached."

"Women. Give 'em good dick and it's like they can't get enough."

Shaine chuckled. "I hear you, man. The struggle is real."

A few more moments of sexist banter and bragging followed until Shaine excused himself to go to the john.

He knew Ramirez had instructed Poppy to get close to Angelo by any means possible, but he couldn't stomach the idea of Poppy sliding into bed with that man. It physically turned his stomach.

So how was he going to keep Angelo from trying to move in on Poppy without jeopardizing the investigation?

Worse, how was he going to keep Poppy from finding out that he'd manipulated the situation to keep Angelo from her? When she found out that he'd only given her lip service earlier...

She'd go ape shit.

That same old argument would surface about him not believing she was capable of doing the job, and all the good stuff that'd come about recently would wash right out the door.

What was the answer?

Leave her be and let Poppy do her job, however she sees fit.

The advice tasted sour on his tongue, but he knew it was simply a bitter pill of truth that he was plainly re-sisting.

Knowing the truth and allowing it to unfold were two separate things.

But he'd have to find a way to let it happen.

Because if he's learned anything, Poppy didn't take kindly to anyone treating her as less than she was.

And damn, he respected the hell out of her for it.

Now, if he could just keep his heart from stopping every time he pictured her in danger, maybe they might be able to survive whatever was to come.

Maybe.

Chapter 18

Selena Hernandez graced the short, stocky female DEA agent with a practiced smile as she slid into her desk with a perplexed expression.

"I'm sorry, what did you say your name was?" she asked, feigning ignorance. She knew exactly who it was and why she was there. *Damn you, Mateo.*

"I'm DEA director Rosa Ramirez, Ms. Hernandez. I'm here to speak with you regarding fellow agent Marcus West."

"Right, yes, and why would I know this Agent West?"

"Because he came to Amerine Labs to speak with your brother Mateo and then that night he was killed. Seems highly coincidental."

"Indeed," Selena murmured with faint distress. "But I still don't see how that affects me or my company."

"May I be frank?"

"I would appreciate nothing more."

"Excellent." Rosa leaned forward, pinning Selena with hard, black eyes. "Amerine Labs was listed on the manifest as the receiver of drugs that were not what was actually shipped from Shenzhen, China. The name was a false identity, tipped off by Customs, which caused them to hold the shipment."

"Yes, my brother informed me of the malicious prank. Let me be frank, as well. While pharmaceuticals may seem like a dry, dusty academic pursuit, drug espionage is actually quite common. We're on the cutting edge of new research and there are many who'd like to take a peek at our formulary. This was simply a nasty ploy to smear our good name, which, judging by the fact that you are here questioning me, tells me whoever did this accomplished their objective."

"I suppose that's true," Rosa Ramirez allowed, though Selena didn't think she bought the story. "I'm sure you can appreciate that we have to follow up on Agent West's last contact."

"Of course."

"And, according to his records, Agent West was last seen with your brother Mateo."

"I find it tragic but nothing more," Selena said with a delicate sniff. The short DEA agent was like a pit bull with a bone. "I am saddened by your loss, but I'm too busy running my company to spend time running some sort of illicit drug operation on the side. At the risk of being rude, I find your implication preposterous."

"Duly noted. However, when it comes to our own, we leave no stone unturned, even when disturbing that stone may unsettle the flow of the river, if you catch what I'm saying."

"Please elaborate. Speaking in metaphor is not my strong suit."

"Fair enough. What I'm saying in plain English is we will pursue any and all leads, no matter whose door it leads us to. Even if it leads us to doors where people with influential friends live."

"I would expect nothing less. I do hope you realize soon that I'm not the enemy, so you can turn your attention to catching *actual* criminals who are turning this beautiful city into a dangerous place."

The agent cast a perfunctory smile Selena's way and rose to leave, but not before dropping one last bomb.

"I've ordered a copy of every customs report with your company listed as the receiver, with particular interest to anything coming from Shenzhen. If anything interesting pops up, I'll be sure to be in touch."

Ramirez's smile widened as if she knew she'd just cast a wide net, figuring something would pop up, and let herself out.

Selena's heart rate tripled as anxiety fluttered her senses.

She stabbed the intercom to ring her receptionist. "Get Mateo in my office, now."

"Yes, Ms. Hernandez," came the swift answer, and within moments Mateo strolled in, looking as if he'd just spent the afternoon on the links, instead of working.

"We have a problem," she stated, rubbing her temples as a tension headache began to pound. "Another DEA agent was just here. And not just any agent, but the director. What the hell did you say to that agent while he was here?"

"I didn't say anything. He seemed to think he knew something and I let him think that. Then, I sent him on his way. Trust me, he had nothing."

"Well, he's dead."

"Yeah, so?"

"Mateo, did you have anything to do with his death?"

Mateo glared. "What kind of question is that? You know I don't dirty my hands in that way."

"Well, that DEA agent is making it her mission to snoop around in our records. She's pulling all our customs manifests and going over our shipments with a fine-tooth comb."

Mateo didn't look as worried as he should. "We're a pharmaceutical company. We traffic in drugs. It's what we do."

"Not the drugs that will show up on some of those manifests and you know it."

"Do you really think that cop is going to know the difference?" Mateo asked, bored. "Sister, you need to relax. Go get a facial or a massage. All this tension is murder on your frown lines."

"Mateo, will you focus for a minute?" she demanded, becoming more frustrated by her brother's lack of concern for the situation. "We could lose everything if they find out."

"They won't."

"I don't have your confidence."

"And you never did," Mateo responded with an airy wave of his hand. "But trust in me that this will all blow over. Now, I have a date with a cute mariachi player. Such adorable behinds. All that shake, shake, shake. I love it!"

Selena watched as Mateo breezed out without a care in the world and she wanted to shake him until his fillings popped out.

If her brother ended up ruining this deal, she would put him in the ground herself.

* * *

Poppy, packed up for the night, was startled by Angelo as she was leaving backstage.

The bar was shut down and everyone had pretty much gone home except Angelo and the janitor.

"You're very talented," he said, making conversation. "A natural."

"Thank you," she said, finding it odd that Angelo was approaching her after hours. "Where's Brandi tonight?"

"She called in sick." He gestured to the bar. "Have a drink with me."

Poppy hesitated for a brief moment, but then realized she was only hesitating because of what Shaine might say. "I could use a drink after tonight's set," she said with a smile.

Shaine wasn't there tonight, having gone to Grind to check out some leads there on his night off.

"What's your poison?" he asked, going behind the bar. "Anything you want."

"Surprise me."

His brow rose as his mouth curved. "A girl who craves adventure...my kind of girl," he said, selecting the finest whiskey in the bar. He poured a shot. "Lagavulin, twenty-one-year-old Special Release, 2012...goes for $624 a bottle."

Poppy hesitated, her eyes widening. "I don't know if I can afford a shot of this stuff."

Angelo smiled and pushed it toward her. "On the house."

"Well, in that case..." She took a tentative sip. "Not bad."

He laughed. "I should hope so. We charge out the nose for this stuff."

"So what's the real reason you've asked me, after hours, for a drink?" she asked coyly. "I mean, everyone knows that you and Brandi are a thing and I sure as hell don't want to end up on her shit list."

Angelo's jaw flexed with annoyance. "I can see I need to have a talk with Brandi and set her straight on our arrangement."

"And what arrangement would that be?"

"Whatever I want it to be."

"That doesn't sound like a very good deal for her."

"She gets what she needs."

Poppy swallowed her disgust. Angelo was slimy—in a slick, suave and ultimately untrustworthy way—and she couldn't imagine why anyone would want to be with him. But he seemed a hot commodity around the party scene, which is why Brandi held on so tightly.

But Poppy was playing a game she meant to win.

"It's just not the same without Capri," she said, trying to draw the conversation to something that might be useful. "She was like a tiny bubble of sunshine with all that blond hair and those blue eyes. I swear she was a pixie or something."

"Yeah, she was a cute kid," Angelo agreed quickly, but moved on just as swiftly. "So where did you learn to dance?"

"Mrs. Danner's Dance Class for Young Ladies," she said, finishing her whiskey. "Classical ballet, jazz and tap."

"That don't look like ballet up there," he teased, and she pretended to blush. "But I like it."

"Don't tell Raquel but I borrowed some of her moves."

Angelo leaned forward to whisper, "You do them better."

Oh, he was a sweet talker, but Poppy saw right through him.

Men like Angelo said and did whatever they had to do

to get a women in bed. They'd flatter, cajole, manipulate and coerce anyone weak enough to buy into their game.

Poppy had always been able to see through men like Angelo, even before she joined the academy.

High school had been interesting.

"So tell me…what was that stuff you gave us that night at the party? Bliss? I've never heard of it but it was wild and I would love to try some more."

"Soon," Angelo said. "But it's in short supply right now. Hot commodity, you know. As soon as I get word of a new shipment, I'll be sure to let you know. Maybe we can take it together. I can show you a few things."

"Maybe so," Poppy said with a flirty smile. "Or maybe I'll show you a few things." *Like how my handcuffs work.* It still hurt to think that Capri had slept with this pig and he couldn't even stand to hear her name. Was it guilt? Or was he that shallow and self-centered that he didn't really care about a dead girl who was too young to be shaking her ass at this club?

Angelo knuckled her cheek softly. "Hey, gorgeous, where'd you go just now?" he asked.

She forced herself not to pull away. "Sorry, I'm just thinking of Capri. I miss her," she apologized, taking secret pleasure in knowing that the subject of Capri made Angelo uncomfortable. "I didn't know her long but she really burrowed into my heart. She was like the little sister I never had."

"Yeah, rough thing, her dying and all. But everything happens for a reason, right?"

That trite statement clanged like a discordant bell inside her, and she immediately thought of Shaine and how he'd hated when people would offer up that cliché when his kid brother was killed.

She wanted to shout, *No, things don't happen for a reason—sometimes they happen randomly because people are shitty to one another*, but she couldn't exactly let that fly from her mouth.

"Yeah, I guess so," she murmured, forcing a yawn. "That whiskey just took what little energy I had left. I'm going to cut out. Thanks for the drink."

"Do you need a ride home?" he asked.

"No, I have my car," Poppy answered, adding, "It's not as fancy as your car, but it gets me from point A to point B."

"So humble. You deserve so much better, baby. You're the kind of woman who deserves to be sitting in a Porsche. All you have to do is ask and I'll make it happen."

Like you made it happen for Capri? She shouldered her pack, flashing a smart-ass grin. "What can I say?" she said as she walked toward the door. "I like to do things the hard way."

"I can appreciate that. But trust me, baby-girl, once you get a taste of prime rib, you never go back to bologna."

Poppy let herself out of the club and walked into the salty night air, glad to be free of Angelo and the threat of his touch.

It was bad enough he touched her cheek.

If you have to sleep with him to get information, you will do it.

The stern voice was a reminder that she was here to do a job, and Angelo was a primary suspect on the biggest case of her life.

If it meant doing the dirty with the dirty scumbag—she swallowed the immediate bile that rose in her throat—then she'd do exactly that.

And then, afterward, she'd scrub her damn skin off.

If only she could also find some way to bleach the memories that would remain…

Chapter 19

Shaine walked into Grind, the music blaring, similar to Lit, and saw that the DJ spinning tracks was the same DJ at the warehouse party as well as the one who'd given Capri the Bliss.

He ordered a drink and milled around, seemingly on the prowl, but he was really covertly watching DJ Raven. The guy was a spectacle with his artificial, pale blue eyes and wild peacock hair. And when he began gyrating his hips in time to the beat, Shaine suspected that he might be on Bliss, as well.

When he'd been on Bliss, his body had ached to move, as if his bones tingled with the need to feel tension. That's why sex had been so sublime. Every sense was heightened to the point of almost madness, and in between that space was the ultimate high.

If Bliss were legal—and didn't cause your heart to explode after taking it too many times—the world would collapse because no one would want to ever do anything but screw and dance.

Shaine made a purposeful drive-by, catching Raven's eye as he walked, even allowing his gaze to linger as if he were appreciating the view and then kept walking.

Shaine knew his covert flirting would get noticed, and, sure enough, Raven openly stared at him with interest.

An hour later, Shaine was sitting at the bar when DJ Raven sidled up beside him with an interested smile. "I've seen you before," he said.

"Yeah, I was at the warehouse party," Shaine answered, motioning to the bartender for another drink and whatever Raven was having.

"Apple martini," Raven supplied, and returned to Shaine with an apprising stare. "I thought I recognized you. You went home with that sassy blonde who came with baby Capri."

"Yeah, good memory," he praised as he took a drink of his beer. "Were you friends with Capri?"

Raven shrugged, flipping his pink, purple and blue weave over his shoulder, his gaze roving the crowd, looking for a conquest. "Baby-girl was like a drop of rain, refreshing, sweet and doomed to evaporate in the heat of the sun."

"Why do you say that?"

"She was addicted to her vices," Raven answered with a dramatic sigh as he returned to Shaine. "I tried to tell her to slow down, but she wasn't going to listen to anyone but that little voice that told her she needed more."

Shaine shook his head, not surprised by the grim picture Raven was painting of the young, troubled girl. "She seemed a nice kid. It sucks that she's gone."

"True, true. She was a good little soldier."

That statement pricked his interest. He smiled quizzically at Raven. "What do you mean?"

"C'mon now, you've been around the scene long enough to know who runs this town. Capri was his favorite. And she was rewarded like a good girl. The only problem was that she didn't know how to keep her hands out of the cookie jar."

"Are you talking about that El Escorpion character I've heard about?" he asked incredulously, trying to seem like he didn't buy that story. "Sounds like an urban legend."

"El Escorpion is very real, baby-boy," Raven said solemnly. "And you never know who is working for him, so watch what you say. The walls have ears, if you know what I mean."

Shaine shrugged, smothering the spark of excitement at stumbling on the first real mention of the shadowy character. "So was Capri dating the guy or something?"

"You sure have a lot of questions for someone who wasn't all that interested a few moments ago."

"Just passing the time," he said, tipping his beer for a quick swig. "I have a night off and I needed a different scene other than Lit."

"Copy that. Lit is filled with overprivileged trust-fund babies who have too much money and not enough sense. And they tip like shit."

"Yeah, I've noticed. All that money and yet they are the stingiest with it."

"Funny how that works," Raven remarked drily, sipping his martini, allowing his gaze to travel up and down Shaine's body. "So how do you like working at Lit?"

"It pays the bills."

"That's it?"

He shrugged. "It's enough for me. And I like the people. Angelo seems cool. The girls are hot and the drinks are good. I'm a simple guy—that's pretty much all I need."

"Angelo," Raven repeated, exaggerating the name as if contemplating something heavy. "That man…ugh. So full of himself. You'd think his piss was the fountain of youth or something. He likes to play like he's in charge but he answers to the boss, just like everyone else."

"Do you mean the owner of the bar or someone else?"

Raven seemed to realize he let too much slip and waved away Shaine's question. "It doesn't matter. I'm just sour grapes right now. Angelo is a greedy SOB and he always has been. Nothing is going to change on that front."

"I like him," Shaine replied, wondering what secrets Raven knew about Angelo. "So, is he, like, some important big shot with this Scorpion character?"

Raven smiled and caressed Shaine's cheek. "You have the most exquisite cheekbones, baby-boy. And those eyes. I could stare for days into those peepers. Tell me…are you available for the night or are you taken?"

Bold and to the point. Shaine grinned, saying, "Taken for now, but you never know what could happen."

He purposefully left it open-ended. Hope loosened more lips. Raven smiled around his glass. "Aren't you the coy one. Maybe I'll see you around when you're *not* taken."

"Maybe so."

Raven finished his martini. "Careful who you play with, beautiful boy. Some people are better at games than most."

Raven sauntered off, melting into the crowd.

Shaine finished his beer, intrigued by the bits of information Raven had spilled.

Was Raven talking about El Escorpion? Angelo? Or someone else entirely?

Hell, maybe he was talking about himself.

Could Raven be El Escorpion? Raven had access to the party scene in a way that would go unnoticed. The DJ slipped in and out, kept to himself and served as a conduit for Bliss traffic. What better way to see and hear everything than by being seemingly part of the machine?

Digging into DJ Raven's past seemed like a good place to start.

The adjoining door opened and Shaine walked in, interrupting Poppy's morning coffee. She glanced up, surprised, but not entirely unhappy to see Shaine.

He looked as if he hadn't slept at all. His eyes were bloodshot and he had that jittery look about him that screamed, *I'm tired as shit but I can't sleep.*

When Shaine went straight to her coffeepot like a zombie in need of brains, Poppy just smiled and continued to read through her emails on the laptop.

Shaine joined her and after a few restorative sips of the hot brew, he said, "Thank God, you have coffee."

"You look like you had a rough night. Business or pleasure?"

"All business. I might've found a lead worth chasing down."

That caught her attention. "Yeah?"

"I went to Grind last night and sparked a conversation with DJ Raven. Seems the guy knows more than he lets on. He let a few tidbits slip that make me wonder if DJ Raven is our guy."

"How so?"

Shaine shared the details of his night and what he'd

found out. Poppy agreed with Shaine; there were definitely some leads to chase down.

"Let's run him through the system and see what pops up." Poppy closed her email program and pushed her laptop to Shaine, where he promptly logged into the FBI database to run a background.

"All we have is an alias. Hopefully, that's enough to grab on to something if he has a record of any sort."

They ran the search but nothing came up.

"Of course it couldn't be that easy," Poppy grumbled. "Let's get in touch with our Miami PD contacts and see if they know him by any other name. Maybe the locals know more than the FBI database."

Shaine nodded and sipped his coffee, exhaling as he settled into the chair, the tension bunching his shoulders easing. Poppy tried not to put much store in the fact that Shaine was more relaxed around her, but she couldn't help the warmth tickling her belly that had nothing to do with her dark roast.

"So, how'd you get DJ Raven to cough up some leads?" she asked, curious.

"I flirted with him."

"Ha! I wish I could've seen that!"

"Hey, whatever works. But he left me with a warning."

"What'd he say?"

"He told me to be careful, that some people play games better than most."

Intriguing. A thrill of excitement chased Poppy's spine. "That's an interesting warning. Do you think it was benevolent or malicious?"

"No clue." Shaine smiled wearily. "So how'd your night go?"

"Angelo invited me for a drink after the bar was closed."

"Did you take him up on his offer?"

"Of course. And I got to enjoy a shot of some very expensive whiskey."

"How was it?"

"The whiskey was great. The company, not so much. He was coming on to me pretty strong. I tried to lead the conversation into areas that were useful, but he was more interested in getting into my pants than actually talking."

Shaine nodded, but his jaw flexed. Poppy knew from experience that Shaine was trying to hold something back.

"Just say what you need to say, Shaine," she said with a short sigh, knowing full well what was going through his mind.

"I'm good," he replied with a brief smile. "Please continue."

All right, that was your chance, she thought. "I asked him about Brandi and he said she had the wrong idea of their relationship, pretty much implying that he was available even though he'd told you that Brandi was his girl and Brandi has told *everyone* that she and Angelo were a thing."

"It could be a classic player situation," Shaine said. "So what'd he try with you?"

"Oh, he was pushing pretty hard. Saying that I deserved the finer things in life and that I deserved someone who could take care of me.

"That kind of line would certainly work with Capri, who yearned for someone to take care of her."

"Exactly what I thought," Shaine agreed. "DJ Raven said something to that effect as well, saying that Capri had been a good little soldier, which leads me to believe that Capri knew more than was safe for her."

"Honestly, she was the perfect pawn. She had that angel face and sweet disposition. No one would look twice at Capri, unlike Raquel or even Brandi who are nothing but hard edges. Capri was soft and sweet and people liked her right away."

"But once she outstripped her usefulness or became a threat to the operation, she was easily cut down. Raven said that Capri couldn't keep her hands from the cookie jar. I don't know if that means she was skimming money from the operation or she just was addicted to Bliss."

Poppy thought of the car Capri drove. "It could be both. I know Capri loved tripping on Bliss. That poor girl wore a happy face but had a sad soul. Bliss made her forget for a short time."

"Makes you wonder what she'd been running from that she thought being a dancer for Lit was a step up," Shaine mused.

Poppy had wondered the same. "Best guess is she was molested at a young age, taught that her only value was in what she could provide for others and then was abandoned, leaving her to fend for herself much too young."

"She was in foster care, so her home life must've been pretty bad."

"And the fact that she fled her foster home makes you wonder if things were bad there, too."

Shaine nodded. "My brother Silas worked a case where the foster parents were worse than the parents the kids were taken from. Reading that report was like walking through a nightmare."

"There are many great foster parents out there, but my guess is that Capri hadn't been lucky to land with one of the good ones."

Poppy drew a deep breath, hating the ache in her chest

when she thought of Capri and how it'd ended for her. Why was she so shaken up about one broken girl? The world was filled with them and yet Capri was the one that stuck like a splinter in her heart.

"We have a debriefing at ten this morning. Are you going to make it? You look dead on your feet."

He rubbed at his eyes and yawned, but denied needing any sleep. "I'll be fine. Just need a shower and more coffee."

"And then a full shift at Lit? You're insane. We need you with a sharp mind, not fuzzed out because you're exhausted," Poppy said, rising to pull him from the chair. "You're going to take a nap."

But instead of pushing him through the adjoining door, she led him to her bedroom where he went without protesting. In fact, he seemed grateful and tumbled onto her bed, crawling to the pillow and cuddling *her* pillow. He went straight to sleep and was gently snoring before she could even blink.

The wild array of dark hair swept across his forehead, making him look younger than he was.

He was beautiful. Poppy sighed. At least that much hadn't changed.

For a long moment she watched him sleep, overcome by nostalgia and the sharp pinch of regret.

Maybe if she hadn't left so abruptly they could've figured things out.

But even as she recognized that leaving had been a re-action to extreme pain, she also knew that staying wouldn't have worked out, either. Shaine had been adamant that she no longer work undercover and it'd been anathema to her to even consider such a dictate.

For one, no one dictated to her.

For two, she required full support from anyone who professed to be in love with her.

So, yeah, leaving had been for the best.

Even if she did miss seeing that man in her bed.

She knew the smart thing to do would be to gently close the door and leave him be, but her feet were moving in his direction and she wasn't stopping herself.

Poppy climbed into the bed beside Shaine and cuddled up against him, wrapping her arms around him, just like she used to.

Immediately, Shaine sighed in his sleep, the sound going straight to her heart.

She missed him so much.

Poppy hadn't planned to sleep, but her eyes began to droop and she dropped off.

She wasn't sure of the time, but she awoke to the pleasurable sensation of hands touching her in intimate places and she knew without a doubt that it was Shaine.

Instead of stopping him, she followed his lead. Their hands touched and explored with drowsy abandon. This had been their thing—sleep sex.

They used to laugh about it, but the fact was, sometimes they'd woken in the middle of the night, lost in each other, and it'd been glorious.

This was no different.

Shaine knew just how to touch her, how to make her shudder with pleasure almost instantly.

His kiss, the feel of his fingers delving, testing, teasing…

Poppy arched into his touch, sinking into a happy place that didn't concern itself with rules or impropriety.

In this place, there was no guilt or shame for indulging in a simple pleasure, just exquisite wonder.

"Shaine," Poppy moaned, loving the way his name on her breathy sigh felt like home. "Yes…"

Shaine rose above her, those beautiful, soulful eyes staring down at her with desire and something else that made her want to cry.

They moved together, their breath shallow as they each worked to reach their climax. With Shaine it'd never been difficult, and within moments, Poppy crashed into her release, crying out as her body clenched around him.

"Poppy," he gasped, losing himself, spending as he shuddered with his climax.

He collapsed against her, pressing tiny kisses against her collarbone before rolling away, his breathing harsh.

"I'm sorry," he said, covering his eyes with his hand. "I didn't mean…"

"Shhh." She stopped him, not willing to let him shoulder the responsibility of what'd happened between them. "I'm not complaining."

He looked at her, his gaze soft. "Are you sure?"

"I'm sure."

But he still appeared as if he were shouldering a mountain of guilt and she couldn't have that.

Poppy purposefully kissed Shaine, showing him with her actions that she neither regretted what'd happened, nor blamed him in anyway. "See? No complaints."

Shaine relaxed but something still troubled him.

"What's wrong?" she asked.

"I know there are still things between us that we should probably talk about and that this doesn't change anything."

Reality was a buzzkill, but she knew he was right.

"Sex is a great stress reliever," Poppy said, trying to make light of what'd happened. "Don't read so much into it."

"I know what you're doing," he said, rising on his elbow to stare down at her. "You don't have to pretend that this was just two people relieving stress. You were never cavalier about sex."

It was true. In the beginning of their relationship, in spite of crazy chemistry, Poppy had held Shaine off for months, trying to run away from the attraction they'd felt for one another. Just falling into bed with each other hadn't been on her radar.

"I liked that about you," Shaine admitted softly. "You were different."

"In high school, I was accused of being a prude," Poppy shared with a small laugh. "If they could see me now…"

"I like that you knew you deserved better. I liked having to work for it."

Poppy blushed. "Well, I might've made you work extra hard."

"You were worth it."

"Stop," she said, blinking back tears. "I can't do this."

"Do what?"

"Bare our souls." She rolled away, irritated at herself for climbing into that bed with Shaine knowing that it would only complicate matters. "I don't regret the sex, Shaine. But I can't pretend that everything is as it was because it never will be. We live separate lives and I'm good with my life. I've moved on as I'm sure you have, too."

Shaine's disappointment was evident as he climbed from the bed and dressed. "You're right," he finally said. "There's no point in scratching at what we've both buried. Sometimes, it's hard to remember why things didn't work out."

It wasn't hard for her. She was reminded every time she awoke in sunny California—endlessly sunny

California—when she longed for an East Coast winter season.

She was reminded every time she closed her eyes in her empty bed that the person she most wanted beside her was the one person who'd broken her heart in the most grievous way possible.

But she wasn't going to say that.

She wasn't going to say *any* of that.

"We have an hour before debriefing," Poppy said, signaling the end of the conversation and cuing Shaine to leave.

He took the hint.

But before he left her apartment, he shared a few final thoughts.

"It's possible you and I will never get each other out of our systems. There's something inside us that keeps that spark alive, and knowing that we can't be together hurts and pisses me off at the same time, because I know we had something great."

"Had. Past tense," she pointed out softly.

"Yeah…" Shaine said, shaking his head, adding as he walked out, "Well, sometimes it doesn't feel past tense."

She couldn't agree more.

It hurt like a bitch but nothing had changed.

And it never would.

Chapter 20

The team assembled in the debriefing an hour later. Shaine was out of sorts. Although he'd slept hard, what had followed afterward was still sitting on him.

Whatever Poppy was feeling, she kept under lock and key because she was the picture of professional.

He envied her ability to shut her emotions off, but he'd find a way to do the same.

"Our officers within Miami PD were able to run down a name used by DJ Raven," Ramirez began, handing out a printed mug shot. "His name is Franklin Brown, age twenty-seven, from the slums in Overtown."

"Looks a lot different without all that peacock hair and weird contact lenses," Shaine noted, as he surveyed the printout. "What's his story?"

"Troubled kid, in and out of juvenile hall, abuse, violence, the usual story. He found the underground Miami scene and reemerged as DJ Raven. As far as I can tell, he supports himself through DJ gigs. He's created quite a name for himself in certain circles."

"Yeah, as the guy who brings the party," Shaine said. "He's the one supplying Bliss at these secret location parties, like the warehouse."

"Did we find out who owns that building?" Poppy asked.

Victoria answered, "The building is vacant. It's owned by a trust and more than likely used as a tax shelter. It's a perfect location for an underground party."

"But the location of the parties always changes, according to Capri," Poppy reminded everyone. "So I'm betting whoever owns that building might know something about the parties that go on there. Otherwise, how else would they know to use that building on that night?"

"Angelo said something about needing time to coordinate the next party," Shaine remembered. "Which tells me there are many players in this game. Even if they don't realize they're part of it."

"I think that's the beauty of El Escorpion's operation…everyone is playing their part but likely they have no idea that they're playing at all. It's built-in plausible deniability. You can't testify about something you know nothing about," Poppy said.

Shaine turned to Ramirez. "Any luck with Amerine Labs?"

"Not much. That Selena Hernandez is one cool cucumber. She didn't flinch or exhibit any signs of stress when I mentioned that we were pulling their customs records, but my intuition said it bothered her. Now we wait to see what move they make next."

Shaine hated waiting. "Let's list what we have so far," he

said, rising to go to the whiteboard. He grabbed a dry-erase pen and started making a list. "Possible suspects—Angelo, DJ Raven, the Hernandez siblings, maybe even Mayor Ferdinand. Who else?"

"I'd definitely put Brandi and Raquel on that list," Poppy supplied, rubbing her chin in thought.

"What about the other girls?"

"The only other regulars are Missy and Tabitha and I'd say a hard no on both of those girls. Big Jane is the only other person in the back and I can't see a middle-aged former stripper with a strong maternal instinct being the mastermind. Besides, I've seen her apartment. She's not exactly living in luxury."

"What did we find out on that stripper Darcy Lummox?" Shaine asked Victoria.

"She's disappeared off the grid. Nothing on her credit cards and nothing on her bank account. For all intents and purposes, Darcy Lummox doesn't exist any longer."

"That sounds like dead to me," Poppy said, sharing Shaine's ominous thought. "We should check the morgues."

Victoria took on that job. "I don't love morgues but I'll do it."

"Vic, you nearly barfed when we took a look at Capri's dead body. I'm not sure you're the right fit."

Victoria didn't argue because it was true. For an agent, Victoria had a decidedly weak stomach.

"Shaine and I will go," Poppy volunteered.

Ramirez wasn't sure. "I don't know if I want you two seen together at the morgue. It's not organic."

"We'll go in the back door. No one will see us," Poppy assured the director.

Ramirez nodded but warned, "Make sure that they don't."

"You know, the best person to ask about Darcy might be Big Jane. She is very motherly toward all the girls who will let her. She might know what happened to her."

"Good idea," Shaine said. "Get closer to Big Jane. If anyone knew what was going on behind the scenes, it's probably her."

"In the meantime, I'll have our forensic accounting department go over the customs paperwork. I'm sure something is bound to pop up that will lead us back to Amerine Labs."

"Why would a lab risk their reputation to mess around with illegal drugs?" Victoria asked, perplexed. "I mean, that's not exactly a struggling business model."

"Yeah, but we're talking about wealth and extreme wealth. The pull can be very seductive."

"Not to mention the tax-free perk of dirty money," Shaine drawled. "Taxes on the pharmaceuticals must be a bitch."

"Are you kidding? They get tax breaks," Victoria scoffed. "Any big corporation finds loopholes that aren't available to the little guys like us."

"All right, all right, we're not going to sit here and debate the merits and deficits of the US tax law," Ramirez cut in. "We need movement on this case. This operation is costing millions and results are expected. Let's make it happen."

The debriefing ended and Shaine and Poppy agreed to meet at the coroner's in an hour. That gave Shaine time to grab a quick bite and another coffee.

He wasn't so dense that he didn't realize that sleeping in Poppy's bed had been the best sleep he'd had in weeks.

The sex afterward had been an unexpected bonus.

The scent of her hair on the pillow had put him right

to sleep. Spending all this time with her had made him realize how much he'd been missing.

But he'd royally screwed up.

There was no fixing what he'd broken.

That much was apparent by how quickly she distanced herself after sex. Going so far as to put a hasty label on their motivation, calling it "stress relief" when, in fact, it'd felt like making love.

But your heart had to be involved in order to make love and that was something neither he nor Poppy were ready to admit to.

The reality was, neither were in a position to open that door.

Poppy was making a name for herself with the DEA and he was really proud of her. If she'd caved to his demands to get out of the field, she would've stagnated and gone nowhere.

How could he have selfishly thought that was okay?

And even if he apologized after having this grand epiphany, what good would it do now aside from complicate an already complicated situation? It wasn't as if an apology was going to wipe away two years of time between them.

Her life was in Los Angeles. His life was in DC.

That's the way it was and he had to be okay with that.

"You two again," the coroner said with a jovial smile. For a coroner, he was a pretty jolly fellow. "I'm starting to think one of you has a crush on me."

Poppy chuckled and said, "No crush, not that you aren't adorable, but we're looking for information on someone we think might've ended up as a Jane Doe."

"Well, let's see what the computer has to tell us," the

coroner said, rolling over to the desk. "Let's start with a name and see if anything shows up."

"Her name was Darcy Lummox. She went by the stage name of Tinsel."

"Tinsel? How exotic." The coroner tapped in the name and waited. Then he brightened. "Well, look at that. Here she is. And yes, she was listed as a Jane Doe until we could get a match on her prints. Her fingertips were badly damaged, so it took some time to decipher the prints."

"Did anyone come to identify her?" Shaine asked.

"Sadly, we went to all the trouble of identifying the poor girl and then no one came to claim her. She was cremated and buried on the city's dime."

"How'd she die?" Poppy asked.

"Strangulation. She had significant bruising around her neck and her hyoid bone was broken."

"Any leads?"

"You know, ordinarily, I wouldn't remember one Jane Doe case over another, but this one stuck in my mind. She was a pretty thing. Long blond hair, blue eyes, but she looked real young. Good genes, I suppose. She died at nineteen but she could've passed for fifteen easily."

Poppy shared a look with Shaine. Was it possible that Darcy was the original Capri but something went sidewise?

"Thank you, Doctor," Poppy murmured. "Was there any next of kin listed for Darcy?"

The coroner rechecked the file. "Yes, a sister. Olivia Lummox. She lives right here in Miami but she didn't come to claim the remains."

"That's curious," Poppy observed, looking to Shaine who seemed to agree. "Why wouldn't a sister, the only living kin, come to claim her only sibling?"

"Hard feelings between the sisters?"

"Maybe. Guess there's one way to find out."

A road trip.

"Got an address, Doc?" Poppy asked.

"Sure do, 1213 Buhach Drive."

"Thanks," Shaine said, and they left to find out why Darcy's sister didn't want to have anything to do with her.

They each drove to a secluded location before dropping off Poppy's car and regrouping in Shaine's car, that way no one saw them leaving together or traveling together near the coroner's office. They couldn't take too many risks with their cover being blown. It was a pain in the ass, but hopefully worth it.

Poppy tried to keep her thoughts centered, but they were all over the place. And when they did settle, they settled on stuff she didn't want to think about.

"You okay?" Shaine asked, noting her pensive silence.

She sighed, deciding to selectively share her thoughts. "I was thinking about Capri the other night and wondering how her life might've been different if she'd been placed in a decent foster home. She was a smart kid. With better people in her life, she could've been more than what she'd ended up."

"No doubt," he agreed. "But isn't that the case with so many people? I hate to echo Ramirez, but Capri's case is pretty common."

"It's easier to be detached from the statistics when you're just analyzing numbers on a piece of paper. It's different when you know the kids getting killed."

Shaine understood. "I know where you're coming from. When I lost Walter, it stuck with me. You never forget, but maybe you can channel that grief and anger into some-

thing proactive, to help a different kid have a better out-
come, you know?"

Poppy nodded in reflective silence. Times like this,
losing so much, she worried that no one was ever going
to manage to change what was wrong with the world.

"Every case leaves a mark of some kind. You never
come out without leaving with something new to regret."

"Is that why you didn't want me going into undercover
work?" she asked.

"Partially," he admitted slowly as if not quite sure he
wanted to have this particular conversation. But he surprised her when he said, "But it doesn't matter. I was
wrong. You're a good agent and you do good work. We
need more people like you in the field, not less."

Unwelcome tears crowded her sinuses. "Do you mean
that?"

"Of course I do."

Dammit. If only he'd just said *that* instead of what
he'd *actually* said that caused them to break up. Everything would've been so different today. "Why couldn't
you have said that years ago?" she asked, almost angrily.

"Because I didn't realize the truth of it until it was
too late."

And that was even worse. Maybe it would've been
easier to stomach if Shaine had continued to be an ass,
doubting her abilities and questioning her experience,
because then she could tell him to piss off and not lose
a minute of sleep.

But that was not what was happening.

The big jerk was contrite.

And each time he looked at her with such stark honesty and raw regret, she wanted to bawl her head off,
which wasn't good at all.

Poppy looked away, her gaze drawn to the passing scenery as she struggled to refocus. "Ain't life a bitch..." she said in a rhetorical murmur, wishing she hadn't brought up the topic.

Shaine seemed to agree and rather than continue to drive nails into each other's hearts, he turned on the radio.

And for that, she was grateful.

Shaine pulled slowly up to Buhach Drive and Poppy saw the older neighborhood still had some charm, though small signs of decay had begun. At one time, the neighborhood had probably been very nice.

The house was surrounded by a waist-high chain-link fence, which had begun to rust. The lawn had patches of crabgrass and bare spots from where an animal had urinated. Poppy whistled softly and a dog bounded from around the corner, a pit bull with a happily wagging tail.

"Hey there, boy, are you going to let us in?" Poppy asked in a soft voice, allowing the dog to sniff her fingers. He licked her fingertips and she took that as a good sign. Slowly opening the gate, she and Shaine walked in. The dog, not much of a watchdog, trotted alongside them, more eager for a pat than to protect his territory.

Poppy knocked on the front door, taking note of the cracked weather stripping and how the door had minor cosmetic damage, as if someone had tried to kick the door down but failed because, in spite of its age, it was solid wood.

"Someone has had some action here," she murmured to Shaine and he nodded, indicating he'd seen it, too.

The door opened slowly and a woman peered out cautiously. "Yes?"

"Olivia Lummox?" Poppy asked in a welcoming voice so as not to scare the woman. When Olivia nodded, Poppy said, "May we come in? We're with the Miami coroner's office. We have a few questions about your sister, Darcy."

Olivia looked unhappy but opened the door and let them in. The dog followed, wagging his butt as he went. "I already told the cops what I knew," she said, leading them into a small formal living room filled with antique furniture. She patted the sofa cushion beside her and the dog jumped up to cuddle beside her.

"That's a great dog you have, very sweet," Poppy started, trying to loosen the tension. "What's his name?"

"Zeus," Olivia answered, pursing her lips ruefully. "He was supposed to be a good watchdog but as you can tell…he's a giant teddy bear. But I love him to death and I couldn't take him back to the pound. So unless someone is afraid of being licked to death, he poses no threat."

"Why did you feel the need for a watchdog?" Shaine asked.

"The neighborhood isn't what it used to be when I was growing up. Our grandmother raised us here and left the house to me and Darcy when she died," Olivia said.

That explained the antique furniture.

"It's a lovely home," Poppy said. "Your grandmother must've had good taste."

"She did." Olivia paused and then asked, "Why did you say you were here? Darcy has been dead for months. Is there a break in her case or something?"

"It's too early to tell, but we're just running down some leads in our spare time. We're not detectives, but when you work with dead bodies all day, sometimes you want to vary the routine."

Olivia nodded but remained puzzled. "I can't imagine what else I could say that I didn't already say to the detectives on her case."

"Sometimes a fresh set of eyes is all one needs to break open a case," Poppy said.

"I guess so. Here goes nothing." Olivia drew a deep breath before continuing. "Darcy was a wild child, always running off to do her own thing. She gave our grandmother more than her share of gray hair worrying about her. I'm just glad Grandma had already passed by the time Darcy started running with that party crowd."

"Did you know that Darcy was dancing at a club called Lit under the name Tinsel?"

Olivia made a look of distaste. "Yes," she nearly spat. "That disgusting place. We were raised better than that. I don't know what came over her. She was obsessed with this guy named Angelo and thought he was in love with her. Then packages started coming to the house. At first, I didn't think anything of it, but then they came every week and each time she would snatch them up, saying they were for a friend. I took a peek at the label and it was from China. I thought to myself, 'What the hell was she ordering from China?'"

"Did you ask her?"

"Yeah, but she clammed up, saying it was none of my business and it was better for me if I didn't know. Of course, that freaked me out and I told her as much, but she didn't care. She was completely over the moon for that Angelo guy and would've done anything for him if he'd asked."

"Did you ever find out what was in the packages?" Shaine asked.

"No, Darcy moved out suddenly, saying she was moving in with a friend and I didn't have to poke my nose into her business anymore. I tried to get her to change her mind but she bailed and I never saw her again."

"Did you try to contact her?"

"Yes, but then she changed her number when she realized I wouldn't stop calling."

"Sounds like you really cared for your sister," Poppy said gently. "Why didn't you claim her remains?"

Olivia's eyes watered and the dog whined, thumping his tail nervously. She soothed the pup with a soft pat on his broad head. "I couldn't bear to admit that she was gone. I know it's stupid but somehow I think I got it into my mind that if I never claimed her body, it couldn't be real. By the time I realized that was preposterous, they had already cremated and buried her and there was nothing left for me to claim. It was over."

So it wasn't a rift between the sisters but extreme grief that had kept Olivia away.

"Do you know who Darcy moved in with? Was it Angelo?"

"No, a woman. That's all I know."

It could be anyone from the club or even someone Darcy had met on the scene. Finding her roommate would be near to impossible.

"Thank you for your time," Poppy said, rising. "I'm curious…how did Darcy meet Angelo?"

"One of her friends from high school started dancing at that club, Lit, downtown, and invited her to try it out. Angelo was the bartender."

"Do you know the friend's name?" Shaine asked.

"Yeah, it was Christine Wilson," Olivia answered, wiping at her eyes. She reached for a framed picture and handed it to Poppy. "Here's a picture of them in high school. It's my favorite."

Poppy stared, unable to believe what she was seeing.

Brandi.

Chapter 21

"How does this make any sense that Brandi and Darcy were friends and we're just now hearing about it?" Poppy asked as they drove back to their apartments.

"It does raise a lot of questions," he agreed. "Do you think she's involved with Darcy's death? She seems hard enough to commit cold-blooded murder."

"Something doesn't add up. Why would she convince her friend to come dance at Lit and then do nothing when her friend goes missing?"

"Maybe she was jealous?"

"Jealous enough to kill?" Poppy asked, shaking her head, not buying it. "I think we're missing something vital here. Brandi is seemingly head over heels for Angelo, which is how Olivia said Darcy acted about Angelo, too. How could two friends fall for the same guy?"

"From my experience women can fall for the same guy

all the time and it can ruin friendships. You mean to tell me you never fought with a friend over a guy?"

Poppy shook her head. "No. If a friend liked a boy or dated him, he was off-limits. It was easier that way, no drama."

"You're in the minority. I remember being at the center of many girl fights."

Poppy cast him a derisive glance. "Oh, and didn't that just feed your already monster-sized ego."

"Hey, you didn't know me in high school. How do you know that I wasn't shy and nerdy?"

She laughed and he didn't know if he should be flattered or insulted, but he grinned, anyway. "Okay, Miss Perfect, what were you like in high school aside from a paragon of virtue who always took the high road?"

"You're mocking me," Poppy said. "I didn't say I was perfect. I'm just saying I didn't chase after boys that I considered off-limits. It wasn't so much taking the high road as taking the less complicated road. I hated girl drama and did whatever I could to avoid it."

"I'm sorry, I didn't mean to mock you. Actually, I think you were pretty wise for a teenager. I wish I'd been as mature."

He earned a smile for that one and he gladly took it. He liked making her smile. But soon enough they needed to return to the case.

"All right, so tonight I'm going to talk to Big Jane and see if I can't get some background information on Darcy and Brandi. Big Jane knows everyone and everything that goes on in the club."

"I thought you already asked Big Jane about Darcy?"

"I did but I didn't press. She didn't seem interested

in talking about her so I dropped it, thinking there were more pressing leads to chase after."

"Why was Big Jane reluctant to talk about Darcy?"

Poppy shrugged. "I don't know, she just changed the subject."

"Knowing now that Brandi and Darcy had history, doesn't it seem odd that she wouldn't want to talk about it?"

Poppy looked troubled. "Yes, it does. I'll definitely dig at that when I see her."

"You know Ramirez thinks our best bet is the Hernandez siblings, but I don't know… Something doesn't feel right with that angle," Shaine said, not quite sure why he didn't think much would turn up with that lead. "I know Ramirez wants them for El Escorpion, but my gut says we're wasting our time with that one."

"They have a legitimate access to a drug pipeline from China. It wouldn't be difficult for them to acquire the raw materials. I can see how Ramirez would think that they're good for it."

"True," he conceded, pulling up to the private location where they'd left Poppy's car. Shaine put the car in Park and turned to Poppy. "Be careful out there. With Marcus gone…this operation feels more dangerous than ever before. I don't like the feeling that maybe we're the ones being played. If our covers have been blown, then we're sitting ducks. I don't like that feeling at all."

Poppy stiffened a little. "Do you think I can't take care of myself?"

"Stop, no. That's not what I'm saying," he said, putting a quick end to whatever nonsense was brewing in her head. He didn't want a stupid misunderstanding to destroy all the good work they'd put in so far. "I'm say-ing, as a fellow agent and your partner…stay sharp."

Poppy relaxed and nodded. "Sorry, I guess I'm a little oversensitive."

"It's all right. I know where it comes from."

Now would've been an opportune time to apologize, to just let himself be vulnerable with Poppy, but he couldn't do it. He wasn't one to embark on useless endeavors and that's what apologizing felt like. They weren't going to fix what'd happened in the past, so why bother dredging it up?

"You're a good man, Shaine Kelly," Poppy said, smil-ing warmly.

A blush actually climbed his throat to heat his cheeks. "Don't be saying that too loudly. I wouldn't want to ruin my street cred."

But then she reached over and brushed a sweet kiss across his lips and a surge of something tender washed over him. He wanted to hold on to that moment forever but it was gone much too soon and he was forced to watch her climb out of the car and drive away.

For a long moment he sat in his car, thinking.

Thinking about how things might've been.

Thinking about how stupid he must've been to let her go.

Thinking he'd give his left nut to go back in time so he could make the right choice this time.

But most of all, he was thinking of that kiss.

And how he wanted a million more just like it.

That night Poppy found Big Jane as she was trying to help Missy into a skintight pleather bustier.

"Good God, girl, stop with the cupcakes," Big Jane ad-monished, squeezing Missy until the girl yelped. "You've gained a metric ton. There's no way you're going to fit in this thing now."

"I've only gained ten pounds," Missy said, sucking in her stomach so Big Jane could yank the enclosures closed. "See?" she said, barely able to breathe. "It still fits."

"You're going to pass out like a Victorian lady with her stays too tight," Big Jane retorted, watching as Missy tottered off unevenly. She sighed. "That girl's dancing days are numbered if she doesn't lay off the sweets. She's eating her feelings, poor thing."

"Yeah, I heard Brandi say something about Missy giving a kid up for adoption?"

Big Jane nodded sadly. "Yes, but it's better this way. Missy is a hot mess and she's in no shape to parent a child. She made the right choice."

"She seems like she might need some help, though," Poppy suggested, wondering if Missy suffered from post-partum depression. "Giving up a baby must be terribly hard."

"Yes, I'm sure it is," Big Jane agreed but shrugged, saying, "Better to give the kid a chance at a good life than to selfishly hold on to it and drag the kid through hell."

Poppy looked at Big Jane. "Speaking from experience?"

"I was never so lucky," Big Jane answered wistfully. "But I always wanted kids. Just never worked out that way."

"You would've been a great mom," Poppy said, playing to Big Jane's soft side. "You're so maternal with all of us. I really feel safe and welcome with you around."

"Why, thank you, honey," Big Jane said with a bright smile. "It's good to be needed."

Raquel stalked out, pushed past Poppy and Big Jane

and hit the stage. It was then Poppy realized that Brandi wasn't there for a second night in a row. "Where's Brandi?" she asked.

"Angelo said she's still not feeling well. Poor kid. Probably caught the stomach bug going around."

But suddenly Poppy got a queasy feeling in her gut. "Has anyone aside from Angelo checked on her?" she asked.

"No, but I'm sure Angelo is taking good care of her."

Somehow she doubted that. Angelo was having fun while the ball and chain was otherwise occupied.

"Big Jane, did you know that Brandi and Tinsel were friends in high school before Tinsel came to dance at Lit?" Poppy decided to just put it out there and see what turned up.

At the mention of Darcy's stage name, Big Jane stilled and, after a long moment, seemed to force a smile. "That's right. I'd forgotten about that. Well, to be honest, she was only here for such a short time I'd almost forgotten about her."

"Did Brandi and Tinsel have a falling-out or something?"

"If they did, it was probably over Angelo. That man seems to have a way with women. I don't see it, personally, but then, maybe I'm past that stage in my life where I need a man to tell me what to do and when to do it."

She was the second person who thought Brandi and Darcy had squabbled over Angelo.

But how did Darcy end up dead?

Poppy decided to leave the questions or else it might seem odd that she kept poking at the subject with more than just passing curiosity. Besides, her set was coming up and she hadn't even applied her makeup yet.

A few moments later, she took the stage and began her usual routine. She allowed the lights to blind her so she didn't see the leering men, and some women, as she worked her set.

The thing was, stripping at the right place was a good way to earn a lot of money, and while she hated that some girls fell into this career, not by choice but by circumstance, she found dancing to be more liberating than she would've imagined.

When she was on stage, she allowed herself to really become Laci Langford, the small-town Connecticut girl who wanted more than her small town could provide.

And when she managed to catch Shaine's eye, she pretended that she was dancing only for him, instead of the throng of people throwing their cash at her.

A part of her wished she could keep her earnings, but she knew it would all go into the department logs and it would be absorbed back into the budget. She was paid well; she didn't need her stripper money.

But it wasn't easy parting with all that sweaty cash.

And because of that, she could understand how girls got themselves into trouble with this lifestyle. The tease of more money was always there. Private dances, escort services, hell, even flat-out prostitution were always options for the right price.

Was that the road Capri had gone down? Poppy knew the girl had done some extracurricular activities, but she hated to think that Capri had sold herself like that.

Poppy pushed thoughts of Capri away, needing to focus. Tomorrow she would check on Brandi, but for now she needed to dance.

Chapter 22

Rosa received an email from forensic accounting later that evening as she was winding down with a glass of wine. She sat up straighter and set her glass down. The smile on her lips growing wider as she read. It was as she suspected; Amerine Labs was up to something hinky.

In the past year several shipments from Shenzhen had been flagged with improperly classified chemical compounds and not one had been investigated, which told Rosa that palms had been greased.

"You better ring up that fancy lawyer team of yours because I'm getting a search warrant, you snotty bitch."

Rosa tried not to gloat but it felt pretty good. Rosa had spent her life being judged by women like Selena Hernandez. She'd done her research and Selena had been born to a wealthy family. It wasn't as if she had ever known what it was like to go to bed hungry, unlike Rosa.

Miami was a beautiful town and she was proud to be a native, but it could be a harsh place if you were born on the wrong side of the tracks.

She sent a quick text to Patrick to let him know of her findings and then went to get the bottle of wine from the kitchen to celebrate their good luck when she was interrupted by a knock at her front door.

Rosa never had visitors this late. She unholstered her gun and went to the door, peeking out the spy hole. No one was there, but a package sat on her front stoop.

Well, that wasn't suspicious at all.

Rosa immediately called Miami PD to make a report. In light of the situation, the bomb squad responded to remove the package.

Using a robot drone, the package was removed from the stoop and x-rayed to determine if there were explosives. When the all clear was given, the package was opened and its contents revealed.

A fashion doll wearing an exact duplicate of Rosa's current outfit was lying in the box with duct tape over her mouth and a note pinned to her breast.

Snitches get stitches and end up in ditches.

"Clever," Rosa murmured, amused by the attempt at intimidation. She thanked the boys in blue for helping her out and then released them.

"Are you sure you don't want us to take that to our forensics department?" the officer asked.

"This may be related to an ongoing case under DEA jurisdiction. I'll have our forensics team handle it. Thank you for your help."

The officers nodded and left, the hubbub of having

the bomb squad in her tiny neighborhood finally set-
tling as people returned to their homes, the excitement
over for the night.

Using gloves, she sealed the doll into an airtight plastic
bag and locked the door, making sure to use the dead bolt
and the chain. Then she closed all her windows, making
sure there was no way anyone could peer into her house
while she slept.

And most important, Rosa made sure her gun was within
grabbing distance. If anyone tried to pay her a visit in the
middle of the night, they were going to discover what a bad
idea that was.

Obviously, Selena Hernandez must know that the manifests were going to show something wasn't right with
their shipments and this was her attempt at scaring Rosa
into backing off.

Yeah, right. Like that was going to happen. It would
take more than a plastic doll with questionable fashion
choices to scare her away from the biggest case of her
career.

But it meant they were on the right track. Someone was
nervous. And nervous people made desperate choices.

And desperate choices led to mistakes.

Bam.

*Can you feel the noose tightening around your neck?
Here it comes, baby. You're going down.*

Rosa fell asleep with a smile.

Poppy found Brandi's apartment and knocked on the
door with her free hand while balancing a bowl of covered soup in the other.

When there was no answer, she knocked harder, saying, "Brandi? It's Laci? Can I come in?"

A long pause followed and Poppy heard shuffling inside the apartment, which told her Brandi was at least home.

When the door finally opened a sliver, Poppy tried not to gasp. Her right eye was black and blue, swollen and weeping, and her lip was busted.

"Brandi…can I come in?" she asked, worried for the girl. Poppy wasn't going to ask if she was okay because she could plainly see that she wasn't. When Brandi reluctantly let Poppy in, she saw that Brandi also walked with a limp.

"What happened?" Poppy asked, setting the soup down and watching as Brandi levered herself painfully into a recliner. "You need to go to the hospital. I think you need a doctor. How long have you been like this?"

Brandi shook her head weakly, tears leaking down her face. Gone was the self-assured, sassy brunette Poppy had first met at the club. This woman was broken.

What the hell had happened?

The smell of old blood and sweat filled the small apartment and Poppy knew she had to get Brandi to the hospital somehow or she was going to go septic from her injuries.

Rising, she went quickly to the sink and wet a clean dishcloth with cool water. She returned to Brandi and gently wiped her face, blotting the dried blood away, trying to get a better idea of her injuries.

"What happened?" she breathed, horrified for the girl. "Who did this to you? Was it Angelo?"

Brandi didn't answer, but tears leaked down her face, confirming Poppy's suspicions.

She peered at Brandi, trying to do a rudimentary assessment of her injuries. "I think you have a broken orbital bone. Your nose may be broken, as well. And what about your leg? It might be fractured, too, judging by the way you're limping. I'm calling for help."

Brandi whimpered, trying to shake her head, making mewling noises in protest as her fat lip prevented her from forming words.

"I can't let you sit here and die," Poppy said firmly, knowing she was taking a risk but she couldn't leave Brandi like this, particularly when it was Angelo who was supposedly her caretaker.

She couldn't carry Brandi on her own and she knew better than to call an ambulance, as it would attract too much attention that would get back to Angelo.

Poppy called Shaine.

"I need you now," she said quietly. "I will text the address. Come immediately and quietly."

Shaine didn't ask unnecessary questions, just affirmed he was on his way. She texted the address and returned to Brandi, who looked nearly delirious with pain.

Honestly, if Brandi hadn't been in such pain, chances were she would've shunned Poppy's help. As luck would have it, Brandi must've been at her limit to even allow Poppy into her apartment.

So much for asking Brandi questions about Darcy.

Shaine arrived fifteen minutes later and Brandi had already passed out from the pain.

"Holy shit. What happened to her?" Shaine asked, frowning as he surveyed the damage. "She's almost unrecognizable."

"Someone beat the snot out of her," Poppy answered. "I think it was Angelo."

"Why?"

"I don't know. Brandi can't talk. Her mouth is too

swollen. Whatever happened, it must've been bad. Can you smell the blood?"

"Yeah, and the bleach."

Chances were Angelo had tried to clean up the evidence of the blood splatter after he'd beaten the shit out of Brandi.

"Can you carry Brandi to the car? We can't call the ambulance."

Shaine nodded and Poppy cautioned, "Be careful. She may have a broken leg."

Brandi's eyes fluttered open and she groaned when she saw Shaine, trying to turn her head away as if she were embarrassed at being seen so vulnerable.

"I got you, girl," he murmured as he gently scooped Brandi up out of the chair, hoisting her up.

A choked cry of pain escaped Brandi's damaged lips, but she didn't fight Shaine.

Shaine carried Brandi to the car and they all climbed in. Poppy sat in the back with Brandi to help her with the seat belt and to keep her upright.

"Why are you doing this?" Brandi mumbled, wincing as her lip began to bleed anew. Poppy gently blotted the blood away as well as the fresh tears that had begun to fall down Brandi's cheeks. "Why?" she croaked.

"Because you might be a bitch but you're still a human being and no one deserves to be beaten and left to die."

Shaine drove quickly to the hospital and the emergency personnel took over.

As Brandi was wheeled away, Poppy resisted the urge to hug Shaine desperately, so grateful he'd been a phone call away. But they didn't know who was potentially watching so they played it cool.

"Want to grab a coffee?" Shaine asked, which was code for "let's talk," and Poppy gladly agreed.

Once they were certain they were alone, Shaine jumped in. "Why would Angelo beat Brandi like that? He nearly killed her. Do you think she was threatening to tell something she knew?"

"I can only imagine. Did you get the text from Ramirez about her package?"

"Yeah, had to be from the Hernandez duo. And if it is, they are stupider than I thought, which tells me, whatever they are, they aren't El Escorpion."

Poppy had to agree. El Escorpion was clever and sneaky. Selena and Mateo were accustomed to using a blunt object when finesse was in order, which is something El Escorpion would never do.

"We can't let Brandi go back to the club. If Angelo was the one who did this, he shouldn't be around her," Poppy said. "I think we should put Brandi in protective custody. Let Angelo think she ran away because of what he did."

"That's taking a big risk to our operation," Shaine warned.

"I know it was Angelo who did it. I've been asking for days where Brandi was and he just kept saying she was sick. He knew she was beaten to hell and he didn't try and get her help because he knew the hospital would be required by law to alert the authorities."

"If we put her into protective custody, she could be there for months, depending on how long it takes to close this case," he reminded Poppy, but she wasn't going to budge.

"My gut says we need to do this."

Shaine considered it, then said, "All right, I trust your

judgment. I don't think Ramirez is going to like it but I know my director will back me if need be."

"She's so hot for the Hernandez brother and sister that she's ignoring what's right in her face. If anyone is losing their judgment on this case, it's her. It feels personal and that's dangerous."

Shaine nodded. "You might be right. I'll discuss our concerns with Hobbs so he's aware. In the meantime, we need to get the paperwork started so that we can have Brandi moved to a more secure location immediately."

Poppy jerked a short nod. "I'll stay here and make sure that no one finds out that Brandi is here. You go start the wheels turning."

"You sure you're going to be okay?" Shaine asked. "What if Angelo shows up?"

"Then I'll handle it," Poppy answered without blinking. She'd love to show Angelo a few moves of her own, teach him that it wasn't nice to beat women. If she got her hands on him, Angelo would be drinking out of a straw for the rest of his life.

Shaine seemed satisfied with her answer but he hesitated, looking as if he wanted to kiss her. For a split second she held her breath, hoping recklessly that he would, but the moment passed and he bailed, leaving her missing the kiss that had almost happened.

Chapter 23

Shaine met Ramirez at the debriefing site, along with Victoria.

As predicted, Rosa wasn't pleased with the newest development.

"There's no need to put Brandi into protective custody," Ramirez said, shaking her head. "The most recent development with the Hernandez siblings points to them acting as El Escorpion. I have a search warrant being served as we speak to collect their records. They're as good as caught."

"El Escorpion wouldn't be so sloppy as to send you a threatening message like that creepy doll. I don't doubt it was the Hernandez siblings who sent you the messed-up message, but they aren't smart enough to be El Escorpion."

"I disagree. I think it's their hubris that is blinding

them to how close they are to being caught," Rosa argued vehemently. "They had motive, means and we have evidence that they're receiving illegal compounds from Shenzhen. Sometimes if it walks and talks like a duck, it's a duck."

"Under most circumstances, I would agree with you, but we're not dealing with your average criminal. Whoever El Escorpion is, they are crafty and used to flying under the radar. That's why no one knows who it actually is. I think we'd be making a big mistake if we didn't put Brandi into protective custody."

Ramirez's gaze narrowed. "I'm aware of your past history with Agent Jones. I hope this is not misplaced trust in action. Agent Jones seems to be getting attached to the girls she's embedded with, which would cloud her judgment. I can understand Agent Jones wanting to keep Brandi safe, but putting her into protective custody would put this investigation at unnecessary risk."

"You're misreading the situation. Jones isn't attached to Brandi—the girl is a bitch. Jones is trying to prevent someone getting killed. That's all."

"Collateral damage is inevitable, you and I both know that," Ramirez said, not budging. "As I told Jones already, you can't save them all."

"She's more valuable alive than dead," Shaine countered. "Whether or not Angelo did this to Brandi, Brandi knows Angelo better than anyone. She's our best bet to finding out if Angelo is El Escorpion."

"We have solid evidence pointing to the Hernandezes as our target," Ramirez argued, leaning on the table with a glower. "I'm sure forensics will come back with evidence that the Hernandezes had that doll delivered in order to scare me."

"That's just it…El Escorpion isn't that sloppy or obvious. You're right in that Selena or Mateo may have sent you that package, but they don't have the mental dexterity to pull off what El Escorpion has been doing for years."

"Are you sure you're not siding with Jones in some misguided attempt at picking up where you left off in the past?"

Shaine flexed his jaw as he tried not to take immediate offense because he knew that would only make things worse. He chose his words carefully. "If I thought Agent Jones was being biased, I would say so. Our past history has nothing to do with my decision to agree with Jones on her recommendation. We believe that by not putting Brandi in protective custody, we are jeopardizing not only her life but also a valuable lead. We discovered Brandi was good friends with another stripper who ended up dead a few months ago. Either Brandi knows who killed Darcy Lummox or she knows something about why she's dead. We need to know what Brandi knows and the only way to do that is to ensure her safety."

Ramirez didn't like what Shaine was putting down but at least she was beginning to listen. Victoria stepped in.

"With Marcus dead…I think we need to be more cautious. I agree putting Brandi in protective custody is the right move."

Shaine sent a silent look of gratitude to Victoria but awaited Ramirez's decision. He knew it wouldn't do any good to gang up on the director. He had to trust that her training would kick in and override whatever personal bias she had working overtime in her brain.

"Fine, file the request," Ramirez finally ordered, not happy. "But I'm still pursuing the Hernandez lead."

There was nothing he could do about that. Shaine nodded, accepting Ramirez's answer.

He looked to Victoria and Victoria nodded. "I'll get it started. You get back to the hospital. I'll have officers Rocha and York on scene to keep out any undesirables until we can have her moved. We'll have the doctor report directly to Rocha or York so they can relay that information to you."

Shaine nodded in agreement. "Thanks, Victoria. I owe you a beer when this is all done."

Victoria rolled her eyes because they both knew he'd never be able to buy enough beer to pay her back for all the paperwork she'd fielded for him.

Shaine returned to the hospital and found Brandi had been moved to a more secure section of the hospital and both officers York and Rocha were posted as sentinels at the door.

"Everything okay?" he asked.

Rocha answered. "Smooth transition and no one is the wiser. The doctor came and took her for X-rays. It's as Jones guessed—broken orbital bone, broken nose and a hairline fracture to her left leg. She's sleeping now. Jones went to get something to eat."

"Thanks. I'll find Jones. You stay here with Brandi. Don't let anyone in or out that isn't wearing a medical badge."

Rocha nodded and Shaine went to find Poppy. He sent a quick text and she replied with her location. He found her in the cafeteria grabbing a snack.

"Well, how'd it go?" she asked.

"Ramirez agreed to put Brandi in protective custody but she wasn't happy about it. She really wants Mateo and Selena Hernandez for our target. She's got years of experience. Do you think we're wrong and she's right?"

"It's possible," Poppy conceded with a sigh. "But I can't escape the feeling in my gut that Brandi is important to this case, whether it's connected to the Hernandez siblings or not."

"She brought up our past relationship," Shaine said, feeling the need for full disclosure.

"Why?"

"Because she questioned whether or not I was being unbiased based on our previous relationship. I assured her my feelings or my past had nothing to do with my decision to back you up."

"Thank you," Poppy said, smiling. "I appreciate that."

"It's nothing that isn't true. If I didn't agree with you, I'd say that, too," Shaine said gruffly. "I mean, you're my partner. We work together. We have to be able to trust each other's instincts."

"And you trust me?" she asked.

"Yes," he said without hesitation.

Her eyes took on a glassy sheen and she looked away with a short nod. "Good."

There was so much left unsaid between them that a simple acknowledgment was almost too much to bear.

And now wasn't the time to scratch at that particular wound.

"Let's go and see if Brandi is awake yet," Poppy suggested as she walked away.

He followed Poppy back to the secure section of the hospital reserved for those with police protection or security, usually for criminals needing medical care before being packaged up for a jail stint, and walked into Brandi's room.

Brandi looked like hell. Nothing like the beautiful brunette she'd been. Whoever had done this had really worked her over.

Brandi's eyes fluttered open and she focused blearily on the two.

"How are you feeling?" Poppy asked, going to the bedside to gently grasp Brandi's hand. "You're lucky I thought to bring you some soup or else you might've died in your apartment."

"Who did this to you?" Shaine asked.

Brandi winced and closed her eyes, trying to fight through the painkillers she'd been given.

"Does Angelo know I'm here?" she asked.

"No. And he won't," Poppy answered. At Brandi's confusion, she said, "You're going to go away for a few days for your own protection."

"What are you talking about?" Brandi tried to frown. "I need to talk to Angelo."

"Did he beat you?" Shaine asked.

But Brandi wasn't interested in talking about that. She tried to sit up but didn't have the strength.

"Damn, even drugged up and beaten within an inch of your life, you're still a pain in the ass," Poppy muttered. "Look, if you want to play the part of the abused lover, you can do it when things are all clear, but for now, your happy ass is going to go into protective custody and you're going to answer a few questions."

"Screw you."

"That's a fine bit of gratitude for saving your life," Poppy retorted, releasing Brandi's hand. "Fine. If you don't want the gentle treatment I'm okay with doing things the other way."

"Who are you?" Brandi asked, her one good eye brimming with suspicion. "What the hell is going on?"

"I'm DEA agent Poppy Jones and this is Special Agent Kelly with the FBI. We're here to take down El Escorpion and end the exportation of Bliss. Now that you know who we are…you are going to go into a building where there are no phones, no cell phones allowed and no communication with the outside world until we solve this case. So, how long you end up in that place depends on how cooperative you are."

Brandi blinked, shocked by Poppy's revelation. "I knew you weren't a dancer," she said, shaking her head. "Too uppity to have ever struggled."

Poppy didn't deny Brandi's assumption. "So tell me why Angelo beat the shit out of you." When Brandi remained stubbornly silent, Poppy followed with, "Okay, how about this… Tell me what happened to your friend Darcy Lummox…the one you brought to the club and then ended up dead a few months ago. Ring a bell?"

At the mention of Darcy, Brandi paled and she actually started to shake. She dropped her gaze to her bandaged IV and wouldn't meet Poppy's stare.

Poppy looked to Shaine and Shaine tried to get her to open up. "We know you were close. We talked to Darcy's sister, Olivia, she said you two were very close in high school. She showed us the picture of you two on the mantel. What happened? Did you have something to do with her death and you're afraid to come forward?"

A tear slipped down Brandi's face and she wiped it away clumsily. "I can't talk about it," she whispered.

"Yes, you can," he assured her. "You're safe now. Angelo can't hurt you. There's no way he's going to get to you."

"It's not Angelo I'm worried about," she said, shocking both Shaine and Poppy.

"Then who are you worried about?" Shaine asked.

Brandi slowly met their stares and said, "*Raquel*. Raquel did this to me."

Poppy stared. *Raquel?* "Why? I don't understand…"

Brandi reached for a tissue and blotted her nose gingerly when it began to run. "Raquel found out that Angelo was sleeping with her and me at the same time and she wanted to get even. She came to my house and we fought, but she overpowered me and the next thing I knew I was on the floor and she was kicking me with combat boots."

"You're saying Raquel did this damage?" Shaine asked, incredulous. "That's a lot of force. Was she alone? Or did she have help?"

"Don't let Raquel fool you, she used to be an MMA amateur fighter. She only started dancing because she tore a shoulder muscle at her last fight. Otherwise, she'd still be in the ring and not on the stage."

How'd they miss that? Poppy tried to regroup. "So you're saying the reason Raquel beat you up was because she was angry at Angelo?"

"Essentially."

"No. I don't buy that," Poppy said firmly. "Try again. What happened with Darcy Lummox? She was your best friend. Tell me who killed her. Don't you think her sister deserves some answers?"

"What does it matter? She's gone. Knowing the details won't bring her back."

"No, but we can give Olivia some closure and maybe some justice to Darcy. As her best friend, don't you think you owe that to her?"

"I don't know who killed Darcy," Brandi said dully, wiping at the tears on her cheek. "Leave me alone. I want to sleep."

Poppy withheld her frustration, knowing Brandi was too muddled with painkillers to think straight. "We'll be back. This isn't over," she told Brandi, and then she and Shaine walked out.

"So what do you think? Raquel? She's certainly vicious enough to do something like this, but to be the person behind El Escorpion? I don't see any connection aside from the tattoo that was probably an adolescent decision geared toward looking badass."

Shaine offered, "Maybe that's the point? The reason we haven't been able to track down who El Escorpion is, is because we're looking for logical evidence. Maybe we ought to start looking at people who have seemingly no motive. Start digging around in some backgrounds and see what we can find out."

"I guess that's a start. I'll be really pissed if Ramirez was right and we just put a ditzy broad into protective custody over a lover's spat."

"That'd be a pisser," he agreed. "But there's still time to figure this out."

Poppy rolled her neck, wincing when it popped. "I feel as if the world is sitting on my shoulders. I could use a massage."

Shaine looked at her quickly and she laughed, realizing that must've come out sounding as if she was fishing for some action. "I'm sorry, that didn't come out right. I just meant I'm ready for a spa day."

"I wouldn't mind giving you a massage," he said with mock sincerity. "I'd promise to keep my hands strictly professional."

And what if I don't want strictly professional, she almost quipped but thought better of it.

They were working so well together, she wasn't about to throw a wrench into things.

Shaine took Poppy back to Brandi's apartment to get her car and then they headed back to their place.

They still had a few hours before their shifts at Lit, and Poppy thought it might be good to use that time to do some snooping.

"Want to do those background checks now?" she asked.

"You sure? It's been a long day and it promises to be an even longer night."

"I'm good."

Shaine smiled. "All right, then, I'm down."

This time they met in Shaine's apartment, giving Poppy a chance to see how Shaine's character, Rocco, lived.

"Ah, I see that Rocco is a slob," Poppy joked, gesturing to the empty pizza boxes and beer bottles on the kitchen counter.

"Hey, I like to stay in character," Shaine countered with a cocky grin that was both adorable and exasperating at the same time. She remembered the epic arguments they would have about their hygiene habits. Poppy liked things tidy; Shaine liked things chaotic.

The best part about their arguments had been the makeup sex afterward.

"Right, so where would you like to do this?" she asked, trying to put her mind back where it belonged.

"Here, let me clear a spot," Shaine said, going to the sofa where he scooped up a mound of clothes, whether they were clean or dirty, she wasn't sure, and disappeared into the bedroom with them. Knowing Shaine…

both. He had a habit of tossing his dirty clothes wherever they landed. And sometimes they landed on a pile of unfolded clean ones. He returned and grabbed his laptop, sitting beside her. "Who are we looking up first?" he asked.

"Raquel. I want to follow up on Brandi's claim that she was an MMA fighter in the past. While I wouldn't put it past her, something doesn't ring true. Brandi might be trying to protect Angelo still."

Shaine punched in the name but they only had her stage name and very little details, until Shaine added the scorpion tattoo. "Let's see what this pulls up," he said, hitting Enter.

"Well, look at that," Poppy said, smiling.

"The FBI database is a scary thing," Shaine said. "But highly effective."

An information sheet with Raquel's name, date of birth, known tattoos and photo popped up.

Under professions, amateur MMA fighter was listed.

"Damn, I really wanted that to be bullshit," Poppy said, disappointed. "So, it could've been Raquel that beat the hell out of Brandi, after all."

"Possible, but not probable. I'm still leaning toward a man who did that damage."

"Why?"

"Because of the bruising on her face. Wide knuckles."

Poppy nodded at first but then realized something. "Angelo has small hands. Almost feminine. I don't think it was Angelo."

"What if someone was setting Angelo up? Everyone knows that Angelo and Brandi were a thing… What if Brandi isn't protecting Angelo's skin but her own? I think she knows exactly who killed Darcy and it's the same person who beat the shit out of her."

"If that's the case, we need to find out a way to get her to talk. Otherwise, whoever it is…might just disappear."

Chapter 24

Shaine picked up the phone on the first ring. He never sent Sawyer or Silas to voice mail, simply because they all worked dangerous jobs and no one ever knew which day might be their last.

"You're lucky, you caught me before I have to leave for my shift," he told Sawyer. "But I'm glad you called. I could use some big brother advice."

"Yeah? What's going on? I heard you took on that big case in Miami. Lots of people would've killed for that detail but you manage to land the high profile gigs."

"What can I say? I'm awesome," Shaine quipped, but he quickly lost the laughter in his tone as he shared, "Man, this case is brutal. El Escorpion is playing hardball. We've already lost one of the DEA agents."

"I heard through the grapevine, which is why I wanted to connect with you. How are you holding up?"

"Okay," he answered. "People are dropping like flies, agent and otherwise. The body count is adding up. Makes me twitchy to close this case, not because I want to add it to my resume but because I don't want to lose any more good people."

"I don't want to lose another brother," Sawyer returned. "Watch yourself."

"Trust me, I'm doing everything I can to stay alive." He paused, then added, "There's something else I didn't expect when I took on this case."

"Such as?"

"My undercover partner. It's Poppy."

Sawyer's stunned silence mirrored Shaine's when he'd first seen her in the debriefing room. "You're kidding me."

"Nope. In the flesh. She's my partner."

"How's that going?"

"Awkward at first, but…she's really good. I underestimated her abilities years ago. I should've just kept my trap shut and took my chances."

Sawyer knew that Shaine had gone through the ringer trying to get over that breakup. "That sucks, man," he commiserated.

"Yeah, I can't help but worry about Poppy getting hurt, but she's kicking ass so I can't complain."

"Matters of the heart, man…reason and logic have nothing to do with them."

Shaine couldn't agree more.

"So, what kind of advice are you looking for? For the heart or the head?"

"I miss her," Shaine admitted with a sigh. "I mean, I always knew that I missed her but I didn't realize how much until I saw her again."

"Nostalgia is powerful," Sawyer suggested, but they both knew what Shaine wasn't saying. It was more than nostalgia. Sawyer sighed. "Look, you never had closure. Everything was just abruptly cut in half when she left. Maybe after the case is closed, you two ought to sit down over a cup of coffee and talk things out. Maybe not to patch things up but to put the issues to bed so you can move on."

"What if…" he trailed, not sure he wanted to say out loud what he was feeling. "Never mind."

But his brother knew. "You still love her."

Shaine didn't want to admit it. Maybe if he never said the words, it wouldn't be true. But he knew that was stupid. "Yeah, maybe," he allowed grudgingly. That was as much of an admission that he could manage.

"No one but you would be surprised by that," Sawyer said. "We've known."

"What do you mean?"

"Shaine, everyone knows you haven't gotten over Poppy. We're not judging you. We loved her, too."

Tears tingled behind his eyes. Ah hell, he hadn't meant to dig so deep. "I'm sorry… I don't know what's come over me. I need to focus on the case, not this crap that's in the past."

"I'm here if you need to talk it out," Sawyer offered. "But in the meantime, get your head in the game. I don't need to bury another brother."

Shaine was never cavalier with his brothers about safety. "I hear you," he said. "Thanks for calling and checking in."

"Of course. That big brother gig, you know."

He laughed. "All right, big brother. Take care of yourself."

Sawyer clicked off and Shaine sighed, feeling lighter after connecting with his brother.

Even though he couldn't share details of the case, just having that momentary connection with home was the mental wash he needed to get back on track.

Sawyer had always been the cool head of the group, which made the white-collar crime division a perfect fit for him. He preferred corporate suits to slumming around in seedy bars with confidential informants.

But Sawyer never acted as if he were better than Shaine for his division choice, like some in the white-collar division.

Silas, their little brother, was the one doing the work that neither Shaine nor Sawyer could stomach.

Child abduction cases.

He'd rather deal with drug dealers, murderers and general scum-of-the-earth than work one case involving a hurt kid.

Shaine headed out to run errands before his shift.

Armed with a search warrant, Rosa stormed Amerine Labs with the forensic accounting team, intent on finding the evidence she needed to pin El Escorpion's many crimes onto their shoulders.

Selena and Mateo watched with cold fury as their employees were sent out of the building and told to wait outside while files were being collected.

"Was this really necessary?" Selena asked sharply. "You're earning yourself a nice lawsuit. I hope you've enjoyed your time as a DEA agent because I'm going to have your job."

"You need to work on your threat department," Rosa said, amused. "You aren't the first and you won't be the last person to threaten my job when I was closing in on their operation. However, I will give you props for the detailed doll. I was pretty impressed, actually. I like it. Once you've been arrested and the case has gone to trial, I'm going to put it up on my mantel. I'm curious, where'd you find someone who can sew such detail? That's a lost art."

"What the hell are you talking about?" Selena asked, genuinely disgusted and confused. "What doll?"

"The nice little package you had delivered to my house. Nice detective work, by the way. My house isn't listed on any database."

"You're insane. I didn't send you anything, nor would I. This is ludicrous. All you're doing is halting important research on drugs that matter. Mateo, call our lawyer. This is a waste of time."

Mateo sent a hateful look Rosa's way and walked outside to make the call.

A shiver of something went down Rosa's back, something that felt a lot like uncertainty, but she pushed it aside, knowing she was on the right track. "Keep talking, I'm sure you're very good at convincing people that you're a paragon of virtue. We already have proof that you've been receiving illegal chemical compounds… drugs often used to make Ecstasy, which isn't far off from the newest street drug, Bliss."

"I don't know what Bliss is and I certainly don't make Ecstasy. However, what you will find is that my company had a significant investment in an experimental drug that had not yet been through FDA approval. I know it will burst your bubble to know that, although perhaps not strictly by the book, our process is completely legal."

Rosa smiled thinly. "We shall see."

The forensics team left the building carrying a multitude of boxes, computer hard drives and external drives and they left Amerine Labs a shell, effectively shutting down their operation until the evidence could be sorted.

Today was a good day, Rosa thought as she drove away, humming a light tune.

Today was an *extra* good day.

Shaine showed up at Lit and followed his usual routine, but he was paying particular attention to everyone tonight, even the people he'd previously dismissed.

But first and foremost, he wanted to check out Angelo and see if the guy acted out of sorts.

"Hey man, how's things?" Shaine asked conversationally. "Anything excited going on tonight?"

Angelo seemed agitated as he went up to Shaine. "Have you talked to Brandi?"

Shaine looked appropriately confused. "No? Why?"

"She's not answering her cell and I went by her apartment and she was gone. It's not like her to split like that."

"Did you guys have a fight or something?"

"No, she said we needed to take a break, you know, after the whole Raquel thing, and so I said sure because, hey, a break sounded good, kinda like a hall pass, but then I haven't heard from her in days so I went to check it out and she wasn't home."

Either Angelo was a good actor or he was genuinely worried about Brandi, which didn't play into the theory that the man had beaten her.

Shaine glanced down at Angelo's hands, confirming what Poppy had said about his small, feminine hands.

There was no way Angelo had done that to Brandi. In fact, his knuckles would be red and chafed at the very least, but they were freshly manicured without a scratch on them.

Shaine clapped Angelo on the shoulder in support, saying, "I'm sure she'll turn up. She's probably just trying to make you sweat. Girls are like that. They like to watch you suffer when you've screwed up."

Angelo nodded, but he looked unconvinced. Shaine frowned. "Is there something else bothering you?"

"Her apartment…smelled funny. Like bleach. And it'd been trashed. Brandi was weird about her apartment. She liked things put back where they belonged. She'd never leave her apartment like that."

"What are you saying, man? Do you think something bad happened to her?"

"I don't know," Angelo said, becoming more agitated. "I just got a bad feeling."

"If you're really worried about her, report her missing to the cops."

"Go to the cops?" Angelo scoffed. "I can't do that. I have a warrant out on me."

"Oh? What for?"

"A bullshit possession charge," he said, waving away Shaine's question. "I missed my court appearance and just haven't had time to sort it out. So they issued a warrant."

"That sucks," he commiserated. Maybe it was the anxiety, but this was the most Angelo had talked since they'd met. He wasn't his usual suave, too-cool self, and Shaine was going to milk it. "Hey, I heard some of the girls talking the other night about another dancer named Tinsel… do you know anything about her?"

"Yeah, she was a friend of Brandi's," he answered distractedly as he flipped through his phone, looking for something. "She had a massive crush on Big Jane of all people. Followed her around like a lovesick puppy. It was weird. Why?"

"Just curious," he murmured, pretending to move on, but his mind was moving quickly. "So did they date or something?"

"I don't know," Angelo answered, irritated that Shaine was still on the subject. "I don't pay attention to who Big Jane is messing around with. Look, I gotta make some calls. Can you hold down my shift for me?"

"Yeah, sure, I got you, buddy. Handle your business."

"Thanks, man," Angelo said, disappearing quickly.

What the hell? Big Jane?

He sent a hasty text to Victoria.

Background check Big Jane. ASAP.

Victoria responded with a thumbs-up emoji.

He grabbed someone to man the bar and then disappeared backstage to find Poppy.

Shaine found her and pulled her aside, out of earshot of everyone else.

"Darcy didn't have a thing for Angelo…she was seeing Big Jane," he whispered.

Poppy's eyes widened in shock. "Are you kidding me?"

"No."

"Why would Darcy say she was all about Angelo when she was really into Big Jane?"

"Maybe her family was ultraconservative and wouldn't be okay with that kind of relationship," he guessed. "But either way, that changes things a bit. And another thing… there's no way Angelo did the damage to Brandi. You're right, his hands…are like a girl's and they are soft. If he'd beat the shit out of Brandi, there'd be marks on his knuckles."

Poppy nodded. "So what are we looking for? Bloody knuckles?"

"That might be a good place to start. Be careful."

That last part came from his heart, not his head, and it'd come out before he could stop it. Thankfully, Poppy didn't seem to notice the difference and didn't take offense.

She waved and returned to her vanity so he could slip back to the bar.

Things just took a confusing turn.

Chapter 25

Ramirez was staring at a report as everyone filed in for debriefing, and Poppy knew by Ramirez's expression that something had gone wrong.

"Everything okay?" Poppy asked, taking her seat. "What's that?"

"We've hit a snag," Ramirez finally admitted. "I've been trying to find some way that the results might be wrong, but it's right there in plain black and white." She met the group's expectant gazes. "None of the discrepancies in the customs manifests can be attributed to Bliss production."

Ramirez pushed the results to the center of the table and Poppy picked them up first. On one hand, she felt privately validated that her hunch had turned out to be correct, but it gave her no satisfaction to know that Ramirez had been off base.

"The forensics team came back with the results of the search warrant…we got nothing. There were some minor infractions, in which they'll be fined by the FDA, but any action will be their jurisdiction. Amerine Labs isn't manufacturing Bliss, that's for certain."

Poppy and Shaine exchanged looks but remained silent.

Ramirez exhaled with disappointment. "So it would seem you were right. Selena and Mateo aren't right for El Escorpion. So what do you have? Please make this day better and give me something to go on."

Shaine jumped in with something productive. "We're pursuing the lead with Brandi. We think she knows something but she's not talking. We need more leverage, something that will make her see that it would benefit her to talk."

"You weren't the only one with a setback," Poppy admitted. "We thought Angelo was our guy but we're starting to rethink that."

"And why is that?" Ramirez asked.

"Because he wasn't the one who beat Brandi and he's not the one she's either protecting or scared of. She blamed Raquel but I don't think it was Raquel."

Ramirez frowned. "So who are you left with?"

"Not much," Poppy answered. "We have a slim lead but it's more baffling than anything else. We followed up on the Darcy Lummox murder and found out that she wasn't in love with Angelo as her sister, Olivia, thought, but Big Jane."

"The club mother?" Ramirez asked, surprised. "Some May-December romance or something? Are you thinking of her as a suspect?"

"Hard to say. On the surface she doesn't present with

a good profile, but there are enough discrepancies that we can't discount the possibility," Shaine said, sharing his confusion. "Big Jane doesn't have motive or means. I don't see how she could possibly pull something like this off."

Poppy agreed, saying, "I've been to her apartment. She's barely making ends meet. I mean, she takes a cut of all the dancers' tips but that's not enough to live high off the hog. And whoever is manufacturing Bliss has money to burn."

"And Raquel's not a good fit?" Ramirez asked.

"Not that I can tell. She's meaner than a junkyard dog but hardly a ruthless businesswoman/chemist."

"Go back to Brandi. Find something you can use as leverage. We need her to start talking," Ramirez said, still sharply disappointed her hunch had been so wrong. Poppy understood that disappointment. When she'd been so off base with the Lachlan investigation, she'd nearly gotten herself killed to prove that she could salvage the operation. But the truth was…she'd known she'd been made. Poppy hadn't been able to admit that simple truth to anyone—pride had pushed her to dangerous decisions.

The phantom ache of her bullet wound reminded her every day that pride was an agent's downfall.

"I really thought we had our man," Ramirez admitted. "Maybe too much time behind the desk has dulled my edge."

"It happens to the best of us," Shaine threw in, and Poppy couldn't help but wonder if he was also throwing her a bone, too.

"That's the problem when a suspect fits the profile perfectly. You get hungry, thinking you're about to eat," Ramirez tried joking to lighten the mood. "But that begs the question, if they're not the ones…who the hell is pulling the strings? And why are they always one step ahead of us?"

That night after their shifts, Poppy and Shaine were both too wired to sleep and Poppy found herself over at Shaine's apartment.

"Mind if I hang out for a little bit?" she asked.

Shaine looked up from making a sandwich. "Not at all. Everything okay?"

Poppy smiled to herself. Shaine had always liked to eat at odd hours. "You know, eventually your metabolism is going to rebel and you won't be able to eat a pastrami on rye at midnight."

"Probably. But that's not tonight," Shaine said, biting into the sandwich and groaning with happiness. "This is just what the doctor ordered. Are you sure you don't want a bite?"

"I'm good." Poppy curled up on the sofa and Shaine joined her. The pastrami was tempting. "On second thought," she said, opening her mouth for a bite. Shaine obliged and she took a generous chunk of sandwich, barely able to close her mouth around the mountain of meat she'd tore off.

"You just took half my sandwich," Shaine complained with a laugh. "Are you sure you don't want your own?"

Poppy shook her head, trying not to laugh with a mouthful. This felt like old times. She swallowed and watched as Shaine made short work of the rest of the sandwich.

"Ramirez was pretty bummed about her lead falling through," Poppy said.

"Yeah, but you and I both had a feeling it wasn't going

to work out. Too easy. El Escorpion is sophisticated and he or she would never do something so obvious."

Poppy agreed, validated in the knowledge that her gut instinct had been spot-on. For Poppy, that meant something.

"I knew I'd been made with Lachlan," she found herself admitting quietly. She met Shaine's gaze. "I went into that situation knowing I was taking a huge risk."

"Then why'd you go?" Shaine asked.

"I was desperate to prove that I could salvage the operation. I thought that if managed to close the case in spite of my mistake…my mistake wouldn't cost me the opportunity to go back undercover."

Poppy knew she was sharing something big. She'd never told anyone about the details of that night. Especially not Shaine.

"Your pride nearly got you killed," Shaine said.

"I know."

A moment of silence passed between them. Poppy let the information sit for a minute.

"The thing is, I always felt I was standing in your shadow, even though you never did or said anything to make me feel that way." Poppy drew a deep breath when she realized she'd begun to shake. "It's not easy for me to admit this."

In response, Shaine gently grasped her hand and held it.

"And then after it all went down… I guess I never really thought about the ramifications. I didn't expect to get shot."

"I don't think any of us expect that to happen," Shaine returned with a small chuckle. "It's a risk we take, though, and something we have to be aware of."

"I know that. I've changed a lot since I was that inexperienced agent," Poppy said.

"I know," Shaine said, surprising her. "I told you you're a good agent."

"Did you really mean it?"

"I wouldn't say it if I didn't mean it. For what it's worth…I should've…" Shaine stopped, unsure of how to continue. Poppy knew how he felt. She squeezed his hand to let him know she understood. Shaine's mouth curved in a rueful smile as he said, "Hindsight, right?"

Poppy nodded. "It's a bitch."

Shaine leaned over and kissed her. He tasted of pastrami and happiness.

But when he murmured, "Stay," she knew she couldn't, even as much as she desperately wanted nothing more than to crawl into bed beside him and forget the past.

"I can't," she answered, pulling away.

"Why not?"

"Because I want to. And because we've already blurred the lines and I won't do anything to jeopardize this case."

"How will staying with me tonight jeopardize anything?"

"Because each time I stay…I fall a little bit more, and we both know that's a dead-end street. It took me so long to get over you, Shaine. I don't think I can go through that again."

"I didn't want you to leave in the first place," Shaine said. "That was your choice."

"I know."

"What if you'd stayed then?"

"I couldn't."

"Why not?"

"You know why."

Shaine nodded, his jaw flexing as if holding back. "I guess that's it then. Can't change what happened."

"No, we can't."

Poppy wanted to tell him that she'd wished a thousand times that she'd handled herself differently, that she hadn't run like a pansy. But leaving had been good for her, even if it'd been painful.

"I've made a name for myself with the DEA," Poppy said, trying to find her footing.

"You've done well," Shaine agreed. "I'm happy for you."

Poppy wanted to shake him. Why did he have to be so agreeable, so understanding? Why couldn't he yell at her so she could feel solid in her decision to break away?

God, why was she such a coward?

She wanted to blame him for everything so that she didn't have to stare at the person responsible in the mirror.

True, he hadn't been supportive. Just like her parents.

"I didn't want to defend myself to the one person who should've had my back," Poppy admitted, caving to the voice inside her head, berating her for taking the coward's way out.

"I was scared. You nearly died. I know the risk comes with the job, but seeing you in that hospital bed... I couldn't bear the thought of losing you like that."

Shaine's quiet response nearly buckled her resolve.

"But you're right, I should've had your back," he agreed. "And I didn't."

So that was it. The apology that should've happened years ago.

Poppy bit her lip to keep from crying.

Now what?

There was nothing to salvage at this point. They lived separate lives on different coasts.

Neither were interested in switching careers.

So that left them with...*what?*

A big fat nothing.

Except heartache.

"I have to go," Poppy said, needing to leave before she broke down in a sobbing mess. "Thanks for the talk."

Before he could stop her, Poppy was in her own apartment, locking the adjoining door between them.

Poppy knew he would follow her if she didn't remove the possibility.

She couldn't take another moment of stark honesty between them.

Not when that conversation should've happened years ago when it would've mattered.

Now, the knowledge just hurt.

No, *hurt* wasn't the word. The knowledge ripped and tore into places that had never truly healed, and now it was bleeding again, only this time, she had no idea how to close the wound.

Because the reality was...Shaine Kelly had been The One and she'd run away.

Too bad destiny didn't give second chances.

Days had passed and Brandi was finally well enough to leave the hospital to go to the safe house.

Shaine and Poppy traveled together to talk with her in the hopes of encouraging her to give up who she was protecting.

They walked into the small, secure house, flashed their badges to the security and entered the living room where Brandi was sitting, her leg propped up on an ottoman, her facial bruising starting to heal.

Her lip was no longer so swollen that she couldn't speak without a lisp and her nose had been repaired but she still looked as if she'd gone a few rounds with a prizefighter and came out the loser.

"What do you want?" Brandi asked sourly. "Come to gloat or something?"

"And to think I made you soup," Poppy said, sitting on the sofa across from Brandi while Shaine stood by the mantel. "I see your disposition isn't any better."

"When do I get out of here?" she asked.

"When you start talking," Poppy answered.

"I don't have anything else to say."

"Bullshit. You're either protecting someone or you're afraid of someone. Which is it?" Shaine said.

Brandi shot Shaine a dark look but remained silent.

"Did you know that Bliss kills people?" Poppy asked, curious. "Causes their hearts to explode. Kinda nasty, if you ask me."

"What are you talking about? Didn't seem to kill either of you," Brandi quipped. "More's the pity. Where's Angelo? Does he know where I am?"

Both Poppy and Shaine ignored that question and posed another.

"Angelo didn't beat you and neither did Raquel. Why don't you tell me who really beat the shit out of you so we can start getting somewhere."

"I already told you, it was Raquel."

"Yes, you told us a lie. Let's try the truth. I don't have time for games," Poppy said, leaning forward to rest her elbows on her knees. "Here's what I think… Either you're part of El Escorpion's operation or you're afraid because you know too much about the operation. Pick your poison. Either way, if you don't start talking, the only dancing you'll be doing will be out in the yard when you're doing time for drug trafficking."

"I haven't done anything wrong," Brandi said, looking swiftly from one to the other. "I'm the victim here, remember?"

"No, you were the victim until you stopped being cooperative. Now you're just a pain-in-the-ass punk who is guilty by association," Shaine said, shrugging. "Either start talking or your comfy stay is going to end with you behind bars."

Shaine could tell she was wavering. The idea of going to jail must've freaked her out more than the idea of holding on to whatever she was hiding.

"If I talk…can you protect me?" she asked.

"Of course," Shaine said. "As long as you're willing to testify."

Brandi hesitated, still unsure, but finally she said, "It was Bear who beat me up."

Bear? "Who the hell is Bear?" Shaine asked. "Are you just making things up to irritate me?"

It was Poppy who spoke up. "Bear…you mean the bouncer guy at the warehouse party?"

Brandi nodded. "He works for El Escorpion. So does DJ Raven. And Angelo. We all do. But we don't know who he is. We just get our orders and follow them. If we do, we get bonuses. If we fail…we get punished."

"And Bear metes out the punishment?" Shaine asked.

Brandi nodded again, swallowing. "Have you seen how big he is? He's like a mountain."

Big enough to crush a girl's windpipe. "Did he kill Capri?"

Brandi didn't answer, but the way her eyes became glassy and wide, Shaine knew it was true. "Why? What happened?" he asked.

"Capri said Bear was a softie," Poppy recalled, frowning with the memory. "I don't understand. Why would Bear hurt Capri?"

"Because he follows orders," Brandi answered fearfully. "Capri broke the rules. Just like Darcy."

Bear killed both women? "What's his real name?" Shaine asked.

"I don't know. All we know him by is Bear."

"Do you have a contact number for him?" Poppy asked.

"In my phone," Brandi answered. "But you confiscated my phone, remember?"

"We know where to find it," Poppy said. "So why did Bear beat you up?"

"I was supposed to pick up the shipment, but I wasn't in the right place. The shipment ended up going back to the sender and the mishap cost time and production."

"Did Angelo know you'd been beaten?"

"Yes, he knew, but he couldn't do anything about it. He works for the same boss. He couldn't do anything to change what had happened and he certainly didn't want the same for himself."

"What a gentleman," Poppy said derisively. "Has anyone ever told you you have shitty taste in men?"

"Yeah, actually Darcy used to tell me that all the time."

"Tell us about Darcy and Big Jane."

"What's to tell? Darcy was into Big Jane. It's not that big of a deal. I don't know why in this day and age anyone would even blink an eye at that, but Darcy was always afraid of what other people would think, so she told her sister she was crazy about Angelo instead. I didn't mind covering for her."

"Were they in love?"

"I think Darcy was. Hard to say about Big Jane. She wasn't exactly open with her feelings."

"How did Big Jane take Darcy's death?"

"I don't know, she was upset. We were all upset. We weren't allowed to go to the cops and we couldn't say or do anything about it. We just had to move on unless we wanted to join her."

"And this whole time you have no idea who you've been working for?" Poppy asked, incredulous. "That seems far-fetched."

"No. We take the cash and we don't ask questions. It's safer that way."

Shaine remarked drily, "I don't know why you're so scared of jail. It sounds like you've already been in prison."

"It's not so bad when you're following the rules. We are taken care of for the most part. Everyone has to work for someone else, right?"

"Yeah, but most bosses don't kill their employees if they don't follow the employee handbook," Poppy said.

Brandi looked tired and a little defeated, as if saying out loud the life she'd been living had finally got to her. "I've told you everything I know. You have to protect me. If they find out I've talked, I'm as good as dead."

"How'd Bear kill Capri?" Shaine asked.

"An overdose. He just kept pumping her full of the bad batch. The stupid kid didn't even know what hit her until it was too late."

That confirmed their suspicion.

"Are you willing to testify that Bear killed Capri and Darcy?"

Brandi nodded but she looked scared as hell.

"For what it's worth, I never would've gotten Darcy involved if I'd known how badly it was going to end."

"Hindsight is a bitch," Shaine said.

"You have no idea," Brandi admitted in a soft voice with a tear tracking down her cheek. "Darcy was a good person. She just wanted to be loved."

Poppy said, "Everyone wants to be loved…that's how people like El Escorpion gets in. They play on basic human need and exploit it."

"What's going to happen to Angelo?" Brandi asked. "He's in danger, too."

Shaine couldn't make promises. The fact was…they were going to have to use Angelo as bait to flush out the real bad guy.

And sometimes bait didn't make it.

Chapter 26

The vibe at Lit seemed off. An invisible tension wound itself around the neon lights and bounced off the oiled skin of the dancers as they writhed and moved in time to the music. It felt like a chemical intoxication without the benefit of the drug.

Tonight Shaine's mission was to get Angelo panicked so that he ran to whoever was pulling his strings. Someone within Lit was watching, using the club as a conduit to the clientele, playing to the party atmosphere and blending seamlessly.

Shaine's intuition said that El Escorpion sensed the heat and was going to disappear. That's why his known associates were disappearing one by one. He was cleaning house to bail—possibly to set up shop in another city, another town where anonymity was easily found.

Of course he had no proof of this...just his gut instinct.

That meant if he was wrong, the whole case could collapse.

They were taking big risks without the security of a payoff.

Shaine found Angelo in the storeroom, leaning against the liquor boxes, looking green around the gills.

"Angelo," he called out, sounding relieved. "I'm so glad I found you!"

Angelo startled, and when he saw it was Shaine, he relaxed. But he looked haggard, as if he hadn't slept in days.

"I have to talk to you. It's urgent," he said, going straight to Angelo. "Brandi called me with some wild story and she told me to find you right away."

"Brandi called you? Why?" he asked, confused. "Where is she? What did she say? Is she all right?"

"I don't know, she sounded scared. What the hell is going on? The things she was saying…it sounds like something out of a movie."

"What did she say?" he repeated impatiently. "Just say it already."

"Sorry," Shaine said, acting insulted that Angelo had snapped at him. Angelo immediately apologized, but he gestured for him to continue. Shaine lost his scowl and continued, "Okay, it was a really quick phone call and all she said was—and I hope this makes sense to you because it sure as hell doesn't make sense to me—she said to meet her at your usual spot with the last shipment. El Escorpion wants you to deliver it personally. If you don't…she's dead." He paused for a minute, watching Angelo's reaction keenly. "Is she serious? What the hell is going on?"

"Ahh, shit," Angelo moaned, bouncing against the box with agitation. "I told her we'd get caught. He'd know we were skimming. He always figures that shit out."

"Who?"

"El Escorpion, you idiot!"

"Who the hell is that?"

"Only the most dangerous drug kingpin in all of Miami. He's smarter than the cops and he's got eyes all over this town. I don't know what I was thinking. Shit." He ran his hand through his thick, black hair, as wired as a drug addict in need of a fix. "Somehow he found out that we took some of his shipment. I don't know how but he did and he's gonna gut Brandi like a pig if I don't deliver. But it's a death sentence if I show up like he wants me to."

"Is that what happened to Capri?" Shaine fished.

"What?" Angelo asked, distracted. Then he shook his head, saying, "Capri got caught messing around. She was the favorite."

"So El Escorpion is a man?" Shaine asked, holding his breath.

"Of course," he answered, irritated. "What's with all the questions? What the hell am I going to do about Brandi? I can't just let her die."

"But you could let her get the shit kicked out of her?"

"What was I supposed to do?" Angelo shot back, his eyes flashing. "This ain't no game. El Escorpion doesn't mess around. Besides, I didn't think she'd get it that bad. I thought she might get it easy because she was a female."

"Why did you think you could steal from him?"

Angelo wiped at the sweat at his brow. "I don't know. We got cocky I guess. The money was insane. Everyone wants Bliss."

"Yeah, except the people who are dead," Shaine muttered, earning a quick look from Angelo. "The drug kills. Capri's heart exploded in her chest."

"What do you know about how Capri died?" he asked with suspicion.

"Because I saw what was left of her heart when she was lying on the coroner's slab."

"What the…" Angelo's confusion was a second behind Shaine's actions as he pulled his gun. "What the hell? You're a goddamn cop!"

"Actually, FBI agent, but let's not split hairs. Here's the deal, you're going to call El Escorpion and schedule a meeting. Tell him you have his shipment and you need to unload it ASAP."

"Where's Brandi?" he asked, narrowing his gaze.

"Don't worry about her. Make the call."

Suddenly, Angelo slowly began to smirk.

"What's so funny?" Shaine asked, beginning to feel the back of his neck prickle.

"I was just thinking…you might be worth a bonus."

Pain exploded in the back of his head as something heavy connected with his skull, and Shaine went straight to the floor.

His last thought was…somehow the bait had become the predator.

And he was the main course.

Poppy stalked into the safe house and went straight for Brandi, jerking her to her feet as she yelped in pain.

"Where is he taking him?" she demanded. Thankfully, the entire conversation between Angelo and Shaine had been recorded, but the connection went dead after a loud thunk, which made Poppy want to climb through the line with panic.

She didn't care about protocol, didn't care that she was

manhandling a witness. Poppy knew Shaine was in danger and she wasn't going to just sit there and hope for the best.

"Who?" Brandi cried, frightened of the rage in Poppy's eyes. "Who are you talking about?"

"Angelo is taking Shaine somewhere. Where would he take him?"

"I—I don't know," Brandi answered, her teeth clacking together when Poppy nearly shook her head off her shoulders. "Put me down! Help!"

"I will rip your head off and feed you to the fish if you don't start talking."

"You need me to testify," Brandi said, her lower lip trembling.

"I couldn't give a shit about the case if anything happened to my partner. Where is he taking him?" She bruised Brandi's arms within her grasp. "Start talking."

"I don't know," she said, tears jumping to her eyes.

"Think!"

"Maybe the warehouse," she cried as Poppy thrust her back into the chair. Brandi winced as she tried to get into a better position. "That's where we did the drop-off of the product. That's all I know! Angelo was always the one who handled that stuff."

Poppy leaned in to growl, "If anything happens to Shaine, I'm going to personally take great pleasure in breaking every bone in your body."

She texted Victoria the location of the warehouse, knowing Victoria would handle the details of getting backup there, but Poppy couldn't wait.

She knew that if Angelo was taking Shaine to the warehouse to meet with El Escorpion…he wasn't coming out alive.

* * *

Shaine's head throbbed as wet stickiness oozed from his injury. His hands were bound with duct tape. Someone had brained him from behind and trussed him up like a Christmas turkey.

How could he be so stupid?

He'd been played.

They'd all been played.

Angelo had gotten them to show their cards too soon. He didn't give a rat's ass about Brandi or what'd happened to her.

The whole point had been to flush out the embedded agents.

Shaine opened his eyes to darkness and realized he was in the trunk of a car.

Enclosed spaces were not his favorite. Panic threatened to squeeze the air from his lungs. He closed his eyes and focused on staying conscious.

The most important thing was to keep his head. If he stayed levelheaded, he would walk out of this alive.

If he panicked, he was already dead.

The car stopped and he heard footsteps approach the trunk. It opened and he squinted against the pain in his head.

Raquel stood next to Angelo, a cruel smile on her lips. "For a big guy, you went down easy."

So Raquel had been the one to clock him. Guess that MMA fighter training was still good for something.

The tattoo, the scorpion… Sometimes the most obvious answer was the correct one.

"Bring him inside," Raquel said, turning on her spindly stiletto heels to walk into the warehouse.

Angelo jerked Shaine to his feet and pushed him in front of him.

"I'm always amazed at how stupid cops must think we are," he said conversationally. "You aren't the first task force to try to take down our operation. Before it was Bliss, we moved Ecstasy, before that, it was heroin. We try to stay on top of the newest trends, the newest party flavor."

"So what's the real reason Brandi was beat up?" he asked, the throb in his head making him nauseous.

"Oh, that was true. The best lie has a bit of truth," Angelo answered. "Brandi was a bad girl and needed to be punished."

"You're a sick freak. Did you watch?"

Raquel gave a sidewise glance at Shaine as she said, "There's a certain finesse to the way Bear does his work. Messy, though." She turned to Angelo. "Next time, you're cleaning up the mess. She's your bitch, anyway."

Angelo laughed. "It was always you, baby. Always you."

Everything had been an act for their benefit. They must've been on to them the moment—or close to the moment—they showed up on the scene.

"Your act was pretty convincing. How'd you know?" Shaine asked.

"You said that you worked at Grind. Miami is a small town. I know everyone who works at the best clubs. No one had heard of Rocco Pacheco. A little digging and, boom…all the references were fake. Doesn't take a rocket scientist to put two and two together."

Raquel laughed. "And there's no way your friend was ever a stripper. Her moves were too refined, too classical to be anything but a good girl pretending to be a bad girl."

Shaine wanted to send a roundhouse kick straight to

Raquel's smug mouth, but his head was still weeping blood and he was dangerously close to passing out. He may even have a skull fracture, which meant he could lose consciousness at any moment if his brain was swelling.

Was the pain because of the blow to his head or because he was in actual danger of dying?

It could go either way with blunt force trauma.

Angelo shoved Shaine and he nearly went flying, but he managed to regain his footing and avoided sprawling to the floor. "C'mon, someone wants to meet you."

They walked onto the empty warehouse floor, not a trace of the party remaining except a few fluorescent lights overhead, and saw a man in a fine linen suit awaiting them.

He turned and smiled with calculating precision. "Ahh, finally, Agent Kelly...or should I call you Rocco Pacheco?"

Shaine stared at the man, swearing under his breath.

Ramirez hadn't been far off the mark.

"Where's his partner?" Mateo asked Angelo sharply. "You were supposed to bring me both."

"He came alone. But we'll get her tonight when she comes for her shift. She doesn't know we're on to her."

"Are you sure about that?" Shaine asked, smiling through the pain. "How do you know you're not being surrounded right now?"

"Good try," Angelo said. "We already know you're sucking air on this case. You aren't the only one with someone on the inside."

Shaine tried not to show his alarm as his mind raced. All of the people brought into this operation had been thoroughly vetted. Who could possibly be working on the inside? Immediate fear stole his breath as he realized

Poppy was completely unaware of what kind of danger she was in.

"That's enough, Angelo," Mateo said, pulling a small baggie from his jacket pocket. "We shouldn't keep our guest waiting. He's come a long way and we don't want to disappoint."

Raquel smirked as Mateo came closer. Angelo gripped him by the arms and held him tight.

"What are you doing?" he tried to keep his voice strong, but there was an edge of fear he couldn't quite avoid. Then he saw that the baggie was filled with pills.

"My sister is a brilliant woman but she doesn't take risks. We were working on a drug that would elevate the serotonin and dopamine levels in the brain for depression, but something went wrong in the trials and instead of lowering the test subjects' anxiety, it left them in a euphoric state. One of the test subjects said it was like 'bliss.' The product had been a total failure for the market intended, but it had huge potential on the black market. One thing led to another and now we have eager customers eating it up. We couldn't keep up supply and demand."

"Except people were dying," Shaine said. "Dead users aren't much for repeat business."

"True. Which is why we were changing the formulary when you showed up on the scene. Unbeknownst to you and your partner, you were the first test subjects for the newest batch."

Shaine felt ill. "And if we would've died? Don't you think that would've ruined your little operation?"

"No one would've found your bodies." Mateo's smile was deadly. "You aren't the first test subjects that had to be disposed of quietly. It's amazing what you can stuff in a fifty-five-gallon drum of chemical waste."

Shaine could only imagine how many dead bodies had been eaten by chemicals and disposed of, none the wiser.

"So what now?" Shaine asked. "How does this end, seeing as how you were on to us the whole time?"

"It ends with you OD'ing on Bliss. I'm sure you can imagine where I'm going with this."

Raquel checked her phone. "It's about that time."

Mateo motioned to Angelo. Suddenly his mouth was wrenched open and pills were shoved inside. Angelo pinched Shaine's nose and held his mouth shut until he had no choice but to swallow them.

Raquel rolled an empty drum over to them. "Look what we have here. A handy container for nosy FBI agents."

Shaine tried not to show fear, but he was terrified of going into that drum. He kicked and fought as Angelo and Raquel dragged him to the drum and hoisted him up to dump him inside. He yelled as the top was slammed down, sealing him inside.

Panic fluttered in his chest as the darkness closed in around him. This was worse than being shot.

This was worse than anything he ever could've imagined.

He was going to die and no one would ever find him.

Worse was the realization that Poppy was walking right into a trap.

Chapter 27

Poppy started to run for the front door when a bullet zinged past her, burying itself in the drywall.

She took cover and grabbed her gun. More gunfire erupted as the security detail returned fire, but whoever was shooting was deadly. Two bodies fell to the ground and Poppy caught sight of a department issue boot.

"She's in here!" Brandi screeched, pointing at Poppy's hiding spot.

Poppy bailed and dove behind the couch just as another bullet exploded the couch cushion, sending stuffing flying.

The sound of footsteps followed as the shooter knew exactly where to go.

"She's behind the couch!" Brandi yelled again, and Poppy wanted to shoot her first.

But as it turned out she didn't need to.

"Thanks," said the shooter dispassionately, shooting Brandi in the head at point-blank range.

Poppy didn't have time to do much more than fire off a round and scramble to another spot, using the wall as a shield. She aimed and fired, missed and the shooter returned fire.

Ducking, she ate plaster as the bullet narrowly missed her face.

Her mind was reeling.

She knew the shooter.

Of all the people…why?

"When did El Escorpion buy your badge?" she called out, angry and sick to her stomach at the same time. "When did you sell out? Was it worth it?"

Victoria Stapp, Shaine's partner for the past six months, was trying to kill her. Rage blotted out any fear as she thought of all the ways she wanted to kill Stapp for betraying the team and, worse, Stapp's own partner.

"How could you do this to Shaine? He was your partner. He had your back."

"You're naive, Jones. The only person who has my back is me. You and Kelly have the same problem. You're both so blind to what's right in front of your face because you think you're so badass."

"Yeah? So is this some kind of revenge to show us up? I'm flattered."

"That's just a bonus. It's all about the money. Lots of it. Let's be real, no one's retiring on anything but a pittance in government work unless you're the director, and I'm done with all this glass ceiling shit. By this time tomorrow, I'll be sitting on a white, sandy beach, sipping a froufrou drink and watching the clouds go by."

"Sounds kinda boring to me," she called out, thinking

fast. "And think of all the sunscreen you'll have to wear to avoid burning that blindingly white skin of yours."

"Somehow I'll manage. For what it's worth…it's not personal. Not really. Kelly was an insufferable ass but we had some jokes, some good times. I don't know you enough to care about you. Sorry about this, but loose ends and all that."

Poppy knew that Shaine had been set up. They'd all been set up. No one was supposed to get out alive.

"Was it you who killed Marcus?" she asked, trying to stall for time.

"Not with my own gun, of course. He didn't see it coming, either."

"You're a piece of shit, you know that?" Poppy said. "Killing one of your own… There's a place in hell reserved for people like you."

"Save it, Jones. Your judgment means nothing to me."

"Apparently, neither does your lack of integrity."

"Screw you, you don't know my life. You don't know what I've been through."

"Cry me a river. Let me get my small violin."

"Yeah, not gonna miss that smart-ass mouth…" Victoria took a shot as Poppy whipped around to take one, too.

Her bullet struck payday, knocking Victoria back. She slammed into the wall, smearing blood as she slid down. The bullet hole was weeping blood as her heart pumped like a geyser.

Poppy kicked the gun away from her nerveless fingers and checked for a pulse. A faint heartbeat thumped sluggishly as she slowly died. The light went out of her eyes and Poppy knew she was gone.

"Traitor," she said to her lifeless face. "If you weren't dead, I'd kill you all over."

She rose, called Ramirez and then jumped in the car to find Shaine.

The last time Poppy had prayed to God, she'd been staring down the business end of a gun, hoping that somehow she lived to see another day.

Now she was praying again…only this time, she hoped she wasn't too late to save the man who meant everything to her.

Shaine was drifting in the darkness. The Bliss was taking over, casting a fuzzy blanket of nothing over the panic trying to eat him alive, and he actually started humming, his voice echoing in the drum.

His hands ached from being tied behind his back, his knees were in his chest but he couldn't bring himself to care about any of it.

Bliss had turned his fear into nothingness. But there was also clarity for the first time in a long time.

Funny how dying had a way of clearing away the cobwebs.

His thoughts went unerringly to Poppy.

He still loved her.

He'd never stopped.

It's why he hadn't been serious about anyone else since Poppy had left. He'd blamed it on the job but, honestly, he'd had plenty of opportunities to make something happen with someone else. The interest just hadn't been there.

His ambition had been a convenient shield for the pain that he couldn't forgive.

And now, he felt nothing.

No pain.

No worry.

No regret.

Just a blinding clarity that made him smile sluggishly.

Poppy had been The One.

And he'd probably always known that, but his stupid pride hadn't allowed him to bare his soul and just admit his fear of losing her, whether it was to the job or to his own ego.

If he could do it all over again, he'd resist the urge to make demands for her safety; he'd ignore that wild fear of losing her and man up to support her when she'd needed it the most. He would've told her parents to shut the hell up, or at the very least, made sure Poppy knew that he didn't agree with those idiots.

The fact that he'd sided with people he didn't even like because of fear was embarrassing.

If given the chance, he'd tell Poppy what a moron he'd been to even suggest that she get a desk job.

And he'd spend every hour given to him to simply savor their time together.

But second chances were in small supply.

Especially when you're stuffed in a drum about to meet your maker.

A drunken smile found his lips even though there was nothing funny about the situation.

There was no dignity in dying this way.

His only hope was that Poppy was okay. If he had to die but she got to live…that would make his death bearable.

As he drifted further down a black tunnel voices echoed around him.

Shots fired.

A scream.

Silence.

And then…there was truly silence.

Because Shaine was gone.

Miami PD, DEA and FBI flooded the warehouse. Mateo Hernandez went down by Ramirez's hand, Poppy took out Raquel as she reached for her gun and then she punched Angelo out, the crunch of his nose under the butt of her gun very satisfying.

But she didn't see Shaine.

She grabbed Angelo and shook him conscious again. "Where is he?" she yelled, shaking the shit out of the man.

Angelo just grinned a bloody smile and Poppy shoved him to the ground. The room was empty except for a drum in the corner.

No.

God. No.

She sprinted to the drum and struggled to yank the cover off. Shaine's dark hair was matted to his head from sweat and he was crumpled in a heap at the bottom of the barrel.

Oh, my God!

Poppy yelled, "Help! Medic!"

Emergency personnel filed in and immediately began working to pull Shaine free.

He was too pale, too still.

Ramirez pulled Poppy away. "Let them do their work," she urged, but Poppy didn't want to leave Shaine's side. Ramirez was more forceful. "Agent Jones, step away. You're not helping him. You're just in the way."

Somehow Poppy managed to listen to Ramirez, but her eyesight was blurred. It took her a minute to realize she was crying.

"I should've realized something was wrong, something wasn't right. I should've known that it was too easy," she said, mostly rambling to herself, but she couldn't stop. "I should've picked up on the signs that Stapp was dirty. How'd I miss it?"

"Stop!" Ramirez shook her hard. "Knock it off right now. Mistakes happen. People screw up. Stop carrying this on your shoulders. None of us saw it coming. Even the best people can miss clues."

But that wasn't a consolation.

Shaine was dying because she hadn't seen the clues. She'd been too focused on her own issues to realize they were all being played.

"I lied when you asked if I could be objective on this case with him. I wanted to prove something. I was hell-bent on showing Shaine that I could handle this job. My ego got in the way of the investigation and now Shaine might die because of my mistakes. You should've taken me off the case the minute you discovered we'd lied about knowing each other."

Ramirez took a deep, steadying breath as she gripped Poppy's shoulder. "Enough. He's strong. He's going to make it."

Poppy had to cling to that assurance or else she might never pull herself together. As it was, she was already rambling, the fear of losing him all she could see or taste.

"I love him," she choked out, finally saying the words out loud. "I'll always love him."

By Ramirez's expression, she'd already figured that out.

Ramirez released her, saying, "When this is all said and done...you're going to have some paperwork to fill out."

Poppy didn't have the strength to smile. Her gaze was on Shaine as they loaded him into the ambulance.

And then her gaze tracked to the officers taking Angelo into custody.

Her jaw hardened as her fist clenched.

The only thing she wished she'd done was put a bullet in that asshole's face.

If Shaine died…she might do it, anyway.

Chapter 28

Shaine's eyelids fluttered.

Sunshine filled the room.

His eyes adjusted slowly until he could make out the utilitarian forms of medical equipment.

Hospital, his brain supplied.

He wasn't dead.

He slowly turned his head to see Poppy asleep in the chair beside him, looking as if she'd been sleeping in that chair for days, maybe even weeks.

It couldn't have been weeks, but she looked rough.

Tears filled his eyes as he lifted his hand to clasp Poppy's.

She awoke instantly.

"You're awake," she said, her voice raspy. Suddenly, tears filled her eyes, too. "Thank God, you're awake."

"How long have you been sitting there?"

"It doesn't matter. I wasn't leaving."

Warmth filled his heart. She hadn't left his side. That meant more than he could articulate. "Thank you."

"Don't thank me. I'll never leave your side again."

He blinked back tears, her answer cracking his heart in two. "I shouldn't have made you leave."

Poppy kissed him gingerly as if he might break, but her hands were trembling as she held his face. "Never again," she promised through her tears. "Never again."

"I'm sorry I didn't support you when you needed it," he said, his voice rough.

"Stop," Poppy pleaded, smiling even as she cried. "I understand it now. That fear of losing the very person you would do anything for…it takes over your brain. I would do anything to keep you safe. Even if that meant doing something stupid. Knowing you almost died… I understand why you did what you did. I can't say that I wouldn't have done the same."

"Are you going to ask me to get a desk job?" he joked weakly.

"Tempting." Poppy laughed, wiping away her tears. "But I know that you behind a desk would drive everyone crazy. So…no, I would never ask that of you."

Shaine swallowed the lump in his throat. The love he felt for this woman was bigger than anything he could possibly put into words.

"And I'll never make the foolish mistake of asking it of you ever again," he said.

"Sounds like a deal," Poppy said, then whispered for his ears only. "Now, you need to focus on getting out of this hospital bed because I have plans for you, Kelly."

He grinned, knowing exactly what she had in mind.

"You really know how to motivate a man, Agent Jones."

Poppy smiled and Shaine let his eyes close.

Knowing that Poppy would be there when he woke up…that was true bliss.

"Angelo Costa struck a plea bargain," Ramirez told Shaine and Poppy a few weeks later. "He's turning over the details of the operation and testifying against Mateo Hernandez in exchange for a lesser sentence."

"Disgusting little worm," Shaine muttered, still not able to say Angelo's name without wanting to curl his lip. "Prison time is too good for him."

"Yeah, well, with that pretty face, I'm sure he'll be popular in prison," Ramirez said with a grim smile.

"Selena Hernandez was found not guilty of her brother's crime. Apparently, she didn't know anything about his extracurricular activities," Ramirez said.

"So, in a way, your hunch was right," Poppy said.

"Yeah, it was," Ramirez said, proud. "I was worried I'd lost my touch. I knew something wasn't right about them. Selena is distancing herself from her brother, trying to save her company from becoming contaminated by the stain of her brother's actions."

"Good luck with that," Poppy quipped. "I don't care what she says, I say she had to know."

"Maybe, maybe not. She considered herself the alpha of that relationship," Ramirez said.

"I still don't understand why Capri was killed," Poppy said. "Angelo said that Capri was messing around but with who?"

"Mateo swung both ways, but apparently, he took quite a shine to Capri. When he found out she was playing with others, he had Bear overdose her so it would look like an accident."

"The prick," Poppy growled. "I hope he becomes the belle of his prison block."

Shaine grinned, sharing Poppy's hope.

Ramirez added, "However, I think Shaine's theory was correct in that Mateo was cleaning house. Eventually, he would've snipped that loose end either way. Capri was living on borrowed time, the poor kid."

Poppy fell silent. Shaine reached for her hand beneath the table just so she would know that he understood.

"I know we can't save everyone, but that one…will always be the one who haunts me," Poppy admitted.

Ramirez surprised them both by saying, "We all have a Capri in our past. All we can do is try to learn from their loss."

It was good advice. Capri would be Poppy's Walter and she'd be a better agent for the sadness their loss left behind.

Ramirez paused and then said to Shaine and Poppy, "It was a pleasure to work with you on this case. I had my reservations, but you both proved that sharing a past doesn't have to mean that it's doomed to fail."

Poppy smiled. "Thank you for taking a chance on us."

Ramirez nodded and gathered up the final paperwork. "I'll make sure Agent West is honored for his work on this case. His was the ultimate sacrifice."

Shaine caught the bright sheen in Poppy's gaze, but he was proud when she nodded stiffly, accepting Ramirez's way of dealing with shared loss.

Shaine murmured, "He was a good agent. I wish I'd known him better."

Poppy nodded and they both stood, shaking hands and preparing to close this chapter.

It was time to go home.

Together.

Epilogue

Shaine carried the last of Poppy's boxes into the new house they'd purchased together and dropped onto the sofa alongside Poppy, exhausted but happy.

"You sure you're not going to miss all that sunny California weather?" Shaine asked just as snow began to fall outside their window. "Just think, right now it's probably a balmy seventy-five degrees in Los Angeles."

Poppy shuddered. "No, I definitely won't miss that. I like true seasons. And, to be honest, I really missed the snow."

Although Shaine had been willing to relocate to Southern California, Poppy took a position with the Washington, DC, DEA office, which included a promotion and a raise.

"You missed bad driving, sloppy roads and shoveling driveways just so you can get to the mailbox?" he asked, not quite sure he bought that story.

"Okay, maybe I don't miss that part," she confessed, laughing. "But I did miss this."

She snuggled up to Shaine, wrapping her arms around him. A fire danced in the fireplace and filled the small living room with cozy warmth.

They'd found the older home in an established neighborhood on the first day of house hunting. Shaine and Poppy had fallen in love the moment they saw it.

And to be honest, they would've been willing to pay more than the list price if pushed.

But they'd lucked out and the house was theirs after a short escrow.

"I missed this, too," Shaine said. "I'll even shovel the driveway if you promise not to be too harsh on my house-cleaning skills."

"Babe, I know you're a slob and I still love you," Poppy said, her eyes twinkling. "But I will take that deal, only because I like to watch you work up a sweat."

"Oh, do you know, now?" Shaine leaned over to nuzzle her neck. "So what say you…should we christen the living room now or later?"

"Actually…I was thinking we should, you know, wait until we get married to seal the deal."

"What?" Shaine drew up, his brow knitting. "Are you saying what I think you're saying?"

"Don't you think it would be romantic to wait to make love until our wedding night?"

"That's in three months," Shaine groaned. "That's inhuman."

Poppy giggled and trailed her finger down his chest. "Oh, c'mon, it won't be that bad… I said we couldn't make love…but we could do other things…"

Shaine swallowed as he abruptly rose and pulled her into his arms.

"I'd do anything for you," he said with all seriousness. "Even if it meant keeping my hands off my beautiful bride-to-be for three months."

Poppy led him into their bedroom with a mischievous smile, saying, "We'll see…"

And then the little vixen put him to the test in the sexiest way possible.

Shaine couldn't wait to be married!

* * * * *

If you loved this novel, don't miss other suspenseful titles by Kimberly Van Meter:

THE AGENT'S SURRENDER
MOVING TARGET
THE SNIPER
COLD CASE REUNION

Available now from Harlequin Romantic Suspense!